Sarah st~~~~~~~ bathed i~~~~~

She walked away from the house, down a shrub-lined path, the night air cool on her hot cheeks. She saw that another person beside herself had found the company tedious. It was Dr Alan Kerr.

He saw her at the same moment that she became aware of his presence, and said, his voice low, 'Did you find the crowd unendurable, too?'

'Yes.' And then in a rush, 'Oh, Alan, whatever could the Governor have been thinking of? I am sure that everyone saw...'

Sarah ran out of words as the implication of what she had just said struck home.

Alan took both her hands and kissed them. 'What did they see, Sarah?'

She lifted her eyes to his. 'You know.'

Dear Reader

A number of my fans have told me that they would not only like to know the story of Dr Alan Kerr and his wife Sarah, who are Tom Dilhorne's great friends in *Hester Waring's Marriage*, but also want to read more about early Australia.

So here is the prequel to *The Dilhorne Dynasty*, in which Tom plays a minor, if significant, part. The novel tells the love story of Dr Alan Kerr, a transported Emancipist, and Sarah Langley, a high-born lady from England. They are separated by their different class and the conventions of the time in which they live. Their first meeting is a stormy one, but as Sarah begins to change under the influence of the new world in which she is living her attitude to the doctor and that world begins to change too.

Those wishing to know more about the pioneering days of early Australia, when New South Wales was developing on the edge of an unexplored continent, and when its Governor could be mocked for predicting that one day Sydney would be a great city, will find plenty to entertain them—all based on fact.

With best wishes

Paula Marshall

AN UNCONVENTIONAL HEIRESS

Paula Marshall

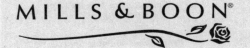

MILLS & BOON®

First published in Great Britain 2003
Harlequin Mills & Boon Limited,
Eton House, 18-24 Paradise Road, Richmond, Surrey TW9 1SR

© Paula Marshall 2003

ISBN 0 263 83502 2

Set in Times Roman 10½ on 12 pt.
04-0403-82795

Printed and bound in Spain
by Litografía Rosés S.A., Barcelona

Paula Marshall, married with three children, has had a varied life. She began her career in a large library and ended it as a senior academic in charge of history in a polytechnic. She has travelled widely, has been a swimming coach, and has appeared on *University Challenge* and *Mastermind*. She has always wanted to write, and likes her novels to be full of adventure and humour.

Author Note

It would take too long to list everything I consulted to make the details of early Australian life as authentic as possible. I used contemporary documents as well as histories of the period. Suffice it to say that both Alan Kerr and Tom Dilhorne were based on real people. There was a ship's doctor who was transported for what Alan Kerr did, and he was an early pioneer of both preventative medicine and the decent treatment of the Emancipists. Lachlan Macquarie was as enlightened as I made him in both *Hester Waring's Marriage* and *An Unconventional Heiress*.

The brick fields, Tom's Emporium, Alan's practice, the lively social life of the Exclusives, Founders' Day and the Governor's Balls and Dinners all featured in contemporary descriptions. The anecdote about the convicts who killed and skinned a kangaroo and the actor who dressed himself in its skin to escape is also a true one. Hyde Park was as I described it. Charles Fraser, the Governor's gardener, was a real person.

Early visitors to Sydney commented on its strangeness and its beauty. It grew with great speed and was a peculiar mish-mash of the grand and the small. Governor Macquarie transformed it by erecting beautiful Regency buildings, many of which are still standing. My son, visiting Sydney recently, took with him a copy of the contemporary map I used, and had himself photographed in front of some of the buildings I had mentioned—on one of them was a plaque commemorating Macquarie.

Chapter One

Why in the world had she travelled here to this strange continent, to a frontier town which was caught between the impassable sea and the equally impassable land? Sarah Langley, whose life seemed to have shrunk down to nothing, asked herself this question for the hundredth time since leaving England nearly six months ago.

All that she could think of, while the long blur which was the coast of New South Wales drew nearer and nearer, was how blessed it would be to stand on dry land again, away from the cramped confines of her cabin and the heaving deck. The state of misery in which she had lived since that last dreadful meeting with Charles Villiers had increased with every nautical mile that the ship had sailed.

Her brother John, who had reluctantly allowed her to come with him on this journey to the Antipodes, was also eager to land, but his was the eagerness of an artist's ambition.

'I can scarcely believe it, Sarah,' he was saying, 'but we have at last reached the promised land. I cannot wait to go ashore, to see the wonders of a new world.'

Somehow Sarah answered him without betraying how

distressed she was. The fact that she had been foolish enough to accompany him on this journey at all was a constant reproach to her and had been from the moment they had left home. Never mind that she had originally joined John in anticipating the beauties of a land lyrically described by the first travellers to it. A land where even the plants and animals were strange and wonderful.

Sydney would need to be Paradise itself to make up for the discomforts of the long journey, which had been hardly alleviated by their stay in Rio and then at the Cape before the last leg of it was accomplished.

When they reached Sydney, however, it was far from being Paradise. They had docked in a place that looked like all the other dismal seaports they had visited on their travels. Crowds of ill-dressed and noisy people had turned out to greet them, together with porters pushing carts, groups of soldiers, and a few, a very few, persons who might be gentlefolk. A ship's arrival was obviously a gala day. Nor could they leave their temporary home immediately as Sarah had hoped. There were formalities to be gone through and officials to be satisfied before they could set foot on the quay.

John, having earlier ordered his man of all work, Carter, to bring his painting materials on deck, was enthusiastically sketching the scene before them. 'Picturesque, so picturesque,' he kept exclaiming. Sarah wished that she, too, had had the forethought to carry her sketchbook on deck with her, but she had wrongly supposed that once the ship had docked they would instantly leave it.

After all, they had both come to draw and paint. John was already known as an amateur of some distinction, although he had been born a country gentleman of great wealth with a seat at Prior's Langley in Hampshire.

Just as Sarah's impatience and boredom reached boil-

ing point—she told herself that she must really learn to
control the temper that she had never known she possessed until Charles's defection—there was a slight commotion on deck. Chalmers, the ship's mate, came towards them, followed by a handsome young officer in
scarlet regimentals.

Chalmers had been one of Sarah's silent admirers on
board ship, finding, like many men, that her chestnut-
coloured hair, green eyes and creamy skin, allied to a
graceful figure, were quite irresistible. Although she was
socially beyond his touch, he was unhappy at having to
hand her over to the company of such a military pea-
cock.

'Miss Sarah Langley, Mr John Langley, I must introduce you to Lieutenant Frank Wright of the 73rd Foot,
the Royal Highland Regiment. He has come aboard to
look after your welfare.'

They all bowed at one another. Young Lieutenant
Wright swept off his black bicorne hat to reveal his
handsome golden head. He was a trifle young, thought
Sarah, who had a taste for more mature men, but good-
looking, very. Lieutenant Wright's eyes approved of her,
too.

'I am here,' he announced, 'on behalf of the Governor,
Lachlan Macquarie, who, I believe, has corresponded
with Mr Langley over his desire to come here to paint
the native flora and fauna of New South Wales.' He
paused and bowed again.

We shall be doing this all day, thought Sarah, who
was suddenly in a fever of impatience to be off the *Pomona*, and found all this punctiliousness wearisome,
even though John seemed to be appreciating it. He always enjoyed pomp and circumstance: Sarah was beginning to think it boring.

'The Governor thought that you would most likely be tired after your long journey, and that you might welcome a few days rest at Government House, before you take up the accommodation which he has found for you in George Street. If this is agreeable to you both, I have a carriage waiting and I will take you there as soon as you have permission to leave.'

'With pleasure,' and 'Most agreeable,' they replied and after further politenesses they made their way along the deck, Sarah on the Lieutenant's arm while he steered her through the noisy bustle of a ship being unloaded.

'They are preparing to bring the convicts on deck,' he explained to her. 'The Commissioner will inform them of the nature of their future life and direct them to where they will be inspected by those needing labourers.'

Still other workmen were coming on board to arrange for stores and supplies to be released from the hold. The Langleys' small party was compelled to wait at the tip of the gangplank since two men were already on their way up it. The first, tall and dark, and well dressed in civilian clothes, Sarah noticed idly, was advancing on to the deck and speaking in tones of barely controlled fury.

'So,' he said to Chalmers, who was directing operations, 'I am to understand that the medical supplies which I ordered, and which I badly need, have not arrived. Your excuse being that there was not enough room for them in the hold. Tom,' he said, turning to his companion, 'which do you think ought to come first? The needs and health of the colonists, or the comfort and convenience of a fine lady and gentleman from England?'

His companion, a sandy-haired man with a pair of striking blue eyes and a humorous, rather than handsome, face, was wearing what Sarah was later to discover were the typical clothes of a Sydney Emancipist. Easy and careless, they consisted of a white-spotted red neckcloth, a loose grey jacket, baggy trousers, scuffed boots and a grey felt hat on the back of his head. He was pulling at his friend's arm to indicate the presence of Sarah and John.

'What?' snapped his friend, turning his head and giving Sarah an excellent view of his eagle's profile and a pair of furious grey eyes that were regarding them both with a look of ill-concealed contempt. John, with his stance and air of a gentleman, and Sarah, the very model of a useless fine lady with her cream silk dress and tiny parasol, seemed to be anathema to him.

Frank Wright could almost feel the Langleys' indignation. 'Steady on, Dr Kerr,' he said cheerfully. 'There's no need to insult Miss Langley and her brother. That won't restore your missing supplies.'

The hard grey eyes swept over him, too. 'Squiring the ladies again, Wright?' he said, unbending enough to doff his straw hat in John and Sarah's direction before he strode off along the deck without waiting to be formally introduced.

His friend, raising an eyebrow, half-bowed, his bright blue eyes hard on Sarah and her brother, assessing them coolly without Dr Kerr's open hostility. In contrast to his friend's taut self-control he was all ease. 'I am Tom Dilhorne, at your service. I hope to see you in my store.'

His voice carried overtones of a rural Yorkshire origin, but he could scarcely have been more confidently sure of himself than if he had been on equal terms with them for years. Lieutenant Wright made no attempt to introduce him, or to acknowledge him in any way when he, too, pulled off his battered felt hat before following Dr Kerr's path along the ship's deck.

'Good God, who in the world were they?' asked John Langley, his voice indignant. He was not accustomed to be spoken to in such a cavalier fashion. To make matters worse, the second, ill-dressed oaf was the owner of a shop!

'Oh, Dilhorne,' said Frank Wright carelessly. 'Dilhorne's nothing. He's an Emancipist. I wonder he had the impudence to speak to you at all. That's not true,' he added, with a laugh. 'I should say that Dilhorne's got impudence enough for anything. The brute has even made a friend of one of the aborigines.'

'Well, his manners are better than Dr Kerr's, even if he is an Emancipist, whatever that is,' said Sarah, furiously. She might not like circumstance, but good manners were good manners the world over.

Frank Wright began to explain to her that an Emancipist was a man or woman who had come to New South Wales as a convicted criminal, and who had served their term or been pardoned. They had no social standing, and were cut off from the colony's elite, the so-called Exclusives, who were those free men and women who had gone out in the service of the Crown as civil servants, the military or the Navy, or who were free traders and farmers, there by choice, not necessity.

'You mustn't mind Dr Kerr,' he ended. 'That's his manner. He doesn't mean anything by it—what's more, he's the best doctor in the colony. The Governor swears by him, although…'

What the 'although' meant Sarah was not immediately to find out, for Carter, who had gone ahead, now returned with the request that Lieutenant Wright should arrange for the transfer of the Langleys' possessions from the hold to the shore as soon as possible.

The Lieutenant, John and Carter left Sarah in the waiting carriage on the quay outside, her parasol up to defend her from the hot sun that shone down brilliantly on this inappropriate November day. 'We shan't leave you long, I trust. Corporal Mackay, the driver, will look after you,' Frank Wright volunteered before he left her. He was invariably cheerful, Sarah was to find.

Sarah was not destined to lack company. First of all Tom Dilhorne emerged from the ship and saw her sitting on her own. He evidently considered himself to have been introduced for he came over to the carriage, pulled off his hat, and said, 'Abandoned already, Miss Langley?'

From anyone else this might have seemed almost impudent, but his cool, laconic manner and his impersonal blue eyes seemed to rob his words of any undesirable overtones.

'Indeed, Mr Dilhorne. But not for long, I hope. There seem to be a large number of ships in the harbour, which I confess surprises me very much. Why is this so?'

He answered her question as gravely as she had asked it without the accents of condescension that most men whom she knew employed towards a pretty woman. 'Why, Miss Langley, Sydney is a major staging post in the Pacific already. There are ships from Macao here and Yankee whalers, too. The nearest one, *The Sprite*, is my own.'

'I understood you to say that you were a store-owner, Mr Dilhorne.'

'I am a trader, as well, among other things. I shall be unpacking some silks from Macao tomorrow. I think that you might like to inspect them.'

'Huckstering away, Tom?' Dr Kerr had arrived while they were speaking. His words to his friend were jocular, but his manner to Sarah was cool if not so brusquely harsh as it had been when they were on board ship. Behind him John, Carter and Lieutenant Wright were also coming down the gangplank, making for the waiting carriage.

'Miss Langley,' he said, 'I must apologise for my earlier discourtesy to you. I fear that my anger at the non-arrival of some of my stores was transferred to your brother and yourself.' He half-turned towards John at the end of his little speech.

Before John could answer him, Sarah lowered her parasol and stared over Dr Kerr's shoulder at Tom, who had retreated and was watching them impassively. Her reply was short.

'Your apology is accepted, Dr Kerr, although there was no need to make one. My brother and I are well aware that our presence is not particularly welcome in New South Wales. However, that is no matter since it is unlikely that our paths will cross again.'

Her tone and her manner to him were as cold as she could make them.

Dr Kerr clapped his hat firmly on his head and answered her in kind. 'You are mistaken, madam. Unless your health is perfect, or you are willing to settle for some half-trained leech from The Rocks, then you and your brother are likely to encounter me on a number of occasions. I bid you good day and good health—you are likely to need both.'

With that, he was gone, leaving Sarah with her mouth open and John amused at his impudence. 'My sympathies, sister. Yonder colonial doctor is obviously made of sterner stuff than the puppy dogs who surrounded you in London. Not that I approve of his manners, you understand: they appear to be worse than those of his Emancipist friend.'

Sarah's face was scarlet beneath her parasol and, although her answer to Frank Wright, who advised her to ignore Dr Kerr's incivility since he was the colony's only decent doctor, apart from a retired surgeon called Wentworth, was a composed one, she was inwardly seething not only at his rudeness, but also at John's amusement. Later she was to admit that it was her own less-than-polite reply which was responsible for the doctor's subsequent insolence. She was dismally aware that it was her own folly in travelling to this barbarous shore, plus the sense of rejection that she had felt since Charles's jilting of her, which had combined to make her less than sensitive to the feelings of others.

At first, the passing scenery which surrounded them on their journey to Government House was a vague blur in front of which she mechanically exercised her forgotten good manners. She recovered sufficiently to ask Lieutenant Wright about something which had puzzled her in Dr Kerr's rejoinder.

'Dr Kerr mentioned The Rocks a moment ago. Are they a street or a district?'

'The Rocks?' Young Lieutenant Wright's insouciance temporarily deserted him. 'It is a district, Miss Langley. It is where the convicts and the rascals of the colony live. No decent person goes there.'

Unspoken was his conviction that Dr Kerr should not have mentioned the place to a lady of quality such as Miss Sarah Langley. For her part, Sarah was now painfully aware that Dr Kerr had been mocking her in recommending to her a physician from such a quarter.

She tried to forget the whole unhappy incident by a closer examination of her surroundings, but her thoughts reverted again and again to the uncivil Dr Kerr. Who would have thought that such a handsome and appar-

ently polished gentleman could have taken against her—
and John—on first meeting them? His behaviour had
merely served to reinforce her conviction that the whole
of the male sex was unworthy of the interest of a woman
of sense.

A woman of sense would try to forget Dr Kerr by
concentrating instead on her journey through Sydney,
which, Sarah found, was composed of a strange mixture
of building styles. There were ramshackle huts, cabins
and lean-tos with children and chickens running around
them, next door to houses that would not have disgraced
a wealthy London suburb. There were flowers everywhere.

Sarah might have felt a little happier if she had not
been suffering from the inevitable consequences of
spending such a long time aboard ship. Her head was
swimming and the ground, when she stepped down from
the carriage, seemed to be moving beneath her. Her
sense of relief when she finally entered Government
House was great. Here, in this attractive, if small, building, she found a haven of rest: a room of her own where
she was surrounded by modest luxury, pure water and
clean linen.

Surely now she could forget both Charles Villiers and
Dr Kerr.

'It's not like you to be such a boor towards a pretty
young lady before she has even set foot in the colony,'
Tom Dilhorne offered mildly to his friend on their walk
back to Tom's gig. 'Got out of bed the wrong side this
morning, did you?'

Alan Kerr could not have said—indeed, he did not
understand—why the first sight of Sarah Langley had
roused such anger in his breast. After all, it was scarcely

her fault that his stores had been left behind, but in some odd way her imperious chestnut-haired beauty had touched a nerve in him that he had long thought deadened by the years which had passed since he had arrived in New South Wales.

Was it that she reminded him not only of the pretty girl he had lost, but also of the life that he might have lived before his own folly had brought him to the other end of the world?

'I don't know,' he said honestly. 'I can't imagine why such a fine lady and gentleman should wish to come here at all. They are exactly the useless kind of gentry the colony could do without. They will want servants, accommodation and care that should be reserved for those who are willing to work to make Sydney a better place for all of us. We could, for instance, really do with another qualified doctor. I am almost run off my feet, as you know. What I also know is that, far from the Langleys working, they will expect others to work for them.

'I do regret, though, that I was so short with Miss Langley. It was not the act of a gentleman, although God knows, I cannot really call myself a gentleman any more.'

'Short,' drawled Tom, 'that's a mild word for biting the poor young thing's head off. Still, I take your point about your stores, although you might have waited to make it later—and more tactfully. You're usually the tactful one, not me.'

Alan Kerr began to laugh.

'Come, come, Tom, you know that you're the devious devil, not me—you ooze tact when you think that it will pay off. Now let's forget the Langleys. With luck, I shan't have much to do with them in future.'

Nevertheless, when he reached his home again, he

couldn't help thinking of Sarah Langley as he had first seen her in the pride of her beauty and wondered again why he had felt such fierce resentment at a sight that should have compelled his admiration, not his anger.

Chapter Two

Sarah was soon to find that in Sydney she and John were curiosities since so few cared to make the long and difficult journey from England, unless compelled by the law, or their duty. That they should have travelled so far to see and record this new fragment of Empire was strange enough: that they should come from the highest reach of English society was even stranger.

Lachlan Macquarie received them with enthusiasm. He had originally been sent out as the Colonel of the 73rd Highland Regiment, but after the mutiny against the previous Governor, William Bligh, in 1810, he had unexpectedly found himself the new Governor on his arrival. A highly competent man of strong principle, he was determined to make his newly acquired fief a land to be proud of rather than simply exist as a kind of dustbin for the unwanted and the criminal.

He was pleased to welcome John and Sarah precisely because they had come to study the colony's beauties, and on the third day after their arrival he gave a dinner party in their honour in order to introduce them to the social life of Sydney. He could also painlessly, through his guests, make the Langleys fully aware of the forms and difficulties of life in this outpost of Empire.

Sarah was careful to dress herself as though she were going to be the guest of honour in the presence of the Prince Regent himself since, after all, the Governor was his deputy in New South Wales. She was magnificent in pale yellow silk. Her only jewellery, a beautiful topaz brooch, which matched the colour of her dress, served to add lustre to the striking beauty that had so overset Alan Kerr.

The officers of the 73rd, both married and unmarried, to whom she and John were introduced before dinner, were impressed by the pair of them. Her looks and John's gentlemanly bonhomie also found favour with their wives and daughters.

'I hear you had the misfortune to meet the biggest rogue in Sydney even before you had left the *Pomona*,' drawled Major Menzies on being introduced to Sarah. 'I understand that his friend, the doctor, was with him, too. I gather that Dilhorne even had the impudence to speak to you without having been introduced.'

'Now, Menzies,' said another gallant gentleman, as blond and handsome as Frank Wright. 'Parker's the name, Madam,' he said to Sarah. 'Tom's not that much of a rogue these days. He's honest with you if you're honest with him. He only cheats the cheaters.'

'Oh, come, Parker,' reproached Menzies. 'Don't be greener than you are. Dilhorne arrived in chains after being sentenced to death at eighteen for God knows what. Once he was released and became an Emancipist, he made himself the richest man in the colony before he reached his mid-thirties—and you call him honest!'

Parker was stubborn. 'Agreed, but you have to admit that the Governor has made a friend of him; say what you like about Macquarie, he wouldn't take up with a thief. At least, not one who's practising now,' he amended.

'Well, whatever Parker says, Miss Langley, I advise you not to have anything to do with him, or his doctor friend, either. Why—' He would have said more, but Parker was pulling at his arm to indicate that the Governor was coming towards them with Dr Alan Kerr at his side.

'Oh, damnation!' exclaimed Menzies, disgusted. 'I see that he's determined to force them all down our throats. Is Dilhorne here, too? No? You do surprise me. Miss Langley, it is the outside of enough for you to have to deal with such people. Tell you later about Dr Kerr,' he finished, just before the Governor reached them.

'Ah, Miss Langley,' said Macquarie with his easy smile. 'I would like you to meet Dr Kerr. He is not only my personal physician, but my friend, and one who has the colony's health at heart.'

'Thank you,' responded Sarah glacially, 'but we have already met.' Her manner did not suggest that the meeting had been a happy one.

'Indeed,' replied Dr Kerr, equally coldly, 'Miss Langley and I have already exchanged opinions on the manners and morals of colonial life.'

'Yes,' said Sarah. The devil inside her that had made her respond to Major Menzies's warning about Tom Dilhorne by secretly determining to meet and speak with him again was compelling her to be as overtly rude to this particular colonial savage as she dare. 'Doctor Kerr has given me an extremely accurate picture of the level of civility that I may expect to find here. I cannot but thank him for it.'

'On the contrary,' Alan Kerr replied instantly, looking

more like an offended eagle than ever, 'it is I who should thank you, Miss Langley, for making me acquainted with the intellectual baggage that great persons from England bring with them to this poor colony.'

Sarah rose to this bait magnificently. 'Pray do not offer me thanks, Dr Kerr. I am only too willing to spread civilisation and culture in whichever part of the globe I may happen to find myself. Particularly when it is so obviously needed.'

They glared furiously at one another. Their hearers were fascinated. Sarah suddenly became aware of what a spectacle she was making of herself and also of what the Governor might think of her own lack of manner, if not to say manners, towards his friend. She also suddenly grasped that the officers of the 73rd were, by their expressions and reactions, cheering her on and she did not really wish to be part of any feud that was currently simmering. She had not only been unladylike, but also unwise—and it was all Dr Alan Kerr's fault. His very presence seemed to provoke her into one excess after another.

She really must try to behave herself in future.

Alan Kerr was, although Sarah did not know it, also regretting his own lack of civility before his friend and patron, the Governor. Like Sarah, he decided to mend his manners.

He bowed.

Sarah curtsied.

The Governor said nothing, although he thought a lot, since saying something might prove unwise. What he was thinking might have surprised both parties and their fascinated audience. He also bowed to Sarah, before taking Alan Kerr's arm and walking him away.

'Oh, well done, Miss Langley,' said Menzies appreciatively. 'Well done, indeed. It's all a jumped-up ex-felon deserves: a real set-down from a fine lady like yourself. It's a great pity that all Emancipists cannot be served so.'

'An Emancipist?' said Sarah, surprised. 'You mean that Dr Kerr was transported here as a convict?'

Menzies was about to refine on his answer when he saw the Governor approaching them again with a respectable Exclusive in tow this time. 'Ahem, Miss Langley, tell you later. I think that you ought to know the truth about Kerr.'

Little though she liked him, Sarah found it difficult to believe that the man with the eagle's profile had arrived here in chains. For what? she wondered. His crime was doomed to remain unknown for the time being since Major Menzies found no further opportunity to enlighten her and she did not wish to raise the subject with anyone else.

She was later to discover that Major Menzies was not the only person to resent Macquarie's friendship with Alan Kerr. Few of the Exclusives shared the Governor's tolerant attitude towards Emancipists, and many of them expressed their anger over it as plainly as they could. This did not prevent them from availing themselves of his medical skills, but it meant that he was cut off from most society in Sydney, such as it was.

Indeed, everyone whom she met that night commiserated with her on her encounter with the two men so early in her stay. Even Major Middleton's wife and his pretty daughter, Lucy, who was near in age to Sarah, and eagerly anxious to make a new friend, were not slow to speak of them.

Lucy's major exclamations, however, were all on the subject of Sarah's lemon silk gown.

'Oh, Sarah, how delightful your frock is. I suppose that it is in the very latest fashion since the waist is so much lower than any you will find in Sydney.'

'That may be so,' said Sarah, smiling and greatly relieved to be gossiping about something as innocent as the dress she was wearing for the Governor's dinner. 'But since it is over six months since I left England I must suppose that it is already out of date there!'

'Never mind that,' was Lucy's brisk reply. 'It is of the highest fashion here and that is all that matters. The colour suits you so well, too. Mama and I are determined to introduce you to all the best people and the places where only the Exclusives are allowed to visit—although even there,' she added, 'one cannot be sure that one will not meet some of the low creatures such as Alan Kerr, even if he is a good doctor—to say nothing of Tom Dilhorne.'

It was becoming increasingly plain to Sarah that Dr Kerr and Tom Dilhorne were like a pair of sore teeth to Sydney's elite since the conversation constantly kept returning to them and their enormities.

The only officer who seemed to have a good word for either of them was a darkly handsome Scot introduced to her as Captain Patrick Ramsey.

He and Sarah chatted together happily about nothing for a few moments before she said, somewhat provokingly, 'I have to tell you, Captain Ramsey, that you are the first person to whom I have spoken who has not spent a great deal of time warning me about Dr Kerr, after commiserating with me for his having been the first of Sydney's inhabitants whom I chanced to meet.'

'Oh, Kerr,' laughed Pat Ramsey cheerfully. 'What the 73rd resents the most about him is his having been sent here for committing treason. To make matters worse, when he and that outsider Dilhorne visited the Chevalier Ince—the fencing master sent here for fraud—to take fencing lessons, they turned out to be better with the foils than any of our officers. They're both crack shots, too. Don't seem fair, does it?'

'But you don't feel particularly resentful about them, Captain Ramsey?'

'No, not I. I can't feel resentful about poor devils sent here in chains. I shall be leaving shortly, while Kerr and Dilhorne are doomed to stay in this Godforsaken hole. Kerr's a good doctor, but one thing worth remembering about Dilhorne is that he's dangerous.'

All this merely served to push Sarah more and more towards meeting again these strange characters who were remarkable enough to set everyone talking. The perversity that ruled her these days drove her towards the dangerous and the forbidden, the permitted and the allowed having let her down so much. Truth to tell, Dr Kerr fascinated her, particularly now that she knew that he had arrived here in chains. Never before had she met such high-nosed insolence—and from an ex-convict, too.

In future, of course, she must not let herself be tempted to lose her temper with him. No, dignified reproof must be the order of the day. He must be left in no doubt of her displeasure should he offend again, but, in future, she must not give him any opportunity to attack her verbally again. By no means.

She really must stop thinking about the wretch.

Fortunately for Sarah, her new life in Sydney was busier than she might have expected. Lucy Middleton arrived on the following afternoon to fulfil the promise which she had made on the previous night to show Sarah all of Sydney's main sights as soon as possible.

Lucy, charming in a young girl's straw hat and a simple muslin dress embroidered with flowers, came to the point as soon as possible.

'I persuaded Mama to let me visit you alone—much more fun for both of us. I do hope that you are not finding Sydney too hot. I know that Mama was very overset by it when she first came here, but one soon gets used to it. She thought that you might be feeling lonely today so she told me to ask you to come to dinner this afternoon. Papa has promised to take us all out to Hyde Park for an airing afterwards. Do say yes. Mr Langley is included in the invitation, of course.'

'I shall be delighted to come, but I fear that John will not be home in time. He has borrowed a horse from Lieutenant Wright and gone to find kangaroos to draw. Goodness knows when he will return!'

'Then you must come on your own. I'm longing to talk to you. It's such a bore having no one but Mama and the children to go out with. There are so few presentable young ladies in the colony, you see.'

Sarah needed no persuasion. A drive to Hyde Park—named after the one in London, presumably—might not represent the height of sophistication and excitement, but it would certainly be better than sitting around waiting for John. Particularly when it would be likely that he would end his day in the Officers' Mess and not arrive home until the small hours.

'One thing, Lucy. What ought I to wear? Formal dress or something more comfortable? A muslin, perhaps—it would certainly be cooler than the toilette I am wearing.'

Lucy gave a jolly laugh. 'Goodness, Sarah, I'm sure you would look well in anything. Mama said after she met you last night that she hoped that I would take a leaf out of your book, you looked so perfectly composed.

Yes, a muslin would be splendid. Papa will send the carriage round for you after nuncheon. We can spend the afternoon together before dinner.'

Later, after dinner, sitting by Lucy and opposite to Mrs Middleton, Sarah was to wonder whether her gown was appropriate after all. Alongside the simple dresses of the Sydney ladies it seemed somewhat over-elaborate. Of course, the many curious eyes that roved over her, both male and female, were, she told herself, solely the result of her being a newcomer. Soon she would no longer be a subject of uncommon interest but would be simply one of the crowd; she could hardly wait for that day to come.

The drive to the Park through streets lined with houses, whose gardens were blazing with flowers, was faintly reminiscent of home, but the stalls of fruit on each corner, and the gaily coloured parrots that hung in cages on every verandah, were not.

Hyde Park, when they reached it, proved to be set among trees and was pleasantly cool. The Regimental Band was already there, stationed beneath the pines, playing popular songs and marches. Men, mostly Army officers, walked, rode and drove about. The ladies sat in their carriages and waited to be spoken to or invited to promenade. Sarah was surprised to find that it really was a miniature version of the Hyde Park she knew in London—and it was none the less pleasing for that.

Major Middleton accompanied them on horseback, and, once their carriage was drawn up, facing the view inland, but near to the band, he left them to visit the Menzies's carriage. The Middletons' was immediately besieged by all those young officers who had not yet seen Sarah, but who had already heard that a rare beauty had come among them and were eager to meet her.

As Lucy and Sarah descended from the carriage, bold eyes roved over Sarah's elegant face and figure, mustachios were twirled at her, as each young fellow jostled for her attention until Pat Ramsey, with Frank Wright in tow, arrived to disperse them all with a word and a look.

'Have a heart,' he exclaimed. 'Besides, you have not been so much as introduced to Miss Langley while Frank and I have.'

'Then you could introduce us,' said one bold young ensign, to be quelled by Pat with:

'Another day, perhaps. Now, Miss Langley, what do you think of our little imitation of London?'

'That it has its own charms, Captain Ramsey.'

'Bravely said. If you look around, you may note how democratic we are here—more so than in London, I think. There are several Emancipists present, and most of them are on good horses, too.'

For the first time since she had arrived in Sydney, Sarah engaged in light-hearted banter with a man as they strolled across the grass. 'Pray tell me, Captain Ramsey, how I am to distinguish them if they are mounted as well as the 73rd's officers?'

Pat laughed, showing his splendid teeth. 'Well, in at least two cases you will find no difficulty at all in detecting them, for both Dilhorne and his friend Dr Kerr are taking the air here this evening.'

'I see that most of the visitors are speaking to one another—will anyone speak to them?'

'Bowing at a distance by the men is as far as most are willing to go. The ladies, of course, ignore them.'

'Of course.'

Pat was about to continue their tête-à-tête when a harassed young ensign ran up to him and saluted. 'Sir, Colonel O'Connell has sent me to ask you to return to Barracks immediately. The matter is urgent.'

Pat gave a great sigh. 'The matter is always urgent. I wonder what bee buzzes in his bonnet this time. Forgive me, Miss Langley, for leaving you. I will escort you to your carriage and perhaps we may continue our conversation another time.'

'Certainly,' Sarah replied, sorry to lose such an easy and pleasant companion, especially since she was doomed to sit beside Mrs Middleton again. Her conversation was scarcely lively and boredom was sure to be on the menu once more.

Well, that was not quite true, Sarah thought ruefully, far from it, for no sooner had she settled herself in the Middletons' carriage again than Dr Kerr on his large grey and Tom Dilhorne on a handsome chestnut rode up. Their daring to approach them was sure to cause even more gossip to run round Sydney.

Tom, after bowing to them all, departed to greet Will French—yet another Emancipist who had made good. Mrs Middleton glared after him, but she could not dismiss Dr Kerr so easily. He was their family physician, for there was no one else as competent as he was, and she was therefore compelled to acknowledge him.

Her manner to him was icy, to say the least, but at least she spoke to him. Doctor Kerr's bow to them was equally cool after he had swept off his hat. Sarah thought furiously how odious it was that such a hateful man should be so attractive, much more so than most of the 73rd's officers.

'Mrs Middleton, Miss Middleton, Miss Langley,' on one side and 'Dr Kerr,' on the other should have been sufficient acknowledgement, and ought to have ended their conversation, but the same devil that had plagued Sarah since she had landed in Sydney provoked her into further folly. She could not prevent herself from adding, 'I am surprised to find you here, Dr Kerr. The occasion scarcely seems sufficiently serious to merit your presence.'

His eyes blazed at her. His head lifted. Alan Kerr had come to Hyde Park quite determined that, if he should find Sarah Langley there, he would do as Tom Dilhorne had suggested and try to be tactful, or at least to moderate his manner to her. Both these good resolutions flew away on his discovering that she was more than ready to take the haughtiest tone with him.

'Oh,' he said, as disdainful as she, 'I came to note the absurdities of high life, or what passes for it here, Miss Langley. I am only too happy to see that you are adding to them.'

His speech was a red rag to a bull. Before she could stop herself Sarah shot her defiance back at him.

'Is that so, Dr Kerr? You may imagine with what pleasure I shall record all the sophisticated delights of Sydney in my next letter home. My friends will be highly entertained with my accounts of the black and white aborigines of Botany Bay.'

He was not to be set down so easily, though, and he offered her yet another of his derisory bows before answering her as harshly as she had spoken to him.

'Our good fortune, Miss Langley, in having you here, is beyond belief. Pray tell us, what *exactly* did bring you to New South Wales? What piece of good, or bad, fortune induced you to confer the honour of your presence on us? After all, you did have the opportunity of choice in the matter, unlike many of us, as I am sure that you are aware.'

To her horror, Sarah felt her eyes fill with tears. She could see Lucy's delighted face, mouth half-open while she followed this exchange of politely expressed savage discourtesies.

And he…he…he had the wit, the impertinence and the acumen to put his finger with deadly accuracy on the one thing that she could endure to think of the least. The reason why, in an impulsive fit of wilfulness after Charles's jilting of her, she had decided to visit this dreadful place where she was being subjected to insults among a crowd of ill-bred commoners.

She lifted her head and looked him straight in the eye, her face ashen. Damn him for his impudence and his percipience, but she would answered him as bravely as she could. He must not know how much he had distressed her.

'We must not keep you, Dr Kerr, from all the friends who surround you. There are surely many present only too willing to be entertained by your ready wit. We must not monopolise you.'

Alan Kerr knew at once that he had hurt her, that the bright armour, which she wore so lightly, had been badly pierced. But he could not stop himself, any more than Sarah could, from continuing the verbal guerrilla warfare that had sprung up between them.

'You are right, as usual, Miss Langley. We are, of course, certain to meet again soon so that I may enjoy the gentle charms of your conversation. I understand that you will be at the Governor's dinner on Saturday week, where I shall be only too happy to discourse with you further on Antipodean, as opposed to European, customs.'

His final bow to her—and the two Middleton ladies— was elaborately formal.

Sarah sat in silence, her face scarlet, and so near to breaking down that she could scarcely breathe. It was fortunate that Mrs Middleton was so angry at Dr Kerr's effrontery that she could not see Sarah's patent distress. She said, her face working, 'The impudence of them. They're sent here as punishment, and when they *are* here they are bare-faced enough to address His Majesty's loyal subjects as though they're no better than themselves, no better than transported felons.'

Lucy laid her hand lightly on Sarah's to comfort her. 'You are not to trouble yourself about what such a creature thinks,' she murmured softly. 'If he were not such a good doctor, he would still be in chains.'

Sarah was too busy musing unhappily about the recent distressing scene to hear what Lucy said. The impudence of him, she thought, echoing Mrs Middleton. He needed taking down a peg or two, that was for sure. Then her common sense, sadly missing since she had arrived in Sydney, took over, and told her that a criminal who had been brought from England in irons had already been brought down by far more than two pegs.

For all that, she thought, he behaves like a Spanish Grandee, which really is the most provoking thing! The next time that we meet I shall try to keep to my early resolution and not speak like an intemperate shrew. After all, it was Charles Villiers who did me the greater injury and not this nobody of an Emancipist doctor! I must try to forget them both.

She looked around. The bright day had been dimmed for her, but just when she had begun to think that everyone was in a conspiracy to distress her, a most unlikely saviour in the person of Tom Dilhorne arrived to take her mind off herself and her troubles. Afterwards, she was to ask herself whether that had been his real intention, rather than the obvious one of his using an opportunity to persuade her to patronise his Emporium. At the time, though, it was not a question that occurred to her.

He swept off his hat in greeting. This time it was an elegant straw one, not the battered felt he had worn on the ship. His dress was rather better, too. He made nothing of Mrs Middleton's open annoyance at his daring to approach them at all, merely saying, 'Your servant, ladies,' before turning his attention towards Sarah.

'Miss Langley, the silks from Macao, of which I spoke when you first arrived here, are now unpacked and in the shop. Not only that, when I inspected the goods, which came from England, there were some fine cottons that might be to your liking.'

'Then you must expect a visit from me—and possibly from Miss Middleton.' Sarah smiled, determined to show both him and the Middleton ladies that she had not been overset by Dr Kerr. 'There are some grand occasions to be attended soon, I hear, and I shall need a positive trousseau.'

Excellent. Whatever that ass, his good friend, had said and done to distress her, it had not succeeded in dampening her spirits completely. Tom thought that he knew why Sarah Langley was having such a powerful effect on Alan Kerr, but it would not do to tell either him or the lady why they were at such odds.

Instead he remarked gravely, 'Happen I can find some new trimmings for you, too.' In front of Mrs Middleton his Yorkshire accent had deepened and coarsened. Whenever he had been alone with Sarah, it had always been slight.

Sarah would have detained him further, but, with the dry remark that 'I am sure that you are finding Sydney of great interest, Miss Langley, particularly since some of our natives are not exactly as civilised as those you have encountered at home,' he took himself off, pausing to inform her that, if she found any problems in hiring servants when she finally set up house, he would be only too willing to help her.

His departure left Sarah appreciative of both his obliquity and his consideration. Oblique, because his comments on her view of Sydney and its inhabitants could only have been taken as an amused reference to her encounters with Alan Kerr. Considerate because he had seen Mrs Middleton turn as red as a turkey cock because he was speaking to Sarah at all, and had left swiftly enough to spare her reproach from the old harridan.

Mrs Middleton did snort at her, 'I wonder, Miss Langley, at you allowing such a creature to speak to you.'

'The Governor told me that his Emporium is well worth a visit. He seems to think highly of him,' was Sarah's only reply to that. Tom's visit had cheered her up no end—a saying of her old nurse's. All the way back to Government House she told herself that now she was in the Antipodes she must try to forget the past for, if she persisted in refusing to tame her own stormy heart, she might as well have stayed in England. She must not repine, but accept the past and try to welcome the future.

Easy to think, but harder to do.

Sarah kept her promise to visit Tom's Emporium on the very next day. She walked there from Government House. The Emporium was quite unlike any shop that she had ever patronised before. It was crammed with a variety of goods as well as a small gathering of Sydney's more respectable matrons, side by side with some whom Mrs Middleton would have dismissed as low. There was no sign of Tom himself: a young man was serving behind a long counter on which even more goods were displayed, when a door at the back opened and he came in, dressed rather like a superior clerk.

He walked the length of the shop, gave her a half-bow, and said, 'Good morning, Miss Langley, have you come to see the silks—or the cottons?'

Sarah was aware that every woman's eye was on her, and that Tom was equally aware of it. She was not to know that these days Tom rarely served in the shop himself, leaving that to the young man and a middle-aged woman who was busy looking after one of the matrons.

He walked her over to a small trestle table on which bales of fabric lay and began to display them to her. There were not only rolls of silk, but of muslin, calico, cotton and the finest lawn. He spoke briefly, but knowledgeably, of them all, even recommending certain threads and trimmings as suitable. He was the complete man milliner, she thought with amusement, as far removed as possible from the dangerous brute that Pat Ramsey and the other officers had reported him to be.

She noticed that his hands, like Alan Kerr's, were beautifully cared for, the nails smoothly cut. This was surprising; even more so was his apparent ability to read her mind, for he said to her, apparently idly, 'Must keep the hands trim, Miss Langley, might damage the goods, else.'

She began to question him further about the silks and he fetched even more bales from the back to show her, together with ribbons, laces and other frippery, which she might wish to choose from. After running out of questions concerning haberdashery, she said, 'I understand that you have many other interests besides this store, Mr Dilhorne.'

Her comment was really a question and he took it as such.

'Indeed, Miss Langley. I run a money-lending business, have connections with stone quarrying and the brick-fields, and own several ships. I occasionally do a little auctioneering and am at the present moment engaged in talks with the Yankee sealers about joining in business with them.'

'You must be a very busy man. I was surprised to see that both you and Dr Kerr had time to visit Hyde Park yesterday.'

'Oh, there's more to life, Miss Langley, than work—as Dr Kerr and I both know.'

How odd it was that she should be enjoying her conversation with a man whom most of Sydney's Exclusives dismissed as a coarse brute. Would Dr Kerr be as interesting to talk to? she wondered. Perhaps even more so, although most people in Sydney would doubtless tell her that she should not be thinking of, or talking to, either of them.

As though he had been reading her mind again, Tom picked up one of the bales of silk and murmured softly, aware that their lengthy tête-à-tête was drawing curious stares, if not to say glares. 'If I may advise you, Miss Langley, it may not be altogether wise to speak overlong with me, or my friend the Doctor. Every tabby-cat in Sydney will be at your throat if you do.'

'Why, Mr Dilhorne,' she said, with a smile as dangerous as his own, 'I know of no one who has the right to instruct me on whom to speak with and how long I may speak to them. I choose my partners in conversation, and my friends, for myself.'

It was not quite simple defiance that she was expressing. She found that she liked talking to him. He spoke

to her as though she were another man, with no airs
either of approval or of condescension. His obliquity
pleased her, too, for he half-bowed to her again and continued their conversation as though he had not spoken
and she had not answered.

Alan Kerr was wrong about her, Tom thought. She
was not your usual fine lady and it was a pleasure to
speak with her about his many interests since she had a
good mind and was not afraid to use it. His intuition told
him that there was something wrong with her, though,
that in some strange fashion her world was awry. It was
as if she were accompanied by a shadow. A shadow that
prevented her from being as easy as she must have once
been, a shadow that set her sparking at his friend every
time she met him.

'There is one question which I should like to ask you,
Mr Dilhorne, if you would not find it offensive.'

'Oh, I rarely take offence at anything, Miss Langley.
Mostly it's a pure waste of time. But should I do so,
then the offender is sure to be told of it in no uncertain
terms.'

His bright blue eyes twinkled at her, but she could
suddenly see in him the danger of which she had been
warned. Nevertheless she ploughed on.

'Why is it that Governor Macquarie appears to favour
the Emancipists when all the respectable folk in the colony think that he is wrong to do so?'

'That is an easy question, Miss Langley. It is because
he believes that the future lies with the people who stay
here, like Dr Kerr and myself, and not with those who
come and go, many of whom are idle.'

'Like myself,' she commented wryly. 'And I am keeping you from your work, I fear.'

He made her no smooth, complimentary answer,

merely said, 'Yes, I am a busy man and time is money, you know. There is another thing that I ought to say— and with no offence taken on your part, I hope.'

'I will answer you with your own words—if you remember them,' she laughed at him, her face soft, quite unlike the virago who had repeatedly berated Alan Kerr.

'Indeed, I do. It is this. There are some of us who have suffered grievously, who lost everything when they were brought here against their will—unlike me, for I had nothing to lose—and who now have an opportunity to gain everything. Do not judge too harshly those who see you as a bright reminder of everything that they have lost and who resent you accordingly. Not all of them will be Emancipists, for there will also be those free men and women who will dislike you for possessing the beauty and intellect that they lack. Be patient with them, Miss Langley, if I may so advise you, for you are one of the fortunate in this world—and there are many in New South Wales who are not.'

Emancipist though he was, Sarah could not take offence at his frankness, since what he had said to her struck home. For the first time she began to grasp that her suffering at the hands of Charles Villiers was as nothing to that which many of those around her, including some in the charmed ranks of the Exclusives, were enduring.

'I will try to remember what you have said,' she offered him at last. She thought that he was obviously talking of Alan Kerr, and for the first time she wondered what it was that the doctor had lost—and why.

'I've been impertinent, I know,' Tom told her with his cheerful smile, 'to speak to you after this fashion, but remember this, I shall always be only too happy to be of service to you, Miss Langley.'

'Miss Sarah to you, Mr Dilhorne.'

'Miss Sarah,' he repeated, before calling over the young man to pick up the silks and trimmings that she had chosen. He made his farewell, not with a bow, but with a hand tipped to his head as though still he wore the battered felt hat in which she had first seen him.

She had made a friend, a strange friend, a man who would never be her lover, but who would treat her as fairly as though no difference of sex existed between them. And if some odd things had begun to happen to Sarah in New South Wales, this was, perhaps, the oddest of them all.

John was predictably annoyed when gossip finally reached him of Sarah's long conversation with the Emancipist to whom he had forbidden her to speak.

'Really, Sarah,' he said, anger plain in his voice, 'he cannot but think that you are encouraging him. It is neither wise nor sensible of you to consort with such as Dilhorne. Who knows how he may behave towards you if he thinks you…light?'

'What I do know,' she flung back at him, 'is that he warned me himself against talking to him, and his manner to me when we did converse was more proper than that of many gentlemen or military officers whom I have met here, or back in England.'

'And that statement merely confirms me in my opinion of your lack of judgement, Sarah. The man is an ex-felon, a thief, a ruffian—you cannot know what you are saying.'

'I know that he is the Governor's friend, as is Dr Kerr—' and why should she mention him? '—and that Lachlan Macquarie is not a fool, whatever you may think of me.'

'I only know that every person of consequence in New South Wales disagrees with him over his attitude to Dilhorne and his friend Dr Kerr—and those like them. You would do well not to offend the people among whom you have chosen to live. No gentleman will respect you if he becomes aware that you are hobnobbing with such a ruffian as Dilhorne—to say nothing of what judgement on you our military friends will pass.'

Sarah felt suffocated. It was a feeling from which she had frequently suffered since Charles's betrayal of her. To overcome it she turned angrily on her brother.

'Gentlemen!' she exclaimed. 'The military! The proper thing to do! I sometimes wonder if we know what we are talking about. Do all these fine words mean that the men who utter them treat women with respect? If I had married Charles, how long would it have been before he took a mistress? As for the military, even innocent little Lucy Middleton knows that the officers, as well as the men, take their pleasure at the houses in The Rocks. Do not look at me like that, John. You know that I am telling the truth. I shall say no more, but I do reserve the right to choose my own friends, now and in the future.'

'My only relief so far,' he returned stiffly, 'is that I am at least fortunate enough not to number Dr Kerr and Dilhorne among them. I can only hope that you will come to see the wisdom of what I have been saying.'

'Oh, let us leave it at that.' Sarah thought that she would begin to scream if this unseemly wrangle continued much longer. 'I cannot say that confining myself to proper gentlemen has been very successful in the past. At least Tom Dilhorne spares me empty compliments and fine, meaningless manners. He talks more sense than all of the beaux I have ever met. Yes, yes,' she added hastily when John began to reproach her again, 'I will not speak of him in future, but I will not promise *not* to speak to him. And that is enough. Do not ask me for more.'

'Quite so, you are determined to go your own way, I see, but do not be surprised if you find yourself left out of Sydney's social life in consequence. I wish that I had never consented to bring you with me.'

Sarah bit back yet another riposte and simply swept out of the room, wishing for the thousandth time that she had never left England. Damn Sydney, damn its social life, damn Charles Villiers and Dr Alan Kerr, too— and damn John for being such a pompous ass. Conversation with him had become impossible.

What in the world was happening to her that she should use such dreadful language even to herself? If she weren't careful, she would find herself saying these unladylike things aloud!

Chapter Three

'So the Langleys have left Government House, I hear,' said Alan Kerr, who was eating a bachelor dinner with Tom Dilhorne in Tom's home off Bridge Street.

'Yes. The Governor not only found them a house, not far from yours, through his aides, of course, but he also had it furnished and managed to conjure up a house-keeper for them into the bargain.'

'A housekeeper? However did he manage that? There's a desperate shortage of such useful creatures in the colony.'

'Indeed.' Tom drank up his port before giving a short laugh. 'Well, if I tell you that he supplied them with Corporal Hackett's widow, you'll gather that he did them no favour. On the other hand, she was probably the only woman available.'

'Mrs Hackett!' Alan nearly choked over his lamb. 'Now that I should like to see. The thought of that high-nosed fine lady, trying to keep in order a woman who has created chaos in every kitchen and drawing room of those foolish enough to employ her, has quite made my day. You know that Major Menzies threw her out of his home after she had reduced the whole household to tears? Yes, any woman who can reduce Mrs Menzies to tears is well worth knowing.'

'Now what should make you think that she'll subdue Miss Langley?'

'Come, come, Tom, you know that in the great houses in which Miss Langley lived all the real business of running a home was done behind the scenes so far as she was concerned. Here, she's living in a little two-storey villa, on top of the kitchen, the cooking and the cleaning. Yes, I can only imagine how hard she'll find it to cope with such a come-down in the world. I am still wondering what odd whim brought her here, so far from the comforts of her English life.'

It was useless to argue with him. He had taken against Sarah Langley from the first moment they had met, and God only knew if he would ever be able to change his mind about her. Tom was sure that his friend was misjudging her badly, that he was unaware of the dark shadow in which the poor creature was living. He also knew that the misjudgement arose from the circumstances of Alan's own sad past, and he could do nothing about that.

Best to say nothing, then. After all, it was likely that the Langleys' stay in the colony would be short, and then there would be nothing to provoke Alan Kerr into forgetting his better self, the self that had rescued Tom Dilhorne from the gutter, and was also fiercely maintaining the good health of Sydney by his tireless hard work.

When Sarah heard that not only had the Governor found and furnished a house for them, but had also appointed a housekeeper to look after it for her, she was overjoyed.

Her joy did not last long. Mrs Hackett was a woman with the build of a pugilist and an expression that was so sour that Sarah felt she probably only had to look at milk to make it turn. If her manner to Sarah was surly, her behaviour towards the servants, also provided by Government House, was downright cruel. Sarah remembered her introduction to them and to Mrs Hackett's malevolence...

She had been seated at her portable writing desk, trying to finish a letter to her best friend and John's sweetheart, Emily Hazeldean, when Mrs Hackett had come in to say that the servants had just arrived in a gig driven by one of the corporals with whom her late husband had served.

'The servants has come, Mam, and most unsatisfactory they are.'

Sarah put down her pen. 'Why, what is wrong with them, Mrs Hackett?'

'Sluts,' she said, balefully, 'and trollops.'

'You are speaking of the servants?'

'Who else, Mam? They're a convict and a convict's daughter, and no better than they should be. They're waiting in the kitchen for you to look at them. You said as how you would.'

She spoke as though Sarah had expressed a wish so outlandish that it scarcely needed to be discussed. Sarah was half-annoyed, half-amused by her insolence, reflecting that from her manner of speaking one might think that Mrs Hackett was the mistress and Sarah the servant!

Settling into her new home had, as Alan Kerr had supposed, taken up a great deal of her time and energy. John, of course, had left everything to her. Not only that, he had departed earlier that morning on yet another sketching expedition and had announced that he would not be back until late since he proposed to dine in the Officers' Mess again. To make matters worse, she was unable to mend her quill pen since he had inconsiderately made off, without permission, with her only sharp knife, having been unable to find his own.

The letter to Miss Emily Hazeldean would have to wait. Sarah set off for the tiny, stiflingly hot kitchen, sighing gently. What appeared to be two bundles of clothing stood waiting for her. The older and larger of the shapeless pair was introduced to her as Nellie Riley; the younger and smaller as Sukie Thwaites. They were both, it seems, untrained and their final roles as assistant cook and maid-of-all-work were to be decided in the future.

Sarah thought that she had never before seen such an unlikely pair. The Governor's aide who had done all the hiring for them had explained that, due to the shortage of women in the colony, it would be difficult to find anyone who wished to be a servant at all, let alone anyone who was trained.

Both women were wearing coarse black-and-red print frocks, gaudy shawls and heavy, clog-like shoes. Their hair was pinned up inside large sun-bonnets, which they apparently wore indoors as well as out. At Mrs Hackett's prompting they both curtsied and addressed Sarah as Mum. She was compelled to admit that Mrs Hackett had not misrepresented their unattractiveness.

She was also eager to inform Sarah of Nellie's disreputable past.

'This here girl was transported because she was a thief, and her brother with her. Best to keep an eye on the silver, Mam.'

What she did not say was that Nellie had supplemented her meagre income at the Female Factory, where

convict women were sent on arrival, by selling herself
to any man who had a penny or some little luxury to
offer her.

'If she don't please, Mam, why, you've only to say
so and we can send her back where she came from and
ask for another gal to take her place.'

Sarah had sometimes been responsible for the hiring
and firing of servants back in England, but she had never
felt the kind of revulsion that she experienced when she
contemplated returning this miserable piece of humanity
to the Factory and its cruel discipline. Sukie, however,
was a free agent, but as she was an Emancipist's daughter Mrs Hackett made it plain that her feelings were not
to be considered, either.

'I hope that you will be happy here,' Sarah said in-
adequately, aware of both the young women's sullen resentment of her for her pampered appearance, as well as
Mrs Hackett's open contempt for what she thought of as
Sarah's softness. She suddenly remembered what Tom
Dilhorne had warned her of in his shop and thought that
it was the most sensible piece of advice she had been
given since the *Pomona* had docked.

At least, back in England her life had been spent at
some distance from that of her many servants, but here,
in this tiny house, their presence would be close and
confining. Never mind, she thought, I have my painting
and drawing to occupy me, and when the weather is fine
I shall be able to ride once John has found me a suitable
horse—and perhaps a carriage.

One thing, at least, was to the good. Since setting up
house she had been so busy that she had not had time
to think about Dr Kerr, the Governor or Tom Dilhorne,
or whether or not she ought to speak to Emancipists.
Their luggage had to be unpacked, their meals overseen,

and John's comfort to be satisfied. He had no intention of looking after himself since in England he had never needed to; a highly trained staff had ministered to his every want. By contrast, in Sydney, all that they had in the way of servants were Mrs Hackett, two unwilling, untrained females and John's man, Carter.

She returned to her writing desk and tried to continue her letter to Emily.

'You would scarcely believe,' she wrote, 'how primitive we are here. All that distinguishes us from the *Pomona* is that the deck no longer heaves beneath our feet...'

She sneezed and looked around the tiny room. Dust was everywhere. Nellie Riley suddenly burst in, waving a feather mop and began to use it with great vigour—which only served to waft it around the room in a red cloud. This started Sarah sneezing again.

'Sorry, Mum,' said Nellie, looking anything but sorry. 'Mrs Hackett was telling me to begin me duties by cleaning the room since it hadn't been done for days.'

Her expression told Sarah, better than words, that the whole business of keeping clean was a complete waste of time so far as Nellie was concerned.

Sarah waved her pen at her. It was no longer fit to write with, but waving it somehow expressed her feelings.

'Good God! Is it always like this? And where does the dust come from—and why is it red?'

'Well, it's allus hot, if that's what you mean, but it's not allus as dusty as this. It's them bricks.'

'Them bricks?' asked Sarah faintly.

'And the wind. Why, Mum, when the winds' southerly the dust from the brick-fields blows across the town. It's the Governor's fault.'

This remarkable demonstration of the Governor's climatic powers intrigued Sarah. 'The Governor's fault?'

'Aye, Mum, cos he's a-building of the barracks and the hospital and they need bricks from the fields. Are ye comfortable, Mum? Can I get you anything?'

Convict she might be, but there was a frankness about Nellie's speech that interested Sarah, who was used to the servility of home. There was almost a contempt in the manner in which convicts and Emancipists alike spoke to the respectable. She knew now why Mrs Middleton had fumed to her about the speech and behaviour of the servants and shopkeepers in Sydney.

She sighed. The letter to Emily must wait. She walked to the window and looked out at the swirling red dust and the brazen sun. On the verandah opposite, not one, but two cockatoos, restless in their cages, squawked their displeasure at the world. She sympathised with them.

It was a relief when there was a knock at the door and Mrs Hackett came in with a letter for her. It was from Mrs Menzies, inviting her to a soirée at the weekend.

Later, looking back on this time, Sarah thought that her first weeks in Sydney passed like a dream. There was so much to arrange, so much to do that in the past had always been done for her. Fortunately for her peace of mind she had not encountered Dr Kerr again. He had been called, Tom Dilhorne told her, to treat a fever which was raging in Paramatta. His absence brought on such an access of high spirits that John feared that the fever had reached Sydney, or so he chose to quiz her, not knowing the true cause.

Sarah had been so busy herself that she scarcely found time to paint, although this had been the excuse she had given for undertaking this journey with John. Her father had encouraged her to develop her talent, but unlike John she had many duties that took up her time. First she had been her father's hostess, her mother having died at her birth, and then, after her father's death, she had performed the same function for her brother.

Coming to Sydney had seemed an opportunity to develop her skills since she thought that she would surely have more time to spend on herself. What she had not foreseen was that the primitive nature of life in New South Wales would create even more demands on her.

'I would never have believed it,' she told Lucy Middleton when they were upstairs in the Menzies's bedroom, inspecting themselves in a long mirror before going downstairs to enjoy the pleasures of a typical Sydney soirée. 'I spent this morning supervising the wash while Mrs Hackett went to the market to buy provisions. She had left Nellie in charge of it, but as you might guess her attitude to cleanliness is best expressed in the old adage, ''what the eye can't see the heart can't grieve over.'' She actually said to me, ''I don't know why we bother, Mum, it will only have to be done again next week. All this dusting and scrubbing don't seem natural to me.'''

Lucy adjusted a curl. 'I really can't understand why you bother with her, Sarah. Why don't you just send her back to the Female Factory?'

Sarah gave a sigh. She knew very well that Mrs Hackett would have preferred to send Nellie back to the factory soon after she had arrived in the hope that she might receive someone more suitable in return. She, on the other hand, found that although she could endure the idea of women whom she did not know being cooped up in prison, it was unthinkable that Nellie, whom she now knew, should be sent back there.

It was her free spirit, which Mrs Hackett could not crush, that Sarah found admirable, with the result that she had ended up being the laundress herself in order to ensure that Mrs Hackett's complaints could not be seen to be justified and Nellie's removal determined on. She found it impossible to try to explain this to Lucy, particularly since she found herself out of sympathy with the rest of the colonial ladies whom she had met. Their preoccupation with precedence, which she had thought to be peculiar to Mrs Middleton, turned out to be common to them all. Being a member of the highest society in England, she found little to choose between all those beneath her in rank.

So she changed the subject of Nellie and Mrs Hackett and commented on Sydney's fixation with precedence and propriety instead.

'You see, Sarah,' said Lucy while she was rearranging the flowers in Sarah's hair, 'you're so grand yourself that you don't understand the differences that lie between a clerk in the Government offices and one of the shopkeepers. What's worse, you're so sure of yourself that you can afford to talk to Tom Dilhorne and Will French, even though they're Emancipists—*and* do the wash, as well. You don't fear that you're lowering yourself, as Mama does. And it's no good saying Pish and Tush to me, either, that's the truth.'

'I like it when you scold me,' said Sarah. 'It's like being scolded by a kitten. No one else, apart from John, ever reprimands me.' Which wasn't strictly true, because Tom Dilhorne had said something similar to her the other day.

'Oh, you may laugh,' replied Lucy, 'but you know that you wouldn't marry any of them. Only one of your own kind.'

She stopped and looked thoughtfully at Sarah. 'I don't know, though. There's a wildness about you sometimes. Look at the way you spoke to Dr Kerr in Hyde Park.'

'Oh, Dr Kerr.' Sarah shrugged. 'Let us not speak of Dr Kerr. Forgive me, Lucy, for saying this, but you amaze me sometimes—you look as though you haven't an idea in your head—and then...' and she shrugged again.

'I know—that's what Mama and the men think, that I'm stupid. It's better that way, Sarah. You don't annoy them—and you can always get what you want if they believe that you're just a dear little kitten.'

Sarah nodded. 'I know who is going to make a good marriage, thinking like that, Lucy. That is, if you don't meet someone devastatingly handsome, and quite worthless, and fall head over heels in love with him. I don't advise you to do that.'

Her tone was so bitter that Lucy looked at her curiously—but said nothing.

'Come on, my love,' Sarah said at last, slipping her hand round Lucy's waist. 'Downstairs with you so that we can try to find these paragons whom we ought to marry.'

They met Pat Ramsey in the little hall. Lucy moved away, probably to try to find Frank Wright, leaving Sarah to entertain Pat again.

'Your servant, Miss Langley. No Emancipists here to amuse you tonight, hey?'

Sarah was annoyed to discover that her friendship with Tom was the subject of gossip, but she refused to betray her feelings.

'I'm sure, Captain Ramsey, that Mrs Menzies's guest list is composed of only the best in Sydney society.'

He roasted her gently. 'Ah, but what is the best, Miss

Langley? The latest *on dit*, from Colonel O'Connell, no less, is that the Governor is thinking of making magistrates of some of the Emancipists. Imagine Dilhorne and Kerr as magistrates, what could be more respectable than that? O'Connell is nearly having apoplexy at the very thought. Now you, I suppose, would approve of at least one of my two names, if not the other.'

Sarah refused to be drawn. 'Tedious stuff, Captain Ramsey—and why should you suppose any such thing? For all you know, I might be willing to support one of the aborigines as a magistrate. It might be what the colony deserves.'

Pat gave a shout of laughter that penetrated into the Menzies's drawing room and turned heads there. 'Oh, Miss Langley, you quiz me cruelly. You make me realise that Sydney's gain is London's loss. Come, take my arm—my stay tonight will be longer than usual for your sake alone, I promise you.'

She took his arm, but her smile for him was cold. 'For my sake, Captain Ramsey? Pray do not put yourself out for my sake.'

He bowed to her again before they entered to make their salutations to the Major and his wife. 'If not for you, Miss Langley, then for no one.'

Sarah forbore to tell him how much such idle badinage bored her. She had heard sufficient of it from Charles to sicken her of it forever, but she supposed that it was the usual way in which men spoke to women, and she must endure it or earn the title of a shrew.

The assembled guests chattered and gossiped for a short time before the main event of the evening—which was a short concert—began, and Sarah found herself being compelled to listen to a great deal of the kind of fustian which Pat had been serving up to her. Not only that, much of the gossip was again about the Emancipists and their goings-on. It seemed that one of Sydney's select gentlemen's clubs—if not the most select—had actually asked Tom Dilhorne to become a member. Worse than that, he had actually accepted their invitation. It became the evening's major topic of conversation.

'I don't believe it', 'It can't be true' and 'Whatever next!' were only a few of the comments that flew round the room. 'They've only invited him because they want to get a finger in his financial pies,' said one knowledgeable old fellow who worked at Government House.

'Ah, but you haven't heard the best part of the story— which also happens to be true,' said Frank Wright. 'You remember Fred Waring?'

Heads nodded. Yes, everyone remembered Fred Waring, the drunken remittance man of good family who had been sacked from his poor post as a Government clerk for drunkenness and incompetence.

'It seems that when Fred turned up and found Dilhorne present by invitation of the committee he made a great scene and said that if Dilhorne, who was nothing but a rascally Emancipist, had been admitted as a member, he would resign and leave immediately. The chairman told him that it was his choice since Dilhorne was staying, so Waring walked out.'

'There's not a decent house in Sydney that will receive him,' Sarah heard one stout matron say. 'And now he's not even got the club to attend. Is his daughter here tonight?'

Frank Wright looked around. 'I don't think so. Only the Middletons receive her these days and not very often, I believe.'

'Do you know his daughter?' Sarah whispered to Lucy who was, as usual, being squired by Frank.

'Who? Oh, you mean little Hester Waring. Not that she's so very little, but she's a poor shy creature, about my age, quite plain. They say that Fred ill treats her. Mama and Papa came across them, by chance, the other night when they were returning home after visiting Colonel O'Connell. He was quite drunk. Hester was trying to help him along and he was cursing her. Now Mama says that she won't have her in the house, either. She could be setting a bad example for me to follow. Oh, look, Mama is signalling to me that the concert is about to begin and I am the first performer.'

Poor Hester Waring, indeed, thought Sarah, and then forgot her. Lucy was opening the evening's bill of fare by singing two old Scots ballads, after which Captain Parker was to delight the audience with some folk songs.

'He has a pleasant baritone voice,' Lucy had told Sarah. The next turn was to be Sarah's: she was to play a short piano piece and then sing some of the songs that had been all the fashion when she had left London.

All in all, once the gossip about the Emancipists had been disposed of, it had been one of the more pleasant evenings that Sarah had spent since setting foot in Sydney. She was flattered by the young officers, and deferred to by most of the matrons and their husbands, even if they did deplore her taste for talking to such undesirables as Tom Dilhorne and Will French. Besides, her brother was a fine figure of a man, and filthy rich, too. Who knows, given a bit of luck he might even decide to take one of their daughters for a wife before he returned home again.

Of course, Sarah soon found that this sense of well-being was too good to last long. Two days after the party she was sitting in the drawing room, readying herself to do some painting, when she heard violent screaming coming from the kitchen.

She put down her unopened portfolio and ran to discover what in the world could be the matter. Before she reached the door, Nellie flung it open.

'Oh, Mum, it's poor Sukie, that old bitch Hackett was downright careless with the kettle and managed to pour boiling water all down Sukie's arm. It's in a right mess.'

Sarah pushed past the distraught girl into the kitchen to find that she was speaking no less than the truth. Sukie, now sobbing gently, was seated in a Windsor chair while Mrs Hackett, ignoring the scarlet ruin of her forearm, and making no attempt to care for it, was berating her at the top of her voice.

'You careless fool,' she was roaring, 'do you never look where you're going? Now you won't be fit to work for a least a week. I've a good mind to turn you off immediately.'

Sukie's sobs redoubled and Nellie shrieked, 'It weren't her fault. 'Twas yours, you old cow.'

Sarah banged a fist on the table.

'Be quiet, all of you. Whose fault it was is of no account, Mrs Hackett. May I also remind you that it is I who turn off servants in this house, not you. At the moment Sukie's welfare is all that matters. Allow me to look at your arm, Sukie. No, don't wince, I shan't touch it.'

Mrs Hackett opened her mouth to defend herself, but Sarah banged the table again, raising her own voice this time. 'Be silent, Mrs Hackett, while I examine Sukie's arm.'

This served to quell the housekeeper, but her malevolent glare was now for the mistress and not the maid. Sarah took no notice of her, particularly when she discovered that Sukie's arm was so badly scalded that she needed the assistance of a doctor.

She looked up at Nellie. 'Is Carter at home—or did he go out with Mr John?'

'At home, Mum—doing some carpentry in the shed at the back.'

'Good, go and tell him what has happened and ask him to run round to Dr Kerr and see if he is able to visit us immediately. I understand that he has returned from Paramatta.'

'Yes, Mum,' and Nellie lumbered off to find Carter, who, she told herself fiercely, wouldn't be best pleased to hear that the old bitch had hurt the girl he had been sparking at recently. Divested of her weird clothing and attired in one of Sarah's old cotton dresses, Sukie had begun to blossom—until this latest mishap had occurred.

'Make yourself useful, Mrs Hackett,' Sarah said sharply, 'and brew us some tea. Drinking it might help poor Sukie to feel a little better.'

She had never felt herself to be so helpless before. She had not the slightest notion of how to treat the dreadful burn, which was beginning to weep gently, so that when the kitchen door opened and Alan Kerr, followed by Carter, came in, carrying his bag, she sprang to her feet to greet him.

'Oh, I am so happy to learn that Carter found you so quickly. Poor Sukie really does need some instant attention. There has been an accident in the kitchen, and as a result boiling water was poured over her forearm.'

Alan Kerr stared at the little scene. At Sarah, who had now seated herself at the kitchen table, her cup of tea before her, at Nellie, holding a cup for Sukie to drink from, and at Mrs Hackett, standing belligerent, arms akimbo, before the kitchen range, glaring her dislike at everyone, including him.

He put his bag down and pulled up a kitchen chair so that he was able to sit by poor Sukie and inspect her arm most carefully before deciding how to treat it. Even so, he still found time to notice that Miss Sarah Langley seemed to be in much finer fettle than usual. She finished drinking her tea before rising and coming over to watch him treat Sukie.

I refuse to stand here helpless, thought Sarah firmly. Mrs Hackett is apparently useless in an emergency, and Nellie would doubtless be little better. I'm sure that he would welcome some assistance, even from me.

'Doctor Kerr,' she ventured, 'if there is anything I may do to help you, pray tell me.'

'Indeed, I will,' he said, without looking up. 'I usually have a young assistant with me, but he is out tending a poor old lady who does not need medical care but whom a little nursing will benefit. If you will pick up my bag, put it on the table and open it, you will find inside it a large blue bottle, some scraps of cotton wadding, bandages, and a pair of scissors. Hand me the bottle and the cotton, and have the bandages and the scissors ready to pass to me when I ask for them.'

Sukie gave a groan on hearing the word scissors. Doctor Kerr said kindly to her while he poured something from the bottle on to the cotton. 'Don't be frightened, Sukie, I don't propose to cut you with the scissors, only some of the wadding and the right length of bandage.'

He worked patiently on in silence, Sukie occasionally moaning a little. After a moment Mrs Hackett snorted. Sarah looked across at her and said, as pleasantly as she could, 'I would be grateful, Mrs Hackett, if you would put a kettle on to boil again. I don't think that Dr Kerr will need any hot water in his treatment of Sukie, but I'm sure that he would be grateful for a cup of tea when he has finished.'

The woman tossed her head, but did as she was bid. Alan Kerr, on hearing this little interchange, smiled to himself, remembering his conversation with Tom Dilhorne. Well, he was seeing Miss Sarah Langley in action against Mrs Hackett and it was quite plain who was the victor. Miss Langley was not going to be driven to tears by the old battle-axe. Not only that, when he said, somewhat peremptorily, 'Bandages!', she was prompt to hand them over, and then the scissors, after another brusque command.

Finally he had finished. Sukie's poor arm had been carefully dressed and her pain relieved a little in consequence. Mrs Hackett needed yet another order from Sarah: this time to make the tea, and offer Dr Kerr some biscuits, which she did with an ill grace. While he waited he held Sukie's hand and tried to comfort her.

'It looks worse than it is,' he said, 'but it is a very nasty scald and you are not to use that arm until I have seen you again in a few days' time. I am leaving Miss Langley a small bottle of laudanum for you to take a few drops at night so that the pain does not prevent you from sleeping. I'm sure she will see the necessity for you to rest until the arm is healed.'

'Indeed,' said Sarah, and then sternly to her housekeeper, 'You heard that, Mrs Hackett—Sukie is to rest until Dr Kerr says that she is fit to work again.'

'Doubtless you'll send her back home for them to look after her,' Mrs Hackett bit back.

'No.' Sarah's voice was as cold as it was firm. 'She sustained her injury here, and here she will be looked after—be in no doubt of that.'

Alan Kerr nearly choked over his cup of tea at the
sight and sound of Miss Sarah Langley treating the town
dragon to the same dismissive manner that she had employed with him. His feelings for her were growing into
a strange blend of admiration and dislike—mixed with
something else which he tried to thrust to the back of
his mind. It would never do for him to begin to feel
anything like lust—yes, that was what it must be, lust—
for a woman so far above him in station.

Sarah was also seeing a new side to him. His care and
consideration for Sukie had been exemplary. He had insisted that she be given another cup of tea—'with plenty
of sugar, mind'—and before he left had given Sarah and
Mrs Hackett instructions about what to do if the pain
increased, or a fever developed.

'You are to send for me at once, at any hour of the
day or night, if you are worried about her condition,' he
ended, immediately before leaving them.

'Well,' said Mrs Hackett when the door shut behind
him, 'I'm glad to see the back of him. It's a great pity
that decent people have to depend for their doctoring on
an Emancipist.'

'That will be quite enough,' said Sarah, tired of the
woman's unpleasantness. 'He dealt with poor Sukie's
scald most efficiently and that is all that matters, not
what label he has been given. Nellie, you must look after
Sukie while I make arrangements for a temporary servant to take her place. If she feels faint, help her up to
bed. If she can't walk, then Carter will be able to carry
her.'

She was surprising even herself, she thought. If she
had been at home, back in England, she would never
even have known that a servant had been scalded, let

alone have helped with her treatment and then been responsible for replacing her!

Not only that, but she was daily performing tasks that other people had done for her. She was beginning to find pleasure in doing them and also that she had an unsuspected talent for organising the work of the house. One drawback, however, was that all these new duties were preventing her from having the time to paint the strange scenery that lay all around her.

After Sukie's replacement has arrived, she promised herself, she would try to remedy that by persuading Lucy to go with her on some afternoon excursions to the more picturesque parts of Sydney. It would be pleasant to spend an afternoon without having Mrs Hackett constantly troubling her with some problem which she should have been able to solve herself.

Suddenly life in Sydney seemed more bearable to her—and why should that be? Who would have thought that handing the surly Dr Kerr bandages and scissors, and looking after Sukie and Nellie's welfare in the face of Mrs Hackett's unspoken antagonism, would make her feel so fulfilled?

Stranger still, who would have thought that she would find herself defending Dr Kerr from Mrs Hackett's unpleasant attempts to demean him?

Chapter Four

It was not the week-end, but the following week before Sarah could make one of the expeditions which she had promised herself. Sukie's arm was healing nicely, but she was not yet ready to work again. Unfortunately their new girl justified Mrs Hackett's daily complaints about her, but Sarah refused to send her back since there was no reason to believe that her replacement would be any better. Sarah, indeed, was beginning to think that they had been lucky to have Nellie and Sukie assigned to them, after she had listened to many of the other Sydney ladies moan about their own servants.

She had decided to walk towards the point, overlooking Cockle Bay, where she could draw the sea, the pines and the everlasting sky. She had hoped to have Carter with her, but John had taken him off into the bush early that morning to finish a picture which he had been painting for some time. Since she was not going very far from the edge of the town and was impatient to be off, she decided that she would be safe enough—and would be happier—on her own. Only Sukie could have gone with her and the heat of the day would have been too much for her in her weakened state.

She walked briskly down the unmade road outside their home, passing on the way a convict gang who were busy paving it. They were dressed in coarse canvas marked with a variety of arrows showing that it was drawn from Government stores. They stared boldly at her when she walked by them without an escort. One nudged another and their laughter followed her until she turned the corner.

The first time she had seen them she had been shocked, but familiarity bred contempt, and now she scarcely noted their presence. What did distress her were the aborigines she saw. They bore little resemblance either to the noble savage of Rousseau, or to the drawings in the folios that had so entranced John and herself. They sat about, half-naked, in the streets, occasionally clowning to entertain those few who might throw them money to buy the drink that degraded them further.

John had told her that they had met some in the bush who looked and behaved like the drawings they had seen back in England, and he could only conclude that it was living alongside their new European masters which had damaged them. What troubled her most was their apparent indifference to the life going on around them.

Nevertheless she walked merrily along, whistling quietly to herself, a low habit that she had learned from one of the grooms back home and had earned her reprimands from her father when she had indulged in it as a child. She wondered why she was doing it, and concluded that it was the result of a kind of mindless happiness brought on by the freedom of the trip that she was taking, the balmy weather and the chores which she had left behind.

She found a natural seat among the rocks on the cliff's edge overlooking the sea, where the trees and bushes behind her offered her a little shade. She loosened the fichu around her neck, and since she was alone, she lifted her skirts to calf length in order to enjoy the breeze which came off the sea.

The scene before her came to life on the paper, and Sarah entered the almost trance-like state that accompanied her practice of the art she loved best in the world. So it was, she later understood, that she did not see or hear the arrival on this idyllic scene of what was to spoil it for her forever, so that she could never again pass it without a shudder.

Her first intimation of danger came with a foul smell accompanied by a low laugh. Startled, she half-turned to see that behind her had crept up a Caliban-like figure, half-naked, half-dressed like a scarecrow in a parody of a gentleman of fashion. He held a black bottle in his hand from which he drank as he staggered towards her. A final grotesque touch was a battered beaver hat which he wore on his filthy curls.

His pleasure on seeing her was unfeigned, but when he spoke his accent was so broad that it was almost impossible for Sarah to understand him. Of his intention, however, there was no doubt. He advanced on her, stopping once to call behind him, when, to her further dismay, another half-drunken, scantily clad figure emerged from the trees to leer at her.

Sarah rose and smoothed down her skirts, which seemed to be revealingly tight and scanty before these nightmare apparitions. So far the only sinister characters whom she had seen had been safely confined in irons, or under the escort of soldiers. She looked around her for help, but could see none.

'I must go,' she said, shakily, 'I am expected back.' Even to her own ears this sounded like a thin and unreal response, and so it seemed to Caliban who continued to stagger towards her.

'Stay a while, my pretty. Jem and me can entertain you.' His grin was wide and cruel.

'No, no, I really must go.'

This parody of drawing-room conversation sounded ridiculous, even to Sarah, and, not surprisingly, had no effect on her tormentor who continued his steady advance on her, throwing away his bottle when he drew nearer. She could not back away from him since the cliff edge was behind her, and his companion had cut off her only other line of escape.

Finally he reached Sarah and caught her by the shoulders, swinging her round and throwing her towards Jem. 'Let's play, my pretty dear. Here, you have her, but you're not to keep her, mind.'

She landed in Jem's arms and when he caught her he kissed her full on the lips. The smell of gin on his foul breath was strong and his whiskered face scraped her soft cheek. Lost between fear and revulsion, choking, Sarah tore her face away. Her lips were already bleeding.

'You'll pay dearly for this,' she cried, abandoning all pretence that she had any control over the dreadful situation in which she found herself.

'Not us, missy.' Jem grinned. 'What makes you think that you will tell anyone, dearie?'

He loosened his grip, pushing her a little away from him so that he might pull at her hair which had fallen, loose, about her shoulders.

'A right pretty doxy for us, eh, Charlie?'

He ran his eyes over her while she struggled to free herself after he had caught her again, secure in the knowledge that she could not escape him. Nevertheless, lost in a torment of fear and shame, she kicked his shins, broke away from him, and tried to run towards Sydney. Was it really possible that she was going to be attacked, ravished and killed on this barbarous coast so far from home and friends?

'Oh, God,' she cried. 'Help me! Help me!'

Jem, laughing, allowed her to run a few steps towards the town before he caught her again, around the waist. He gripped her by her streaming hair and kissed her brutally, one hand roving over her body. 'Stay still, my dearie. Old Jem'll pleasure you right enough, after Charlie has had a go at you first. Here, Charlie, you have her again, but not for good, mind,' and he threw her back to his mate with such force that Sarah lost her balance and landed in the dirt.

Charlie pulled her to her feet. She pushed him back, panting, 'My brother is rich. He'll reward you well if you take me home.'

'Take you home? Now, why should we do that? Your filthy money's no use to us in the bush. No, me duck. You can pleasure us here and now, and then the fish can have you.'

He pulled her to him: his intention was unmistakable. Sarah tried to fight him off, but in vain, and with Jem cheering him on, he began to bear her to the ground, shouting, 'Oh, I likes a lass of spirit!'

It was hopeless: death and dishonour now seemed inevitable and a great sob burst from Sarah's throat...

Doctor Alan Kerr had been visiting a shanty in The Rocks where a ragged Emancipist, who had been dividing his time between honest work and thieving, needed treatment for a leg broken in an attempt to burgle one of the poorer grog shops that existed only to serve such outcasts from society as he was. He had been part of a

gang that had dragged him home rather than leave him
for the watch to find lest he inform on them.

Alan had a good idea of how the fellow's injury had
come about, but he set his leg, left him some laudanum
and took as payment a bottle of the grog, which the gang
had liberated after the accident. After that he decided to
ride home, having been on duty since sun-up when he
had been called out to assist in a difficult birth.

He was travelling along the cliff path towards Sydney
when, on nearing Cockle Bay, he heard the sound of
shouting voices and laughter. He turned a corner to see
before him two men and a struggling woman whom they
were undoubtedly attacking. He had no doubt about what
was happening—or was about to happen.

He swore to himself, spurred his horse, and charged
at the men.

Jem and Charlie were so intent on their pleasure that
they were not aware that a man on horseback was arriving until it was too late for them to take any evasive
action.

Sarah suddenly found herself sprawled on her back,
abandoned involuntarily when the oncoming rider's
whip descended on Charlie's head to the cry of, 'Let go
of her, damn you!'

For a moment the watching Jem was stunned into im-
mobility, and then, with an incomprehensible shout, he
fled back down the path by which he had come. Charlie,
however, although half-stunned, sprang forward and,
shouting abuse, tried to pull the rider from his horse, but
was prevented by another blow from Alan's whip which
sent him, unconscious, to the ground on the very spot
where Sarah had lain a moment earlier.

She had scrambled away, pulling her dress down, and
vainly trying to pin up her fallen hair. She turned to her

rescuer, panting at him, 'Thank God, thank God that you arrived in time. They meant…they meant…' She ran out of breath.

'I know what they meant,' said Alan Kerr grimly, shocked that it was Sarah Langley whom he had rescued in this outlandish spot. What the devil did she think that she was doing here, and alone?

For the first time Sarah grasped that it was Dr Kerr, of all people, who was her saviour; trembling and fearing to fall, she stretched out her hands to him, only to hear him say brusquely after he had dismounted from his horse, 'Pull yourself together, Miss Langley. You are quite safe now.'

The knowledge that it was Dr Kerr who had found her in this condition and had rescued her from dishonour and death increased her misery, rather than lessen it. Whatever would he think of her now?

Mute and still shaking, she picked up her fichu and tried to fasten it around her neck, something which her trembling hands found difficult. Alan walked over to where the half-conscious Charlie lay and, pulling him to his feet, began slapping him into awareness.

Numbly, she watched while Alan, shaken himself by what he had seen when he had come upon her desperate struggle, finally brought Charlie to his senses and methodically began to beat him with his whip, punctuating the blows with the statement that this would have to serve as punishment since he had no intention of exposing Miss Langley to the shame of a trial in which her ordeal at his hands would have been revealed.

Sarah, now huddled on a rock, her portfolio in her hands, said faintly, 'Pray stop, Dr Kerr, I cannot bear this. After all, you did prevent the worst.'

On hearing this, Alan gave her attacker one last blow

before he threw down his whip, and turned his attention to Sarah. Charlie, relieved that he was not to be hauled before the beak and then summarily hanged, ran off towards the bush, lest worse befall him.

The anger and fear that he might have been too late, which Alan Kerr had experienced when he found her being assaulted, now spilled out over Sarah herself.

'Oh, you may say stop now, Miss Langley, now that you have been rescued, but what, in God's name, prevailed on you to go running around the wilderness exposing yourself to the riff-raff of The Rocks?' His angry gaze swept over her. 'And in the most provocative clothing, too. Have you no common sense? Where is your brother—or his man—who ought to be here guarding you?'

Whatever happened she must not cry! She would not, must not, give him that satisfaction. She might owe him everything, but she did not need to be so addressed. In her misery and distress she forgot that while she might have thanked God for her delivery she had not properly thanked Alan. More than that, she had no idea that relief at her narrow escape was fuelling his anger.

'I forgot,' she said, lifting her head proudly, 'I forgot that I was not at home in England, but was in this barbarous country. I shall not forget again.'

She turned away, to pick up her scattered painting materials: it was almost as though she were dismissing him.

Alan barked at her back, 'Good God, madam, you surely don't expect me to leave you here to find your own way home after this? Come, let me help you up on to my horse immediately. You must overcome your dislike for me long enough to allow me to see you safely back home. The two whom I have driven away are not the only ones around here who prey on helpless women.'

Sarah felt as though she were living in a dream—or rather in a nightmare. In an almost trance-like state she allowed him to help her up into the big grey's saddle so that he could lead his horse to the Langleys' home. Slowly, she began to recover from the mental paralysis caused by the attack, becoming sadly aware of her dirt-streaked face and torn and grimy clothing.

Luckily they met few people on the way back but, to her horror, when they neared her home she saw that John was outside, remonstrating with Mrs Hackett who stood, stiff with righteous anger, at the front door.

He ran to meet them, saying, 'Thank God that you are safe. I have just learned from Mrs Hackett that you went out on your own, without any attendant. Whatever could have possessed you to do such a thing?'

He took a harder look at her. 'Good God, Sarah, is it possible that you have been attacked?'

Before Sarah could speak Alan answered him. 'Yes. I am happy to inform you she has come to no harm, but her common sense ought to have told her that she should not have gone wandering around the cliffs above Cockle Bay. She appears to be stupidly unaware that she now no longer lives among the tame peasantry of the Hampshire countryside. Fortunately I came upon them before the rogues who were attacking her had done more than give her a severe fright.'

His voice was dryer and harsher than Sarah had ever heard it before. He speaks as though I were asking to be attacked, she thought resentfully. The tears, which never seemed to be far away in Dr Kerr's presence, were threatening to fall—but she would not let them, never.

John Langley was reassured by Alan's calm authority.

'You are not hurt then, my dear.' It was more of a statement than a question. He turned to Alan again. 'Do I understand that I have to thank you for saving Sarah from physical assault—or worse?'

This time Sarah forestalled Alan. 'You are correct, John. I owe him my life—and my honour—and I have not even thanked him properly yet. If you will let me down, I will do so.'

What an absurd figure I must cut, she thought when she finally stood on firm ground again. She turned her dirty face towards Dr Kerr.

'I know that you think me an idiotish creature who goes cavorting idly around the countryside, a fine lady who should not even visit New South Wales, and deserves to be attacked for her folly. But I owe you more than I can ever thank you for.' To her horror she was so near to tears that her voice faltered.

'No more of that,' she said, regaining her self-control. 'Perhaps, one day, we might meet and speak without quarrelling. And now, I must go in and try to mend my ruined self.'

She bowed to Dr Kerr and walked slowly into the house, bedraggled but gallant, with her head high and her gait steady.

Alan, listening to John Langley's thanks, looked after her. He did not insult Sarah's brother by saying that he had done nothing, nor did he seek to exaggerate his rescue of her.

He heard John out in silence and then said gravely, 'I must inform you that I think that your sister may feel that, because of the antagonism which lies between us, I was overly harsh in my treatment of her after the attack. I was harsh at first out of the shock of discovering that it was she who was being attacked.

'I must also inform you that I have treated many women who have been assaulted thus and I have invariably found that to be too sympathetic may drive them into hysteria and later into despair. It may seem cruel, but it is the right—and the only—thing to do in these cases since there is no medicine which might help them. It pains me to have to be so hard but needs must, I fear. Fortunately your sister possesses a resilient character which responds to firm treatment. I hope that I did not come on too strong with her, but she rallied rapidly and showed no signs of falling into the vapours.'

He added, a little wryly, 'On the contrary, she was so busy being angry with me that she had less time to refine on what had so nearly happened to her—which, all things considered was, medically, a good thing.'

John grasped him by the hand. 'Yes, she is a strong-willed creature, that I will allow. And you, you took no hurt yourself, I trust?'

'None, but I must warn you that your sister may show some adverse reactions to her unfortunate experience. You must watch her carefully and send for me if her spirits seem unduly low.'

He refused John's offer of a glass of sherry. 'No, I will not come in, thank you, Langley. Make sure that your sister has a proper escort in future. Send your man Carter round to my surgery and I will give him a cordial that will help her to sleep.'

He brushed aside any further thanks. John watched him ride away and could only think that it was a pity that the man was an Emancipist—he deserved better—and that Sarah had taken him in such dislike. He understood why Governor Macquarie respected Kerr, not only as a doctor, but as a man. There were many worse back in England who had not suffered transportation and he resolved to find out what misfortune had brought him to Sydney.

Sarah lay in bed, covered only by a thin sheet, her brain and body both burning. John had come in a moment ago with a glass containing a cordial that Dr Kerr had sent to soothe her. There had not yet been time for it to work, only for the sickly taste to add further to her bodily discomfort. But this was as nothing to her mental agony.

Mixed up with her memories of the afternoon, and her encounters with Alan Kerr, were those of her last six months before she had left England. It was as though they had been a prologue to all that had happened to her since she had set foot in New South Wales. Prominent among them were her recollections of Charles Villiers, of whom she had resolutely refused to think ever since she had left England. The attack, however, had broken down the barriers she had erected and she sank into a reverie in which the dreadful present gave way to the hurtful past.

She had met Charles at a dinner given by their neighbours in Hampshire. Their daughter, Emily, her best friend, had arranged for her to sit by him. 'I'm sure that you are going to like him,' she had said earlier. He turned out to be charming as well as handsome. From the crown of his neat fair head to the heels of his well-polished shoes he was all that a gentleman should be, turned out *à point*, but not overdone: Brummell himself would have approved of him. He was well read. His conversation was just the right mixture of chaff and sense, and his attention to Sarah was flattering without being fulsome. What was better than best was that he seemed to be as taken by Sarah as she was by him.

Although he was old Lord Amborough's nephew and heir he made no secret of his relative poverty. Amborough had little beside his shabby mansion and some bare acres to leave him, but Charles had a minor sinecure in the Foreign Office, and an income from his late mother's estate which, while not large, was sufficient to keep him in reasonable comfort. None of this added up to wealth. His modesty about himself and his prospects was not the least of his charms. John liked him, too, which completed Sarah's pleasure.

For several months Sarah and Charles contrived to be together as much as possible, so no one was surprised when, one bright spring day, he proposed to her and was eagerly accepted. The only fly in the ointment was an overheard comment about Charles having hooked his heiress at last, but Sarah put that down to the jealousy of a disappointed suitor.

All that happy summer they enjoyed themselves while the lawyers began their legal dance over the marriage settlement, but bit by bit, as time went on, the pleasure in his company that Sarah had originally felt slowly diminished. Charles, she found, did not entirely approve of her painting. He hinted that when she became Lady Amborough there would be more important things for her to do. Exactly what they would be, he never said.

Her high spirits, which had seemed so charming to Charles before they were betrothed, did not seem quite so attractive when they conflicted with his somewhat conventional view of life. He expected her to agree with all he said, without any discussion—which he called argument and disliked.

Perhaps none of this would have mattered had not John and Sarah's lawyers insisted on protecting Sarah's rights quite so energetically when drawing up the marriage settlement. Charles's financial situation turned out to be rather poorer than he had claimed: he had not been entirely frank with either his own, or Sarah's, advisers and Sarah's own wealth was such that her lawyers felt bound to protect her. Charles made his resentment plain, casting a further cloud over her happiness.

Matters might yet have been mended, but at this juncture they found themselves staying with a distant cousin of Charles at a house party in Norfolk. Sarah was never to forget that week. She found Charles's cousin inimical, the other guests boring, the house cold and draughty and the food deplorable. To make matters worse, she contracted a heavy cold and was confined to her bed with a high temperature, leaving Charles to his own devices.

One of the guests was a rather plain young woman named Caroline Wharton. She had attached herself to Sarah and was fond of making comments, which Sarah realised afterwards were unpleasantly barbed.

'I envy you, Miss Langley, you have such determined opinions,' she said one afternoon. 'Now I find it difficult to make up my mind…' and she drifted away down the room where she could be heard plaintively asking Charles's opinion of Tom Moore's latest poem.

'I don't like her,' said Sarah's friend Emily Hazeldean. 'She's like a leech where you are concerned and she positively fawns on Charles.'

'Oh,' said Sarah carelessly, secure in Charles's affection, 'she's harmless, poor thing.' Words that she was later to recall with a pang.

Most shared Emily's opinion, though. Sarah discovered that Caroline was enormously wealthy, but of no birth at all, and it was rumoured that she was hunting for a husband and a title.

Sarah recovered from her malaise to come downstairs

to find Charles hanging on Caroline's every word. He explained apologetically, for explanation was needed, that he felt sorry for her, and in Sarah's absence wished to make her a little happy. Sarah laughed, complimented him on his kindness to her friend and forgot the matter.

Even when, back in London, Charles cancelled several engagements with her at short notice, and John had told her, quietly, that on one particular day when he had cried off, John had seen him in Hyde Park, squiring Caroline, Sarah had replied easily, and, as she later understood, blindly, 'Oh, I know about that. Charles is too kind.'

The legal formalities dragged on and the wedding day drew no nearer. Charles's caresses, which had at first possessed an ardency which faintly frightened Sarah, now diminished. Her half-awakened senses resented this sudden cessation, and she became a little irritable.

One afternoon, reading, for painting had become unattractive to her in the face of Charles's disapproval, she heard the doorbell ring and Charles was announced. She remembered that it had been raining and his hair was damp. The new dark fashions suited his blond beauty and he had never looked so handsome. Her pleasure at seeing him for the first time in several days was unfeigned.

'Pray sit down, my dear. Today has been a dead bore: your arrival has brightened it for me.'

To her astonishment he refused. 'Thank you, no, I prefer to stand.' His manner was constrained and abrupt. 'What I am going to say to you is very difficult for me, but it is important for both of us.'

'Yes?' she queried, somewhat puzzled. Even then she had no notion of what he was going to say. The memory of her innocence was so painful to her that even now, over a year later and thousands of miles away, she writhed as she recalled it.

'I think that you will agree with me that we have made a grave mistake.'

'A grave mistake,' she echoed, mystified.

'There is not that between us which would make for a satisfactory marriage. Be honest, Sarah, you must know that what I am saying is true.'

'No, you be honest, Charles,' she flashed back at him. 'What are you trying to say? Until this minute I thought that we were happy together. I know that the lawyers have been making trouble, but John has assured me that the matter has now been settled.'

Charles assumed an expression of great virtue. 'This has nothing to do with the lawyers, Sarah. It's the two of us. The first false glow of our affair has died away. I honestly believe that we would be better apart. As friends, if you like, but not married.'

This cannot be happening, she thought wildly. Who is this stranger who has taken Charles's place and is saying these things?

'You can't mean this,' she said, her face drained of colour and her whole body trembling as though she had suddenly been afflicted by an ague. Even to herself she sounded childish and futile. 'Why, only last week you assured me how happy we were together.'

His expression grew even more noble. 'I was trying to spare you, Sarah, and trying to convince myself that we could enjoy a successful marriage. But I was wrong. I think that you would be better off with someone who shared more of your interests.'

'My painting,' she said bitterly. 'It's my painting, isn't it? Or is that only an excuse? For what, Charles, for what?' If only he didn't look so insufferably noble, as though he were somehow conferring a favour on me.

He did not answer her directly, simply said. 'If you promise to release me, Sarah, I would say that the break was at your bidding. No discredit would rebound upon you.'

'But you are jilting me.' Sarah came out with the horrid word at last. 'And everyone will know the truth, whatever you say. I have been besotted with you and you have been avoiding me. Why, Charles, why?'

Something in his face, some memory, some half-heard comments that she had refused to acknowledge, brought the truth home to her in a sudden blinding flash.

'It's Caroline Wharton, isn't it?' Her voice rose. 'Isn't it, Charles?'

His face told her everything. She whirled away from him, trying not to cry. 'Oh, go to her. Get out of my sight. Be friends! Friends! I never wish to see you again. You disgust me. I disgust myself. Say what you please, but go—at once.'

She had run from the room. It was at an end. He had gone. He had left her for Caroline who was richer, more biddable and would do everything he wished so long as she ended life as Lady Amborough. She was Sarah Langley, spinster, rejected and found wanting, the butt of gossip and smiling behind hands. The unpalatable truth, that he had left her, was plain to all who knew them. Her love for him had been so openly expressed, and his sudden preference for Caroline so obvious to all but herself, that there was no deceiving society.

Now, here in this barbarous country she had narrowly escaped being soiled goods into the bargain. Why, even Alan Kerr would have rejected her if Jem and Charlie had had their way with her.

Gradually the cordial did its work and she fell into a troubled sleep. Her last thoughts were that there was tomorrow to live through and John and Dr Kerr to see again.

For several days Sarah remained in her room. Dr Kerr visited her and his manner towards her was strangely gentle. She thought ruefully that it had taken a brutal assault on her to bring them to some sort of a truce. She wondered how long it would last. At first she dreaded going out into colonial society for she was well aware that the servants' grapevine would have spread around Sydney what had happened on the cliffs. In retrospect she was grateful to Dr Kerr for his reticence in punishing her assailant on the spot rather than subjecting her to the humiliation of a trial.

Her total recall of the disastrous end of her betrothal to Charles, so long buried from view in her memory, had in a strange way enabled her to face life again without worrying overmuch what others thought of her. Her near death on the cliffs made her earlier experience seem more trivial, even though it still hurt. Whatever the reason, with John and Lucy Middleton by her side, she faced the knowing looks of the Sydney matrons and the colony's officers without feeling quite the scalding shame she had expected.

Lucy's staunchness, kindness and tact helped Sarah to recover. She might have almost come to believe that she had dreamed the whole thing had there not been certain unforeseen consequences of her ordeal.

The Governor's New Year's Ball was the next great event in Sydney's social calendar and the pair of them went shopping for silks again in Tom Dilhorne's store.

He happened to be present that day and greeted them with, 'Your servant, ladies, and what may I do for you?'

'Silks again, Mr Dilhorne. We have come shopping for silks so that we may look to our best advantage at the Governor's Ball.'

'Then you have come to the right place.'

He began to pull bolts of cloth from a stand behind the counter, saying to Sarah when he returned with them, 'I trust that you are feeling well, Miss Langley.'

There was nothing in his expression or tone to suggest any double meaning in his question, but when he walked towards her Sarah found that she had a strong impulse to dash to the door.

Since her misadventure her only contact with men, apart from Dr Kerr who was always careful not to touch her, or to come too near to her, had been with John and Carter. The latter always kept a respectful distance from her when he accompanied her on her sketching expedition.

In Tom's proximity—and she had never experienced such a thing before when she had been with him—she felt her breathing quicken and a feeling of suffocation come over her. She moved away from him to a counter where ribbons and cords were on show and began to examine them closely.

Tom looked keenly at her pale face and shaking hands and made no attempt to move nearer to her. On the contrary, he retreated to the other side of the counter to continue his conversation with them.

'Ye'll be making the gowns yourself, ladies. That should be a new experience for Miss Langley.'

'Yes,' said Lucy brightly. 'Sarah has promised to help me with my lace trim.'

'Aye.' He was laconic. 'Happen Miss Langley knows the latest London fashions.'

Sarah made an effort to be civil, although her voice sounded strange to her ears. 'Any London fashions which I know are, I fear, already a year out of date.'

'But newer than Sydney fashions,' said Tom. 'I think you'll make the fashions this year, Miss Langley.'

Sarah was aware that he was trying to be kind, and that the effort was proving too much—for her, not for him. She was sure that she was about to choke. Luckily, Lucy saw her pallor and her distress, and covered it with her seemingly artless chatter. Sarah was beginning to grasp that Lucy's chatter was seldom artless. She managed to joke with Tom, before she left, that any dress which she made would be remarkable for being finished at all.

Once out of his shop Lucy led Sarah home and made her drink some of the Madeira which John had brought from England.

'I'm a fool these days,' Sarah muttered. 'Thank you, Lucy.'

She forgot her malaise when it did not return. Dr Kerr had told her not to overdo things so she spent most of her spare time at the Middletons, or in the little studio that she and John had set up in one of the upstairs rooms. Dr Kerr stopped visiting her once she seemed to be on the way to recovery. John told her that he had gone to one of the tiny settlements between Sydney and Paramatta where there had been yet another outbreak of fever. The Governor was hoping that he would return in time for his ball. Sarah was a little surprised to discover that for the first time she could view meeting Dr Kerr again with equanimity.

* * *

Sarah set out for her first colonial ball having completely forgotten her uncharacteristic behaviour in Tom's store. John escorted her and she wore the deep cream silk that Tom had recommended. Lucy was demure in pale blue, and despite her mother's glowering looks ran to meet Sarah after she had been received by the Governor.

Mrs Middleton was not entirely certain that she approved of Lucy's friendship with Sarah, but her family's place in the best society in England more than made up for Sarah's odd notions about the treatment of Emancipists in Sydney.

The band of the 73rd Highlanders was playing in the vast ballroom that was Government House's most remarkable feature. There were great bowls of flowers everywhere and the Governor's welcome of Sarah had been as warm as he could make it. He assured her of his sympathy, and of his relief that she had taken no real harm from her unfortunate misadventure. Her reply was muted because either the scent from the massed flowers, or the heat of the ballroom, was making her feel a little breathless. He had taken her hand and bent to kiss it: it was only with difficulty that she prevented herself from wrenching it away.

Somehow she managed to retain an outward composure that enabled her to enjoy the airs which the band was playing. Her dance programme was soon filled, and compliments on her appearance were profuse, but she soon discovered that the ball, to which she had looked forward with almost feverish anticipation, was not proving the happy occasion which she had imagined.

She was once again on the edge of the malaise that had afflicted her in Tom's store. Frank Wright was her partner in the quadrille, and on taking his hand she felt her breath shorten. The end of the dance brought her some relief, and she moved gratefully over to where John and the Middletons sat. She saw that Dr Kerr had already arrived and was talking to an animated Lucy.

Captain Parker, her partner in the next dance, a waltz, came up to claim her.

'Miss Langley, charming as ever,' he murmured when he bent over her hand. Sarah's inclination was, as it had been with the Governor, to wrench it away, but she controlled herself with an effort, saying, 'One might almost imagine one's self in London tonight, Captain Parker.'

'Indeed, Miss Langley. The Governor certainly knows how to give a ball.' To her dismay she found herself retreating from him as he spoke: the air in the ballroom seemed stifling and she brought her fan into action—which he took as an opportunity to flirt. Mercifully—or so it seemed—the band began to play, to which Captain Parker's immediate response was to say, 'By Jove, Miss Langley, the waltz, let's show them how it's done in London!' He seized her round the waist and pulled her towards him.

The stifling sensation that had threatened her all evening became overwhelming. Stephen Parker's laughing face turned without warning into that of the whiskered Charlie. She had barely time to register her fear and her revulsion before she felt herself falling forward into blackness...

Sarah had never fainted before, and when, later, she returned to consciousness she had little idea of what had happened. Captain Parker and the ballroom were gone, and she was in an anteroom, lying on a sofa. An anxious Lucy, holding a glass of water and Sarah's shawl, was standing by the door, while Dr Kerr was at a little distance from where she was lying, his face grave.

'There, Miss Middleton,' he said, 'I told you not to worry. The heat of the ballroom overcame Miss Langley, and now that she is out of it she has recovered.'

Sarah stopped herself from saying, 'It was not the heat,' when she caught Dr Kerr's eye on her: an eye that almost held a warning.

She took the water that Lucy offered, and swung her legs off the sofa: an unwise move for her head began to spin again, and Lucy put out her hand to steady her glass.

Once her head stopped spinning, Sarah noticed that Dr Kerr made no effort to touch her, and after Lucy had steadied her glass, gently discouraged her from putting an arm around Sarah's shoulders. Now how does he know that? Sarah thought. How does he know that I think that I should scream if anyone so much as laid a finger on me?

Almost as if in response to that unspoken thought, Dr Kerr turned to Lucy and said, 'Miss Middleton, I wonder if you would be so good as to try to find Miss Langley's brother. I collect that he had arranged to play cards with some of the officers and the Governor's aides in one of the drawing rooms immediately before Miss Langley's fainting fit.'

When Lucy had gone he knelt down beside Sarah, and said gently, 'Miss Langley, I know that you cannot bear to be touched, and that you are strongly affected by the nearness of my own sex. I assure you that this is no uncommon consequence of such an attack as you have suffered. You must believe that this reaction will pass in time—but time is what you need.'

Sarah raised her head and looked at him unsteadily.

'I'm a fine lady,' she said simply. 'You told me so once. Aren't I allowed to have a fine lady's vapours?'

'Come,' he said, smiling, 'that's better. I shouldn't know you if you were not firing broadsides at me.' But his eyes were anxious. She could not help noticing that the delicacy with which he avoided touching her, or coming near to her, reflected a depth of feeling of which she had not thought him capable.

Her own smile in response to his riposte was a watery one.

'I'm afraid that my ship is quite sunk, Dr Kerr and the cannon ceased firing before it foundered.'

'I do not believe that, Miss Langley. Gallant spirits are never completely overset, and yours, I am sure, are gallant.'

To her disgust, on hearing the kindness in his voice, Sarah's pent-up tears fell at last. She could not control them. She had never wept over Charles's desertion of her, but it was as though the loss of Charles, of home, and the recent attack, added to Alan Kerr's changed manner to her, were all too much. She did not know which of her hurts was causing this storm of pain, nor did it seem to matter. She only knew that at last she could give vent to her feelings.

Alan Kerr, watching her, shared her distress. At what point in their relationship he had come to see the true Sarah Langley behind the stony façade with which she faced the world he was never sure. He was only sure that his feelings towards her had changed. He had now acquired a fierce desire to protect her, to shield her from the world's despite.

He rose, and made sure that the door was firmly closed so that he could hear—and deter—any person who sought to enter. He still made no effort to touch her—as much for his own self-control as for hers. He handed her his handkerchief which she took without a word, abandoned to everything. Pride and decorum were alike forgotten. In the months since her betrayal and her humiliation she had never once allowed her self-control to slacken. Even on the cliffs she had refused to let herself collapse—and now, suddenly, all her self-control was gone.

Alan Kerr found himself staring at a portrait of the late ill-fated Governor, William Bligh. Ever since his taunt to her in Hyde Park on the afternoon she had gone there with the Middletons, about her reasons for leaving England, he had become aware that something more than a mere flighty spirit lay behind her urgent and biting manner.

He had seen her quail while he spoke, watched her lift her head to confront him, and, on later reflection, he would have given much to recall his own careless words. They had seemed so idle at the time—though even then, perhaps, he had sensed some loss, some deep hurt. The attack on the cliff could not be solely responsible for the agony that she was suffering, although it had undoubtedly stripped her of her defences.

Presently a small voice behind him said, 'Thank you, Dr Kerr, for your recent kindness to me.'

He turned. Sarah was looking at him, tremulously, her eyes red-rimmed, but her expression had lost its hopelessness. He went to the side-table beneath Bligh's portrait where a decanter of red wine and some glasses stood. He poured out a short drink and handed it to her. Sarah took it gratefully, and, on lifting it to her lips said, shyly for her, 'Will you not take a glass with me, Dr Kerr?'

He stiffened slightly and his previous haughty reserve

was almost on him again. 'You must excuse me, I fear, Miss Langley, but I never drink alcohol.'

In ordinary circumstances Sarah would have felt this as a rebuff, but as things were she inclined her head and gratefully drank the harsh, red liquid. He saw her grimace and smiled. 'The wine we drink here does not travel well, I am told. But it is probably better than the illicit whisky and gin brewed in illegal and secret stills.'

Sarah was happy, for once, to engage in small talk. 'I'm not likely to partake of those, Dr Kerr.'

'No, indeed, Miss Langley. Though we must remember what the Bard says: "We know what we are, but we know not what we may be."' Perhaps, he thought, a little glumly, not the most tactful of comments in the circumstances. But she smiled back at him over the rim of her glass, before raising it to say, 'Bravo, Dr Kerr. To quote Shakespeare in the ballroom—or more properly, the anteroom—is the mark of your true, educated Scotsman, is it not?'

She was offering him a flag of truce, no doubt of that, and in that sense he accepted it.

'Indeed, Miss Langley—a correct and proper observation, if I may say so.'

She handed him her empty glass and he replaced it, saying, 'Shall I send to find what is delaying your brother? I think that you are sufficiently recovered to return home. I advise you to take matters quietly for some days. Do not hesitate to send for me, should you feel the need.'

After he had gone Sarah lay back on the sofa. What a strange being he is, she thought, such a mixture of sentiments. One does not know where one is with him.

It did not occur to her that the same words could be used of her, but for the first time Alan Kerr had left her, not in strife, nor in indifference, but in amity. That, at least, must be worthwhile. She did not ask herself why Dr Kerr's approval of her should be so important that she should treasure it.

Chapter Five

'Sarah, my love,' said Lucy a few days later, 'you seem to be making heavy weather of that.' The pair of them were sitting in the Middletons' drawing room engaged in repairing the dresses which they had worn at the New Year's Ball.

'Hmm,' said Sarah, sucking the finger that she had just pricked for the third time in five minutes.

Lucy looked up again and laughed. 'I shall never know,' she said, 'how someone so useful as you are with a paintbrush can be so clumsy with a needle. Why don't you give up and read us some more from *The Mysteries of Udolpho* instead?'

Sarah's laugh in reply was rueful. She was slowly beginning to understand how cushioned her life had been back in England. There had always been a host of poor relations like her old Great-aunt Drusilla, who was so anxious to please that she was only too ready to mend a torn hem, insert some lace or trim a bonnet. In Sydney, if she did not do these many little tasks herself, they did not get done at all. The mere idea of asking Nellie or Sukie to do them was laughable.

She shook her head, 'No, Lucy, I am determined to

master the art of sewing a fine seam. Who else will do it if I do not? Pray do not volunteer yourself, I am determined to be useful.'

She paused before adding lightly, 'Think how much Dr Kerr will approve of me when I am quite transformed from being a useless fine lady. Perhaps I ought to venture into the kitchen and ask Sukie to teach me to make a milk pudding to complete the picture.'

Lucy said, apparently idly, 'You have made up your quarrel with Dr Kerr, then?'

Sarah shrugged. 'Was there a quarrel? We got off on the wrong foot when we first met. Now perhaps we are on the right one.'

She was disinclined to say anything critical about Alan Kerr since the humanity that he had shown to her on the night of the ball. Instead, she tried to concentrate fiercely on her sewing, which, to her disgust, the more she tried to keep her stitches small, grew increasingly grimy. What was really making concentration difficult was that that she could not forget what John had told her about Alan Kerr earlier that day.

Governor Macquarie had invited John Langley to an informal dinner for the two of them in his private rooms in Government House. He wished to see the drawings and watercolours that John had completed in the first months of his visit.

After dinner, the drawings having been admired, the Governor had fetched a bottle of port, cigars and a small table set for chess and challenged John to a game. Drinking and smoking companionably together, they were halfway through it when John touched on something that had been puzzling him.

'I know, sir, that it is not done to enquire why someone arrives here as a convict, but I must confess that I wonder why a man as sterling and as gifted as Dr Kerr appears to be should have come here in chains. Who better than yourself to ask discreetly? I know that what I say to you, or you to me, will not reach the man himself. The fact that he is your valued friend only adds to the puzzle.'

The Governor leaned forward to make his move. 'You may ask, and I will answer you. It is a sad business. You know that Dr Kerr has a kind and compassionate heart behind his dour exterior?'

'I have begun to suspect as much,' said John, wondering at the relevance of the reply.

'Perhaps we had better leave our game for a minute.' The Governor refilled John's glass. 'The point is that it was his compassion that brought him here. He comes from an old Border family of good repute—but the family is poor and he was the second son. He wished to be a surgeon, and the easiest way for a poor man was for him to be attached as one to a ship in the Royal Navy.

'I said that he has a kind heart. He rapidly ran foul of his Captain who was a martinet of the old school. He thought that the Captain's cruelty, rather than the needs of discipline, were resulting in an inordinate number of over-brutal floggings. His Captain was not best pleased when his First Officer supported Kerr and he was compelled to reduce his rate of punishment. But he did not forget, or forgive Kerr for his intervention.

'Some little time later the mutiny at the Nore broke out. One night, in his cups—you must understand that he was very young at the time—Dr Kerr went so far as to say in the Mess, in front of his Captain, that he sympathised with the mutineers, one of whose grievances was the brutality of naval discipline. His Captain saw an

opportunity for revenge. He accused him of supporting
and fomenting treason, and had him thrown into irons.

'This was at the height of the French Wars. No mercy
was shown to the men at the Nore and little to Kerr.
Despite the efforts of his fellow officers, who were horrified by the Captain's harshness, the Admiralty took the
Captain's part, feeling that an example should be made
to discourage others. He was tried for treason and sentenced to death. That sentence was later commuted to
transportation for life. On top of that his family disowned him, as did the young woman to whom he was
betrothed.

'I am told that when he arrived here he was wild at
the injustice of it. He claimed to be a loyal subject of
King George III, but was so headstrong on the voyage
over that he was sent to the penal camp on Norfolk Island. I understand that on the journey from Britain he
met Tom Dilhorne, who became his friend and mentor
in the convicts' world and helped him to survive in it.
Kerr even succeeded in training Dilhorne to be his medical aide on Norfolk Island. Some time later they were
transferred to Sydney by my predecessor since New
South Wales was so badly in need of doctors. Dr Kerr
is now a valued servant of the colony while Dilhorne
moved on to exercise his undoubted talents in the com-
mercial and business world.

'That, Langley, is Dr Kerr's sad history—and a little
of Dilhorne's, too.'

'A sad story, indeed,' agreed John. 'You would not
object, I trust, if I told my sister of this? I should like
her to know that Dr Kerr's reason for being transported
is not to his discredit. It also explains his refusal to drink
alcohol.'

'I should be most happy for Miss Langley to know of

it. You must tell her what you think fit.' The Governor
smiled. 'Your sister is a most resolute lady and I would
like to think that she and Dr Kerr were friends.'

There was something in the warmth with which the
Governor said this that made John Langley look across
at him sharply, but Macquarie's handsome face wore its
usual bland mask. The Governor's enemies often accused him of scheming to attain devious ends. It was the
usual Exclusive comment on his attempts to integrate the
Emancipists into the social life of the colony. So far,
however, John had found him to be a man of great integrity and vision.

After they had finished their game, John had taken his
leave; and on the following morning, at breakfast, he
had told Sarah enough of Alan Kerr's sad story to explain his presence in a penal colony.

Sarah had listened carefully and had said little, though
she thought that it went a long way to explain Dr Kerr's
bitterness. She said nothing of it to Lucy but stitched
steadily on until the maid arrived with the message that
Captain Ramsey and Lieutenant Frank Wright wished to
know if the Middletons were at home.

Lucy put down her work. 'Pray tell them to come in.
Quick,' she ordered Sarah, snatching her sewing up and
bundling it, together with hers, to thrust it into a bureau
drawer. 'Now you are reading *Udolpho* to me and we
have nothing to do in the world but be fine ladies.'

She fell into a languishing posture on a sofa so that
no one should know that she had been stitching away
for dear life until the maid had come in. Sarah, hardly
able to contain her amusement, began to render Mrs Rat-
cliffe's masterpiece in her best Mrs Siddons-like voice.

'Oh, how pleased we are to see you,' Lucy exclaimed
when the two officers entered. 'Sarah and I have been

positively rigid with boredom. We have absolutely nothing to do. Pray tell us all the news from the garrison and the town.'

Neither officer needed much encouragement. In a society where women were in a small minority, to enter a room and find in it two females as attractive as Sarah and Lucy eagerly waiting to be entertained was an opportunity few encountered.

'Little news,' said Pat Ramsey dismissively. 'Fred Waring was carried home drunk again, and a couple of convicts have escaped into the bush.'

His tone was so casual that Sarah looked at him in some surprise. 'Do you not follow them, Captain Ramsey? Or do you simply leave them there? I confess that I am not conversant with the nature of the bush.'

'No need for you to be, Miss Langley,' said Frank, 'since you are never likely to be lost in it. When convicts escape, so long as too many do not go at once, we leave them there. The bush will do for them soon enough—great heat and little water, you know. Some say that there are small camps to be found there, lost to our knowledge, but one doubts that. Few ever come back.'

'Frank's right,' said Pat. 'Some of the poor fools who escape think that if they can cross the Blue Mountains they will immediately reach China and freedom.'

'Surely not,' said Sarah, who had spent several days trying to paint the Blue Mountains satisfactorily. 'The Pacific is in the way.'

'Oh, you're a clever lady and you know that,' said Pat gaily, 'but they don't. They believe anything. Why, I do believe that most of those who have been transported are as stupid as the aborigines.'

'But not Tom Dilhorne,' said Sarah, teasing him.

'No,' conceded Pat. 'Whatever Dilhorne is, he's not stupid.'

Frank decided to change the subject. 'How the dooce did we get into this boring line of talk?' he asked. 'Miss Lucy will be yawning, and you too, Miss Langley. Do tell us that you will both be coming to Race Day.'

'Race Day?' exclaimed Sarah and Lucy together, with Lucy adding,

'I thought that the Races were over for this year.'

'So they are,' explained Pat. 'But some of us have decided that life in this benighted hole needs a little cheering up and the 73rd have decided to run a special Race Day—with O'Connell's blessing, I may add. And you, Miss Langley, are to bet on my Hercules.'

'No, indeed,' interjected Frank Wright. 'By no means. You are to bet on my Vulcan. Hercules is past his best. He was last year's winner. You'll only lose your tin, Miss Langley, if you bet on such a spavined creature.'

'I never bet on any horse until I have seen it,' said Sarah, ignoring the fact that she had never bet on a horse before. 'Who will be your jockeys?'

'No jockeys,' said Frank heartily. 'We are our own jocks, you know. Gentleman riders all.'

'And ladies? Are ladies allowed to compete?'

Both men laughed. 'You are funning us, Miss Langley,' said Frank. 'No offence, we know that you are a fine horsewoman.'

'Your brother, though,' said Pat. 'He could be a jock. He has bought Menzies's two blacks, has he not? Castor and Pollux.'

'Oh, I doubt that John will take part in the Races,' said Sarah. 'He would be too worried that he might have an accident which would prevent him from painting.'

'Speaking of that,' said Pat Ramsey, 'the organising

committee wondered if your brother would consider giving one of his recent oils of Sydney as a prize for one of the races. It would make a change from the usual piece of cheap plate.'

'You must ask him,' said Sarah. She wondered if something by herself would do instead, but since Charles's dismissal of her painting she had been shy of showing it to, or discussing it with, others—particularly men. She would always be worrying if they secretly despised her or considered her unwomanly.

'A penny for your thoughts, Miss Langley?' queried Pat brightly. He was wondering why she had suddenly fallen silent.

'I was just thinking,' Sarah said, not prepared to tell the truth, but needing to say something, 'what a varied life you live in Sydney. The Park in the afternoon, races and balls and drives to the Point. Just like Hyde Park and Ascot and celebrating the King's birthday at home.'

'Home,' said Frank Wright, and then was silent. They were all remembering home. They were contrasting it with the wilderness that was New South Wales once one left Sydney. Every effort they made to reproduce home, thought Sarah, merely served to point up the difference.

She looked through the window at the brilliance outside: at the Middletons' washing flapping in the slight breeze, and at a wallaby that had broken through the fence and was staring at her. It was as strange to her as she was to it.

Time started again. Sarah promised to bet on Hercules and, as some consolation to Frank, agreed to let him squire her at the Races. The aversion to men that had so afflicted her at the Governor's Ball had almost disappeared in the weeks since the assault, but she was still warier than she had been before it. Further idle conversation followed until the convict servant brought in the tea board, and they took tea as gravely and ceremoniously as though they were in Grosvenor Square.

Later, dining on her own, since John was dining at the Officers' Mess, and busily engaged in eating a pudding of uncommon stodginess, Sarah asked Sukie if she had read Mrs Glasse's cookery book. She had brought it from England on the recommendation of a friend who had heard that such things were lacking in the Antipodes.

Sukie blushed and did what she always did when confused or embarrassed: bobbed an inadequate curtsy. 'Lor' bless you, Mum, I ain't got no letters.'

'Oh!' said Sarah. 'Then perhaps you could ask Nellie to read it to you?'

'She ain't got no letters neether, Mum.'

Sarah was used to a staff that, even if recruited from the children of tenants and villagers, had been instructed in the rudiments of reading and writing.

'Pray fetch Nellie to me.'

A flustered Sukie returned with Nellie who, Sarah noted with disapproval, was fatter and more unkempt than ever. Even John had noticed her appearance and had said, 'That girl looks exactly like an unmade bed.' Mrs Hackett had overheard him, sniffed, and later asked Sarah, yet again, to send Nellie back and get another assignee.

'Nellie,' asked Sarah, 'is it true that you are unable to read?'

Nellie dredged up a sniff and said something which sounded like 'yessum'.

Sarah considered them both. 'I am prepared to teach you to read and write if Mrs Hackett agrees to free you for a short time each day.' She was surprised at the reception of what she thought was a magnificent offer.

Nellie gave vent to a positive cannonade of sniffs. 'Oh, no, Mum. Me'n Sukie, we don't want to able to read—t'ain't natural. T'ain't for the likes of us. Thankee, Mum, thankee.'

She took Sukie by the hand and half-dragged her from the room, before Sarah could reply.

Well, she thought indignantly, that should teach me not to try to help my inferiors!

Later, however, while Sarah sat sewing, waiting for John to return, Sukie crept into the room.

'Please, Mum.' She twisted her hands in an agony of embarrassment. 'Please, Mum, I should like to learn to read and write. I want to cook proper, be more of a lady like…like Mrs Hackett.'

'Tomorrow then, in the afternoon, when the washing up for nuncheon is over, we will start you on your ABC.'

Sarah felt as though she had climbed a mountain— and it was only poor Sukie, wishing to learn her letters, who had created that feeling of accomplishment.

Sukie turned at the door. 'Mum?'

'Yes?' Sarah wondered what was coming.

'There's lots of poor girls like me that'd like to learn to read, Mum.' On that she left the room, leaving Sarah with her cry for help.

All in all it had been quite a day. John's tale of Dr Kerr, Lucy's sewing bee, and now this. Did Sukie really think that she, Sarah Langley, was going to set herself up as the unpaid dame of a charity school to teach convict girls how to read?

Why was it that she, Sarah Langley, did not laugh, or grow indignant or dismiss the notion, but sat there wondering if, after all, this might be a better use of her time than pining after Charles Villiers, or thinking about Alan Kerr?

Now, how on earth had he entered her musings again? Drat the man!

Over the next few weeks the whole colony seemed to be thinking about nothing but Race Day. Even Alan Kerr, when Sarah met him in the street, Carter behind her, carrying her painting materials, had a cheerful word with her on the subject.

'Shall we see you at the Races, Miss Langley?' he enquired, after he had asked after her health and she had assured him that the feelings with which she had been afflicted were beginning to pass away. Alan, looking at her, knew that she was speaking the truth. She was looking radiant again, her complexion was brilliant and her green eyes were shining at him—in friendliness now and not in disdain.

Whenever he had had a free moment she walked into his thoughts, and he could not walk her out again. She was nothing like the girl he had lost, but perhaps that was her attraction.

Her attraction! What was he, an Emancipist in a colony that demeaned them, doing pining after a lady like Sarah Langley?

Sarah, for her part thought that he looked tired. All Sydney knew how hard he worked, how tireless he was in the care of his patients. She did not tell him that her days, too, had become very full. She wondered if he knew about her latest venture.

With Tom Dilhorne's amused help—and despite her brother's disapproval—she had taken over a small room at the back of his store where, three times a week, she taught Sukie and some of the Emancipists' children their letters. Even Lucy, she found, did not totally approve of what she was doing, partly because she was losing a little of Sarah's company, and partly because her sympathy towards the Emancipists was more theoretical than practical. It was really a small rebellion against her mother's strict ways.

Teaching, Sarah soon discovered, was not easy. She made too many assumptions about the state of knowledge of Sukie and the others. She had few books, few slates, few slate pencils and little paper. Her own chalks and pencils had to be used and she occasionally found herself resenting the time it took from her own interests. Her stubborn determination not to be bested drove her on, though—she would succeed, she would.

Now, smiling freely for the first time at Alan Kerr, she was unaware that her new interests had given her a glow and a vibrancy which contrasted strongly with her recent apathetic state. Elasticity had been restored to her step and her manner to him was lightly playful where previously it had been antagonistic.

Before they parted Sarah told him that she was engaged to visit the Races with Lucy and Frank Wright, Pat Ramsey being fully employed in the necessary task of turning an unpromising field into a race track.

Sarah thought that Dr Kerr looked a little disappointed on hearing that she was already engaged, but persuaded herself that she must be mistaken. She was not to know that the last flash of her green eyes stayed with him all the way down the street and round the convict gang that had almost completed paving the corner.

Sarah had been correct. Alan had half-thought of asking her to accompany him to the Races, but common sense had prevailed. He might have once been a gentleman—now he was an Emancipist; and if the Governor chose to favour him, few others did. John Langley had been kind, but Sarah was another matter.

She was a lady, a fine lady, almost certainly assured of a great marriage back in England, and the Mrs Middletons of this world were outraged enough that he spoke to her at all. To wish to squire her to social functions was quite another matter. Even John Langley's kindness might wilt at such a proposal.

Besides, there was Sarah herself. What would she say to him if he made her such an offer? It was further foolishness to suppose that she saw this visit to New South Wales as more than a mere interlude.

Tom Dilhorne's laconically transmitted information that she had opened a charity school in a room behind his store, in order to teach Emancipists' daughters and illiterate servant girls like Sukie to read and write, had surprised him more than a little. He had not thought her sufficiently serious enough to embark on such an undertaking, and he wondered how long she would persevere with it.

He sighed impatiently before walking on. Miss Langley took up far too much of his thoughts. He would have been surprised to learn that Sarah was telling herself the same thing about him.

Sarah found Tom Dilhorne waiting for her when she rounded the corner that separated Sydney from the bush. It was not the first time that she had come across him unexpectedly, but it was the first time that she had asked herself whether his appearance was as accidental as she might once have thought. He tipped his hat back a little on seeing her.

'Your servant, Miss Langley. I have a favour to ask
of you.'

'Indeed, Mr Dilhorne? You have done favours for me.
It is time that I repaid your kindness over the room.'

He waved that on one side. 'That was nothing. No
need for thanks, as I said at the time. Now, I know of a
little lass whose mother died recently and she needs the
kind of help that I think you can give her. I wondered
whether she could join your class.'

Once before she had heard Tom Dilhorne speak in
this measured, almost gentlemanly tone, so different
from his usual lower-class mode. There was more to him
than she might have thought. For the first time Sarah
wondered what story lay behind Tom's arrival in chains.

She smiled back at him, saying, 'Of course she may
join my class, it will be a pleasure to help her. Bring her
along this afternoon.'

His thanks were brief, but heartfelt. He tipped his hat
again and walked away. His bearing, she thought amusedly, was still as ungentlemanly and as unmilitary as it
could be. John had told her that, for a colonial, he was
amazingly rich, but you would never guess it from his
manner.

Chapter Six

Race Day dawned fine and clear. John left early in the morning, having been invited to breakfast at the Officers' Mess. The Middletons were due to arrive shortly after nuncheon in order to drive Sarah to the course in their carriage.

She dressed herself in the gown that, with Lucy's assistance, she had made: yet another new experience for her. It was a delicate blue muslin, with a high waist and tiny puffed sleeves. Her straw bonnet had been decorated by Lucy with tiny home-made forget-me-nots and Sarah herself had stitched on its wide blue ribbons. 'The work of my own fair hands,' she had proudly told John.

She had just pulled on her dress and was carefully smoothing it down when she became aware of an extraordinary hubbub coming from downstairs. Mrs Hackett's angry voice was predominant. Someone was crying and Sukie's shrill whine cut across the other noises. Sarah sighed. Such scenes had been common in her early days in Sydney, but she had thought that those unhappy times in the kitchen were over and done with.

The uproar did not die down. Quite the reverse. Just when Sarah had decided that she really must find out what on earth was happening, the door flew open without ceremony, and Sukie burst in. Her face was scarlet and her excitement was such that she could not speak without stuttering.

'Oh, M...m...mum, you m...m...must come down. She m...m...mustn't... M...m...Mrs Hackett mustn't...'

She ran out of words and began to wring her hands together in her desperation.

Sarah put down her new bonnet. 'Really, Sukie,' she said, annoyed that her last-minute preparations were being so rudely interrupted. 'You must slow down and tell me exactly what is wrong.'

This stern injunction had the effect of rendering Sukie even more incoherently urgent. She grasped Sarah by the hand and began to pull her towards the door. This manoeuvre succeeded in convincing Sarah that something must be very wrong if the normally apathetic Sukie was so strongly affected.

She threw her bonnet back on the bed and ran lightly down the stairs and into the kitchen.

There she found Nellie, purple in the face, and moaning loudly, hanging on to the back doorknob and Mrs Hackett trying to drag her free of it and shove her towards the open doorway.

'You bad girl, you wicked girl!' she was shouting. 'You must leave at once. At once, do you hear.'

Nellie's moans turned into shrieks and cries of, 'No, I dassn't, I dassn't!'

Sarah attempted to take control of the situation by trying to make some sense out of what was happening.

'Mrs Hackett, tell me at once what is going on. Why are Nellie and Sukie screaming, and why are you trying to push Nellie out of the back door?'

Mrs Hackett let go of Nellie, who at once fell to the floor, clutching her stomach, and redoubling her wailing.

'You may well ask, Miss Langley,' replied Mrs Hackett, 'and I will tell you. This wicked girl is with child and is trying to give birth in my kitchen. I will not have her here. She must take the fruit of her sin to the workhouse to be born. I want no sluts having by-blows here, and nor will you, Miss Langley, if you have any sense of decency. Out with you, my girl,' and she advanced on the shrieking Nellie again.

'Stop, stop at once,' said Sarah firmly. 'Am I to understand that Nellie is on the verge of having a baby and that you are turning her out into the street?'

Before Mrs Hackett could reply, Sukie cried out, 'Lor' bless you, Mum, you have the right of it. Don't let her send Nellie away. She'll die, Mum. It's Race Day and there'll be no one about to help her.'

'She should have thought of that when she was misbehaving herself,' cried Mrs Hackett in an ecstasy of righteousness. 'She's an offence to all decent women. I'll be bound she doesn't even know who the father is.'

On this Nellie crawled across the floor towards Sarah and began to pull frantically at the hem of her dress. 'Don't let her turn me out, Mum. The baby's nearly here. Oh, Gawd, Mum, I don't want to die in the street.' Her writhings redoubled and even Sarah could see that she was in the last stages of birth.

In the whole of her previously calm and ordered life she had never found herself in such a position as this. It was obvious that she was going to receive no help from Mrs Hackett, but in all humanity she could not allow her to turn Nellie out. That unfortunate had now begun to sob unremittingly, lost to everything but her own pain.

To make matters even more complicated the Middletons were due to arrive at any moment.

She took a deep breath, and said to Mrs Hackett with a calm that she did not really possess, 'Mrs Hackett, under no circumstances are you to turn poor Nellie out.' Since this did not appear to be enough to prevent the woman from beginning to argue with her again, she added sternly, 'I warn you, Mrs Hackett, your own position here is at stake if you disobey me.'

She looked across at Sukie. 'Are you sure that Nellie is really about to give birth?' At Sukie's nod she added, 'Then you must go to Dr Kerr's surgery and ask him to come here immediately.'

Sukie's response was a 'Lor' bless you, Mum', before running out of the back door at the double.

Now, thought Sarah, if Dr Kerr can arrive soon I might be able to accompany the Middletons to the Races, leaving Nellie in good hands. She addressed the stiffly disapproving Mrs Hackett. 'If you are not prepared to do anything else, please put some water on to boil, ready for the doctor, should he need it.'

Sarah had some dim memory that this was the correct thing to do at the birth of babies, calves and dogs. She bent over Nellie, who was briefly silent and tried to help her to her feet. 'Come, let me take you up to bed.'

Unsteadily she hauled her up the stairs, reflecting wryly that Nellie's bulk had been the consequence of the baby rather than of layers of clothing. She lifted her on to her own bed, throwing on one side her splendid new bonnet, with a dry internal query as to whether she would wear it that day.

Mrs Hackett, still stiff with disapproval, arrived shortly afterwards with a kettle of hot water, and unwillingly helped Sarah to free Nellie from her carapace

of grubby clothing, and dress her in one of Sarah's fine
cambric nightgowns. She gave a martyred sigh when
Sarah told her to wet her flannel so that she could bathe
Nellie's sweating face and her hands, which were grimy
from struggling around on the kitchen floor.

The minutes crept by, with no sign of Dr Kerr or a
returning Sukie. Nellie seemed to have settled down into
a cycle of low moaning interspersed at regular intervals
with agonised writhings.

'Mrs Hackett,' said Sarah when it became apparent
that Nellie's baby was about to be born, 'you have as-
sisted at births, surely. After all, you were Mrs Corporal
Hackett for a number of years.'

Mrs Hackett averted her face. 'I have always made
certain, Miss Langley, that such tasks were always given
to others. My sensibilities would not allow me to take
part in such a delicate operation.'

'Oh.' Sarah contemplated her housekeeper's igno-
rance as well as her own. She guessed that the wretched
Sukie was likely to be the only one of them, apart from
the helpless Nellie, who had actually been present at a
birth.

Some little time later the doorbell rang. It almost certainly heralded the Middletons' arrival. Sarah stripped
off her overall and ran downstairs. She opened the door
to find that Mrs Middleton and Lucy were waiting for
her in their landau. She advanced rapidly to the carriage,
composing herself and putting a cheerful expression on
her face.

'I fear that you must excuse me. It is the most annoying thing. I have had an accident to my dress, as you
see, and I must stay to change it. Pray do not wait for
me. I will send for one of Tom Dilhorne's gigs and join
you later.'

Mrs Middleton simply looked suspicious.

'Oh, dear, whatever has happened to your beautiful dress?' lamented Lucy. Sarah's excuse sounded uncommonly thin even to her, but there was no telling Mrs Middleton the truth. She had the uncomfortable feeling that she would certainly approve of Mrs Hackett turning Nellie away. Sarah had already been made aware that nothing indecorous must pollute Lucy's ears. She could only imagine what Mrs Middleton's middle-class gentility would make of learning that Miss Sarah Langley was preparing to act as midwife to her own immoral kitchen maid!

'Pray present my excuses to Lieutenant Wright and Captain Ramsey,' she added brightly, retreating to the door, still talking gaily, 'and tell them that I hope to join you all later.'

Sarah felt compelled to rush away since she had the uncomfortable feeling that if her absence were prolonged Mrs Hackett might take the opportunity to push Nellie out of the house. She knew that Mrs Middleton did not believe her excuses even if she could not guess at the unlikely truth—which, sooner or later, she was nevertheless bound to discover. She watched the Middletons' carriage depart, taking her afternoon's pleasure with it and, once indoors, resumed her overall and took up her place at Nellie's side.

That unfortunate had subsided into a half-sleep punctuated by moans—something which alarmed Sarah since she had had a vague notion that once birth had started to take place it went forward briskly if all was well. Another cause for worry was that Sukie had not returned. To try to distract herself and also to remove her grimly disapproving housekeeper from Nellie's bedside, Sarah ordered the still grumbling Mrs Hackett to go and make tea for the three of them.

Mrs Hackett had just come back with the tea when they heard the kitchen door bang. Sarah put down the cup she had just been given and set off downstairs in order to see what in the world could be happening now. Halfway down she met Sukie running up, and the first sight of her face was enough to tell Sarah that Dr Kerr had not been found.

'Oh, Mum,' she wailed. 'I went to Dr Kerr's lodgings as you said. But he wor'n't there. His landlady said as how he'd gone to the Rocks to set a convict's broken arm. An' when I got there he'd been and gorn.'

Her agitation was so extreme that she had to stop for a moment to get her breath back before continuing her story in the voice that she had always used until she had been employed by Sarah.

'They said he was orf to a farm on the edge of the bush where the farmer's wife had gone into labour. Oh, dear, I couldn't go all that way on foot, but then I saw Mester Dilhorne in his gig. He stopped and asked me what I thought I wuz doing there, so I told him. An', oh, Mum, he said that he would fetch the Doctor for you and that I was to go straight home with the news. He said that he knew that we would both be brave gels and help Nellie and the baby until he arrived with the Doctor. I'd already told him that ole Hackett would be no use. He said he'd come to help if he couldn't find Dr Kerr.'

She ran down at last to sink gasping and panting on the chair beside the bed. Sarah picked up her cup and handed it to Sukie who obviously needed it more than she did, since she had spent the last three-quarters of an hour running around Sydney. Sukie drank it down in one giant gulp.

So, Tom Dilhorne looked as though he might be her unlikely saviour if, God forbid, he couldn't find Alan Kerr. And how long would it be before either of them arrived? More and more it looked as though the task of birthing and saving Nellie's baby was to fall to her.

'Sukie,' she asked, trying not to let the very real desperation that she was beginning to feel to affect her voice, 'Have you had any experience in birthing babies?'

'Lor' no, Mum. I were there when my little sisters were born, but I was only a young'un then, and I can't rightly say that I remember what happened.'

Sarah sighed. It was plain that she was going to have to summon up all the resolution of which she was capable if she was not going to allow Nellie to suffer needlessly should the baby arrive before either Tom or Alan Kerr did.

Nellie had begun to shriek again, and this time it was plain to even the untutored Sarah that the baby was already being born. She bent over the bed and examined Nellie—to discover that the baby's head was already showing! After that she had no time for thought. Mrs Hackett promptly had hysterics when she realised that the baby was actually being born, and only behaved herself after Sarah had slapped her, hard.

Sukie, on the other hand, was only too willing to help, and between them they brought Nellie's baby girl into the world unharmed, even if her cries and Nellie's were enough to wake the dead—as Sukie gleefully commented to Carter later.

At the last moment, just before the baby was born, Nellie put her hand into Sarah's, and after she and the baby had been washed, she took it again, and slept, still clutching at it. Almost as though sleep were infectious, Sarah dozed off herself in her bedside chair, after she and Sukie had swaddled the baby in towels and laid it in its makeshift cot.

Sukie went downstairs to be ready to greet Dr Kerr when—or if—he arrived. She didn't want Mrs Hackett letting him in and telling him some lying story about how she had birthed the baby on her own while Sarah and Sukie stood about, helpless. Oh, yes, life had taught Sukie some hard lessons and knowing what the Mrs Hacketts of this world were capable of was one of them.

She did not have long to wait.

Tom Dilhorne was as good as his word. He gave up his afternoon's pleasure and finally discovered Alan Kerr at a farmstead on the edge of the bush, drinking tea on its veranda while a new-born baby squalled inside the house.

'The third today,' sighed Alan on hearing Tom's news. 'At this rate Sydney's population will be likely to rival that of Europe's towns. I suppose that by the time we reach the Langleys' home our fine lady will already have gone to the Races. Never mind, I'll make my way there as soon as possible.'

If Tom thought that his friend misjudged Sarah Langley, he did not say so. Nor did Tom twit him when they arrived at the Langleys to be admitted by a triumphant Sukie.

'We done it! Miss Sarah and I done it. That Hackett was a useless old bitch—she tried to turn poor Nellie out of the house when the baby started to come, but Miss Sarah was a brick. You'd have thought she'd birthed babies all her life! Nellie and the baby are doing fine. They're all upstairs.'

Alan took the stairs two at a time, leaving an amused Tom at the bottom. He reached the bedroom to discover there a most sentimental tableau. Nellie and Sarah were sound asleep, and the baby, too, in an improvised cot made from a drawer out of one of Sarah's tallboys: its original contents had been emptied on to the carpet.

He paused for a moment. Sarah awoke on hearing the door open and stared at him. She was immediately conscious of her appearance: her hair had come down and her overall was bloodstained and crumpled.

'Oh, you came, at last.'

Alan was quite overcome. Whatever he had expected it was not this. For a moment he could say nothing, and then managed, 'Yes, I'm sorry I took so long, and you did stay with Nellie—Tom said that you would.'

'What else could I do?' she said simply. 'I couldn't let Mrs Hackett turn her out and you couldn't come. I can only hope that I haven't done all the wrong things.'

Alan looked at the sleeping child. 'I'm sure that you didn't.' To his astonishment he had a strong desire to take Sarah into his arms and kiss her weary, dirty face. The face of a woman who had forgone her own pleasure to help her erring servant. He shook his head to clear it before saying, 'I don't know another woman of your station who would have done what you did for Nellie this afternoon.'

'Oh, come,' she returned spiritedly. 'You must know that I've run a great household since I was a girl—although I must confess that my duties didn't include acting as a midwife until today.'

She yawned. 'How do you manage it, Dr Kerr? One afternoon of only half-doctoring and I feel nearly as exhausted as the poor mother herself.'

'And you missed the Races, too,' he said softly, still overwhelmed by his insane desire to kiss a woman whom he had previously thought of as a selfish termagant, but who had displayed a compassion for a poor amateur prostitute and her illegitimate child that had led her to forgo her own pleasure and risk the contempt of the respectable when what she had done became known.

'Oh, the Races,' Sarah said, almost with a yawn. 'What do they matter compared with Nellie's safety. You *are* going to look at Nellie and the baby, aren't you?'

'You remind me of my duties,' returned Alan, amused. 'Yes, if you promise to rid yourself of that over-all, and rest a little.'

Sarah went downstairs, still yawning, stripping off her overall on the way. She entered the kitchen to discover Tom Dilhorne there, drinking tea with Sukie. He rose to greet her and his expression on seeing her was an admiring one. 'I've been hearing of your accomplishments, Miss Langley. Sukie is full of them.'

'They were Sukie's as well—you mustn't forget that. I couldn't have managed without her.'

Sukie had risen in order to pour her some tea, but Sarah waved her down and picked up the pot herself, saying, 'Let's drink to the baby, shall we?'

'She's got a name,' Sukie told Tom. 'Nellie wants to call her Sarah—that is, if you don't mind, Mum.'

Sarah was conscious of them all looking at her, and of the amusement on Tom's normally impassive face. 'Of course I don't mind. I shall be delighted.' She laughed inwardly when she thought of what her London friends might have found to say on hearing that her name was to be given to a convict girl's by-blow after she had delivered it herself. What would they think if they could see her now?

'That was well done, Miss Langley,' murmured Tom,

'but what is going to happen now to Nellie and the baby?'

Sarah did not immediately grasp what he meant. He smiled. Miss Sarah Langley might now fancy herself a great woman of the world, but she had a charming naïveté in some matters.

'Well, leaving aside Mrs Hackett, who has flounced off to the market, I can't see your brother being very happy at the acquisition of an invalid mother and her crying baby to the household.'

Sarah sat down. She suddenly felt very tired. 'Of course, I really am being stupid. You are right. What in the world am I going to do with Nellie and the baby? I feel so responsible for them both.'

Before Tom or Sukie could answer her, Alan Kerr walked into the kitchen. 'Everything's A1 at Lloyds upstairs,' he told them. 'I've given Nellie something to help her sleep.'

'And you need a cup of tea,' Sarah told him, conscious of how tired he looked. He had probably been on the go since early morning.

'Thank you,' and he sank gratefully into Mrs Hackett's armchair.

'We have been discussing what to do with Nellie and the baby,' Sarah told him, handing him his tea.

'I could look after her,' offered Sukie.

Alan shook his head, 'No, that won't do. Tom will know, won't you, Tom?' and he smiled knowingly at his friend.

'Oh, aye,' Tom riposted. 'Pass the responsibility on to Tom Dilhorne as usual,' but his eyes were twinkling. 'Now Miss Sarah's a practical lass, but it's not possible for her to help here. Yes, I've an idea or two, but you must leave me to think them over. You'll not be able to move Nellie and the baby yet, but by the time you can I'll have thought of something.'

'I'll drink to that,' smiled Alan, raising his cup to toast Tom.

Sarah had failed to notice that Tom had, for the first time, not used the formal Miss Langley when speaking to her. This was because she was too busy grasping that, seated in her kitchen, and mingling with those whom she had always previously thought of as her inferiors, she was feeling happier than she had done since Charles Villiers's defection.

Tom's downright practicality seemed to be affecting her, too. 'They're in your hands, then, Tom,' she offered. 'I'm going to have some explaining to do to John, anyway.' She laughed ruefully. 'I suppose that what happened here today will be all over Sydney before I can turn round.'

Alan was gazing at her in admiration. Here was quite a different creature from the one he had first encountered in Sydney Harbour. He leaned forward. 'One thing of which I am sure, Miss Langley,' he said, 'is that such gossip will not affect you. When you decided to save Nellie you did the right thing, and that matters more than all the malicious chatter in the world.'

'I second that,' added Tom, raising his teacup first to Sarah, then to Sukie and finally to Alan.

Sarah coloured a little, and flashed her green eyes at them. 'The pair of you did the right thing, too. I'm mindful of the fact that you both gave up your chance of a day's pleasure in order to help Nellie.'

Alan, overcome, thought that he might drown in Sarah's glorious eyes—and failed in consequence to notice that his observant friend was well aware of his reaction. 'It was our duty,' he said. He could not tell Sarah that it wasn't only for Nellie that they had done it, it was for her, because he was becoming aware that Tom shared his admiration for the beauty sitting so pleasantly with them in her kitchen.

What Alan was beginning to feel for her was more than admiration. He had believed that the ability to respond so strongly to a woman had deserted him after his unhappy experiences back home, but no such thing. Sarah Langley, without even trying, was sounding a chord in him that he had long since thought silenced.

Sukie decided that they all needed another pot of tea, and also brought out a barm loaf, which Mrs Hackett had made the day before, and buttered it vigorously. Soon they were all, including Sarah, enjoying themselves immensely, eating it and listening to Tom telling a comic story about one of the convicts who had wandered through the bush and thought that he had reached China until a party of soldiers arrived to disillusion and arrest him.

He was an excellent mimic and they were all laughing heartily at its riotous ending, when John, somewhat overset, after spending the day drinking with the officers of the 73rd, made an arrival home so noisy that it woke the baby.

He roared into the drawing room, shouting, 'Sarah! Where have you been all day? The Middletons told me some nonsense about your clothes. Why is Dilhorne's gig outside?'

He finally entered the kitchen and looked about him in surprise, his red face growing redder.

'Where has a crying baby come from? And why are you all in the kitchen? And what are Dilhorne and Kerr doing here?'

Sarah rose. 'Which question would you like me to

answer first, John? We have had such a commotion today as you would not believe. We can have a fête day
of our own—that is, if you dare indulge yourself any
more.'

Her tiredness was such that her high spirits were verg-
ing on hysteria.

Tom and Alan Kerr had also risen when John Langley
had burst into the room. It was Alan who spoke first.
'Your sister has behaved extremely well, Langley. She
will tell you about it when Tom and I have left. After
that, you must be sure to see that she gets some rest.'

'I'll look after Miss Sarah.' Sukie's experiences that
day seemed to have unlocked some reserve of character
in her never before displayed. John stared at her as
though one of the kangaroos had been gifted with
speech.

'Well, you all seemed to have had a good time even
if you didn't go to the races. But that doesn't explain
the baby.'

He was astonished at the reception of these simple
words. When Sarah had stopped laughing, she took her
brother by the hand. 'Come into the drawing room, John,
and I will tell you everything. Doctor Kerr and Mr Dilhorne you will excuse us, I am sure.'

Alan and Tom put their heads together and found a
solution to the problem of what to do with Nellie's baby.
Mrs Grimes, the farmer's wife whose baby Alan had
delivered on the same day as Nellie's, needed a kitchen
maid and she agreed to take in Nellie and the baby. 'Two
will be no more of a problem than one,' she said, untruthfully, but kindly.

The day after the baby's birth Mrs Hackett called

Sarah into the kitchen. There she found a tall young Irishman, his battered felt hat in his hand.

'This is Kevin Riley, Nellie's brother. He would like to see his sister and the baby, if you will so allow.'

'Certainly.' Sarah had not known that Nellie had a brother, let alone one so personable as Kevin Riley appeared to be. Sukie ushered him upstairs where he remained for about half an hour, and when he returned to the kitchen he asked Mrs Hackett if he might speak to Miss Langley alone. Sarah received him in her pleasant drawing room. Fortunately, John, who would have disapproved of such a liberty, was absent, and although Riley refused her offer of a seat he spoke to her in tones of frank equality.

'Nellie has just told me that she owes her life and that of her baby to you, Miss Langley, when that dragon of a housekeeper would have turned her into the street.'

'I only did my Christian duty,' Sarah said.

'More than that, I think, considering everything. I know that what she says is true. It is the talk of Sydney today that you acted as her midwife. You have my undying gratitude, Miss Langley and if there is anything I can ever do for you, then I will do it. I consider it a debt of honour.'

His manner was so oddly formal that Sarah felt constrained to answer him in kind.

'There is no need, Mr Riley. In common humanity I could not abandon Nellie when she was threatened with eviction nor when the doctor was unable to arrive in time.'

'But you did it for my sister, and that I shall not forget.'

'I suppose that Nellie told you that Dr Kerr and Mr

Dilhorne have arranged for her to work at Grimes's farm.'

'Yes, and I shall not forget that kindness, either. Nellie will be better out of town—there will be few temptations in the country. God knows that I have not been able to protect her in Sydney.'

'Let us hope that the baby will steady Nellie,' said Sarah hopefully. He seemed a most worthy young man, of a different calibre from his sister, and she respected his independence in a way that would have been difficult for her before she had come to New South Wales. In England she would have offered him money, but delicacy restrained her.

A proud reticence was written in every line of him, and she was relieved that he had visited her during John's absence. Her brother's most frequent complaint about the natives of Sydney was of their lack of the proper respect due to his station. His disapproval of the whole affair was manifest. He had made it plain to Sarah that, while he would not have gone so far as Mrs Hackett and turned Nellie out, he thought she ought to have found some solution that did not involve her in the actual birth.

'You mean that I should have gone to the Races and left her to Sukie,' retorted Sarah, exasperated.

'Well, not exactly, that,' John began, harassed, if resigned to the fact that Sarah had managed to land herself in yet another scrape.

'Then what did you mean?' exclaimed Sarah, indignantly.

'I only know,' said John, 'that most people in good society here will not approve of what you did. Think of what Nellie is—and think of your reputation.'

'Oh, pooh to that,' said Sarah—and left the room.

* * *

She found, though, that he was right. The news ran round Sydney and lost nothing in the telling.

'I wonder at you, Miss Langley,' said Mrs Menzies, 'but I take it that a gel as young as you did not stop to think of what kind of creature she was assisting to give birth.'

'Do you take me for a fool?' replied Sarah fiercely, before she could stop herself. 'Of course I knew how Nellie came by the baby. All that she did was sell herself to the privates of the Regiment for a few pence before she found employment with me. At least she didn't set herself up in Madame Phoebe's establishment and cater for the officers. Or are you pretending that you don't know of Madame Phoebe? Where do you think half the children in my school come from—and your own servants?'

Two red spots appeared on Mrs Menzies's cheeks. 'Well, really, Miss Langley, I never thought to hear such a speech from a lady of quality. Your brother should speak to you.'

'I am sorry,' replied Sarah, stiffly. 'I should not have spoken to you as I did. I helped Nellie in the name of common humanity, as I would have cared for a servant at home. The only difference here is that I had to do the work myself instead of ordering someone else to do it for me. Is that so very wrong?'

Mrs Menzies refused the olive branch which Sarah had offered her. 'My dear, no lady should know of such things.'

Sarah was exasperated all over again. 'You cannot expect me to pretend that I do not know that the young servant girls are not safe from half of the men who visit us—and also that I am not aware of the consequences, be they never so distant. If I had Race Day to do again

I would do nothing differently. Pray, let us turn to another topic.'

Her escapade, however, as John chose to call it, could not be so lightly dismissed. None of the young officers of the Regiment referred to it when she met them, but she was agonisingly aware that they knew of what she had done.

She half-expected Mrs Middleton to prevent Lucy from visiting her, but that lady, whilst deploring Sarah's behaviour, was too proud of the Langley connection to forfeit it. Lucy came to see the baby before Nellie moved to the Grimes's farm. She hung wistfully over the cot, which Sarah had bought from Tom's shop, the drawer having been returned to its rightful place.

Sarah had been surprised by the quality of wood used in Sydney. Her chest of drawers, and now the baby's cot, had been made of cedar, and the heavy doors, well bolted, which hung in every room of the house, were of a weight that would have been envied in England. They were odd luxuries in a place where much else was primitive and makeshift.

'Are you sorry that the baby will soon be leaving, Sarah?' asked Lucy, trying to force a bone rattle into baby Sarah's unresisting fingers.

'Yes,' she replied, 'but John will be relieved. She's rather noisy at night and John needs his sleep. He was quite shocked when I rose the other evening and walked the baby in order to quieten her. He said that he had never thought to see me act as a nursemaid.'

'Oh, the men are all the same,' said Lucy, easily. 'They prefer babies to live in the nursery, well away from their quarters, and there aren't many nurseries in Sydney.'

Sarah walked to the window. 'I suppose that a great

deal of gossip about Nellie and me is running around Sydney.'

'Yes, but it's not all unkind. I overheard Papa tell Mama that Frank threatened to knock down one of the officers in the Mess the other night for saying unkind things about you—and Pat Ramsey is quite fierce in your defence.'

'It's very good of them and I'm sorry that I need to be defended at all,' said Sarah glumly, 'but I don't honestly see what else I could have done.'

'Well, *I* think that you're wonderful,' said Lucy fervently. 'I couldn't possibly have done what you did. I should have died. Even the sight of blood makes me feel quite ill. And you ruined your pretty dress, too—after all the work you put into it.'

'To say nothing of all the blood I spilled learning to sew whilst I made it!' Sarah answered her friend lightly, but she was exceedingly grateful for Lucy's kindness, which soothed her sore heart a little after John's criticism and that of the regimental ladies. She would not forget, either, the open admiration with which Dr Kerr and Tom Dilhorne had treated her. She thought it odd that a pair of ex-convicts seemed to have more generous hearts and minds than their supposed betters.

For his part, Alan Kerr was struggling to come to terms with his feelings for Sarah Langley. Tom had twitted him about them and, as usual, Tom was telling the truth as he saw it. The problem for Alan was the vast gulf that lay between them. How could he, transported and disgraced, dare to aspire to capture the heart of Sarah Langley? Yet every time he met her she fascinated him the more, with the result that his errant body was likely to betray him.

And here he was, visiting her again, this time to examine Nellie and the baby in order to find out whether they were well enough for Tom to drive them to the farm.

Sarah received him with every appearance of pleasure: indeed, she was extremely gratified by his recent changed manner to her. He thought that he had never seen her look so well and his heart leapt at the sight of her. To suppress its ill behaviour he asked, in his most doctorly manner, 'I trust that I see you well, too, Miss Langley?'

'Very well. In fact, I flourish. I am supposing that birthing babies agrees with me,' and her green eyes shone at him.

Her frank manner, so different from that of the other women he met, delighted Alan now that he was no longer the target of her anger. To stop his errant mind from betraying him as much as his body, he looked for a neutral topic of conversation and saw it in an oil painting, which stood on an easel in the corner of the room.

'Is that John's work?' he asked. 'May I look more closely at it?'

'Certainly.'

Sarah watched him walk across the room and bend a little to examine it. No, he was not conventionally handsome, nothing like Charles, but there was a strength and power in his face, as well as in his body, which Charles had lacked. His voice, with its slight Scots burr, added to, rather than took away from, his attractiveness to her. She wondered how he had managed to remain single when simply to look at him made her feel breathless, and (confess it, Sarah!) rather shivery.

He turned, and she blushed a little, as though what she was thinking was reflected in her face. 'Your brother has excelled himself in this, Miss Langley. It is Watson's Bay, is it not?'

'Yes, and thank you for the compliment.' She debated for a moment on whether to tell him the truth. She decided that he deserved it. He had been kindness itself to Nellie and could not have been more so if she had been a lady and not a poor servant girl of dubious morals.

'I had better admit to you, Dr Kerr, that you are looking at my work, not John's.'

'Your work!' He swung back towards the painting. 'Then I must compliment you again. This is a very fine piece. John himself has never done better. There is a wildness about it that is typical of the scene. You have not painted a piece of England transplanted.'

Sarah could scarcely contain her pleasure. 'You are very kind.'

'I am not kind at all. You have a remarkable talent. Did you paint much back home?'

'A little. I had the same teacher as my brother and we learned together. However, as you must know, Dr Kerr, a woman trying to paint seriously is regarded as a very odd thing.'

He waved a hand dismissively, finding himself admiring her more than ever. 'Not when a woman paints as well as this.' He looked across at her again. 'You are a remarkable woman, Miss Langley, you have many talents and an admirable courage and determination. Not many persons of your station would have cared for Nellie as you did. I honour you for that.'

'Thank you, Dr Kerr.' Sarah's voice was unsteady.

He continued, 'I know that you are suffering for it. Every tabby cat in the colony must say her malicious piece. You must not mind them, though: their opinion is of no value.'

Her laughter was unforced. 'I only wish that they could hear you. You hearten me. Of course, you are right, they disapprove of me exceedingly, particularly because I have been stupid enough to speak my mind.'

She began to laugh again. 'Now, why should I tell *you* that? I have spoken my mind to you often enough.'

Alan had resumed his seat. He leaned forward, 'You are honest, Miss Langley. Don't forget that I have frequently spoken my mind to you. I hope that we may now meet in peace.'

He felt a shocking compulsion to kiss her, there, on the corner of her enchanting mouth. What could he be thinking of? Her delightful freedom of manner would disappear very quickly if she had the slightest notion of what he was coming to feel for her. Desperately, to try to recover himself, he added, 'You must understand, Miss Langley, that for every person who disapproves of you, there is another who honours you for what you did.'

'You must not over-refine on my conduct,' Sarah told him, but she was pleased nevertheless. She found that she did not wish him to leave, for she had never yet been able to speak so freely to a man as she was now speaking to Alan Kerr.

Neither did he wish to leave. His eyes roved the room and he saw a portfolio propped against the book case on the far wall.

'Yours, Miss Langley?'

Sarah nodded agreement. For the moment, and for a reason which she did not understand, speech seemed suddenly beyond her.

'May I inspect it?'

Again she nodded.

Alan picked up the portfolio, opened it, and examined its contents, exclaiming as he did so. He found Nellie and Sukie there, engaged in household tasks. Mrs Hackett, her face hard, stood disapprovingly in the kitchen doorway. John was caught in a few vivid strokes: talking to Lachlan Macquarie, drawing a kangaroo, his face screwed up in concentration. Halfway through he found something that Sarah had forgotten: himself, talking to Tom Dilhorne, both of them in characteristic poses. He was leaning forward a little and Tom's billycock was on the back of his head.

Alan looked up at her. 'I was right,' he said slowly. 'You have a rare talent.'

He rose and she rose with him. He put the portfolio down on a side table and stretched out his hand to take hers. Sarah's lips parted and he bent his head, whether to kiss her hand or her cheek she never found out.

A door slammed. Baby Sarah could be heard crying, John was calling for Carter. Face to face, they broke away.

'I must see to John's dinner.' Sarah stammered, and Alan ground out,

'I must be off to the Macarthurs. Their baby has the colic.'

They were awkward together where a moment before they had been on the verge of something true and different.

I must be mad, Alan thought, riding down the street, quite mad. She is beyond me. For a moment there I thought that she returned my feelings. I thought…oh, to the devil with what I thought. I cannot think anything, I am a disgraced ex-convict and she is a lady and that must be the end of it.

Deep down, though, he hoped that it was not.

Chapter Seven

Governor Lachlan Macquarie was not popular with the 73rd Highland Regiment or the free citizens of New South Wales. Some of the officers defended him a little, but since he continued to favour the Emancipists, with whom he considered that the future of the colony lay, his unpopularity grew.

John liked him, but shared the general opinion of his policies and avoided conversation about them as much as possible. Alan Kerr he liked and respected, but he disapproved strongly of Tom Dilhorne because Tom offered him none of the deference which he, a Langley of Prior's Langley, considered to be his due.

Privately he thought that Sarah had been encouraged in her reckless behaviour by Tom, and Sarah's frequent attempts to point out that she had involved Tom in Nellie's trouble, rather than the other way round, went unheeded.

For many reasons, including her brother's obvious prejudice, Sarah, who had at first accepted the Exclusives' view of the Governor, came to understand that his vision of a colony run by colonials, even if they were convicts, and the descendants of convicts, must be correct.

'After all,' she said one day to John and Lucy when they, and the Middletons, were picnicking at Watson's Bay, 'the soldiers and the clerks come and go. Only the Emancipists like Dr Kerr and Tom Dilhorne stay.'

'Then the colony will never come to anything,' was John's riposte to that.

Since this was obviously the popular view of the matter, Sarah, for once, held her tongue. She thought, ruefully, that she was growing up a little in being more cautious of airing her opinions. It was something that she was learning from Tom Dilhorne. What he said, and what he thought, she was beginning to understand, were often two quite different things, although she also realised that he was always honest with her. Doctor Kerr, of whom she was seeing more and more, since he was frequently a dinner guest of the Langleys, was a quite different man: his moral sense and his honesty were his most distinguishing characteristics.

Sarah was becoming used to topsy-turvy seasons, so picnicking in the open in what in England would have been late winter had ceased to amaze her. Lucy accepted the weather as the norm and Sarah wondered how she would manage in England when, as was inevitable, the Regiment returned home.

The nine-days' wonder of Nellie's confinement and Sarah's part in it had died down. Tom had driven Nellie, the baby and Sarah—much against John's wishes—to Grimes's farm where a genuine welcome awaited them. Sarah was fully accepted again in colonial society and Governor Macquarie made it quite plain that she had always possessed his confidence and his support.

The latest subject of gossip was the perpetual problem

of the Irish. They numbered a large part of the convict population, having been transported after the failure of the Irish uprising. They were also the most rebellious since they were political prisoners and had little in common with the prostitutes and thieves with whom they were classified.

Their recalcitrance earned them frequent floggings, and exile to Norfolk Island or Van Diemen's Land where discipline was brutal. There had been some loose talk that they might be considering another uprising—there had been one in 1804—and that some of the more hardened and long-term English convicts might join them. The Governor's attempts to moderate the harsh discipline under which they were compelled to live had met with no favour from the military or the Civil Service, and many of the convicts themselves despised him because they thought him to be, in their words, 'an easy mark'.

Sarah was telling Lucy of Kevin Riley's visit. She had asked Alan Kerr whether he could account for the difference between the slovenly Nellie and her trim and apparently educated brother. He had told her that Riley was self-educated, was free on licence and was determined to get on in life despite having been sent to the colony for involvement in the same robbery as Nellie.

He was also something of a political rebel as a consequence of having been taught by Father Harold, one of the priests transported for his part in the Irish Rebellion of 1798.

'How like you, Sarah,' Lucy remarked, 'to find out about such things. I must confess that most of the convicts look and sound pretty much the same to me, rather dirty.'

'But not Tom Dilhorne and Dr Kerr,' said Sarah, a trifle naughtily.

'Oh, them, they're different,' proclaimed Lucy, but she could not have said wherein the difference lay. Instead she added, 'Let's talk about jollier things like the Governor's Banquet and Garden Party. You'll need a new dress for them.'

'Surely not,' Sarah said. 'I thought that they were mostly outdoors.'

'Not at all. It's only the most stand-up and knock-me-down event of the whole year.'

Sarah laughed. 'Grander than the New Year's Ball,' she teased. 'I can't imagine anything grander than that.'

'Don't fun, Sarah. I know that you've been to reviews, galas and balls back in England, but for Sydney the Governor's last grand party of the summer is really the season's highest point.'

'Well, the last gown I had made for a great occasion came to a sad end,' sighed Sarah. 'What do you think will happen if I make another? An earthquake, perhaps?'

'Or a hurricane,' said Lucy brightly. 'Not that there won't be lots of great occasions in the future. Life here is never dull.'

Sarah suppressed her amusement. She had already been surprised by the frantic nature of the pleasure-seeking in Sydney. It seemed that in an effort to compensate for their isolation and distance from home, everyone was determined to pass the time as entertainingly as possible.

She often wondered how this hectic life struck the compulsory visitors to New South Wales who plodded around Sydney paving the roads, building the bridges, hospitals and barracks, and installing the essential services that made the Exclusives' lives so easy. Alan Kerr,

on a recent visit, had expressed impatience at this constant pleasure-seeking and had praised Sarah for running
her little school and her expeditions to paint and draw
the countryside and its many strange animals. Most of
Sydney's inhabitants showed little interest in what lay
around them.

John looked up from his work and said, 'I think that
it's time we were going home. With all this talk of a
possible uprising, we ought not to invite trouble.'

General agreement to this followed. While she and
John packed up their painting equipment, Carter began
to collect the remains of their picnic. Sarah, watching
him, thought that he, like herself, had changed since they
had arrived in Sydney. Whilst his manner to John remained respectful, there was no doubt that it was more
free. He had taken to slipping out to the nearest grog
shop to drink with the Emancipists and Sarah had been
amused to notice that there was more than a hint of Tom
Dilhorne in his manner.

It suddenly struck her that he might not be so happy
to return to England as John had assumed. Her brother
had recently begun to talk more often of their going
home. He was finding England, in retrospect, more attractive than it had seemed when he had left it.

Sarah, absent-mindedly climbing into the carriage,
asked herself how she felt about returning home. Sooner
or later, they would leave. I would miss this, she almost
said aloud, while the carriage rolled them back to their
temporary home through the geranium hedges and the
stalls laden with the last fruits of the season.

She avoided thinking that what she would miss most
was not the scenery, nor the weather, but her growing
friendship with Alan Kerr, and yes, Tom Dilhorne, too.
They were totally unlike the men she knew back home,

and not for the first time she contrasted Charles unfavourably with them. His charming idleness suddenly seemed intolerably empty.

What, after all, had he ever done, or hoped to do, but inherit?

Lucy's forecast that Sarah would need a new gown was correct. Mrs Middleton supported her daughter, and after visiting Tom's store, where he ordered bale after bale of muslins and silks to be unrolled and displayed before her, Sarah finally decided on a turquoise silk whose colour was to be its only adornment. He also produced a box of tortoiseshell head combs decorated with fake diamonds, made of paste, and a fine lace shawl for her to wear, mantilla-style, falling from the crown of her head to her shoulders.

For such a cold-seeming, practical man, his interest in female haberdashery seemed extraordinary. She said as much to Alan Kerr one evening while they drank tea after he had dined with the Langleys.

Alan, who found these meetings with Sarah both a delight and a strain—her nearness troubled his errant heart—said, 'Well, he's a merchant and a successful one. Everything is grist to his mill. Don't underestimate him, he's probably the cleverest man you'll ever know. Does this question mean that you've been buying for the Governor's Banquet?'

'Yes,' Sarah always found herself a little shy with him. It would never do for John, or any other guest, to know of the extraordinary effect that Alan Kerr was beginning to have on her. 'I suppose,' she added slowly, 'that you scarcely approve of such an event.'

'On the contrary. The Governor is celebrating the

founding of the colony. That must be something of which we all approve.'

'All of us—?' began Sarah, and then stopped, aware that she was touching upon the forbidden topic—how and why he, and so many others, had arrived in the colony at all.

Alan enjoyed her rosy confusion and the delicacy that had prevented her from ending her previous remark. 'Why not? I didn't choose to come here, but now that I *am* here, I must make the best of it as many others do. God knows, the colony needs doctors. Besides, even if it were possible, I would not now return to my old home, even if I thought that a welcome awaited me if I did.'

He stared into the fire, the first of the season.

John, who was sorting through one of his portfolios to find a watercolour of a wombat that he wished to show Alan, looked up.

'Forgive me for asking, Kerr, but do I infer from your words that you would have nothing to return to in Scotland?'

'Of course you may ask. The answer is simple. I collect that you know my story—Macquarie is sure to have told you of it. My family threw me off after my trial. My father made it plain that I was no son of his, and that I was not to pollute the family home should I avoid hanging.'

The words were lightly spoken, but Sarah could guess at the bitterness that lay beneath them. Impulsively, she put out her hand to him. 'Oh, shame, forgive me for saying this, but for a father to treat his son so cruelly...'

He looked at her gratefully. 'I thought that I had lost all feeling over it long ago. Tonight I find that I was mistaken—but you must not condemn him overmuch, Miss Langley. What I did and said was unforgivable, even if it was drunken foolishness, not treason. I was a silly, opinionated boy who deserved to be punished—although not perhaps as greatly as I was.'

'Do I take it that you have heard nothing from them since?' asked John.

'Nothing, but my father was a martinet and I suppose that it was he whom I was rebelling against when I attacked my Captain's unthinking cruelty. My mother feared him, as did my brothers and sisters. He was proud of me, too, which I suppose made my offence seem worse.'

He gave a mirthless laugh. 'Well, all that is long gone. I have a new life here, and one which is in many ways more worthwhile than the one I lost.'

'All the same, though, your story is a sad one,' John said. 'Would you like me to use my influence to help you to return home with a good name? I have many powerful friends in high office and, God knows, it would be little enough to do for you after your rescue of Sarah.'

'You are very kind, but no, my home is here. I am happy and to return would only serve to reopen old wounds.'

'Nevertheless,' John told him, 'my offer stands. You have only to change your mind, and I will do what I can.'

Sarah was proud of John's gratitude. She sometimes thought him too cold, too inclined to be Langley of Prior's Langley, but his kindness to Alan warmed her heart.

She took Alan's teacup from him. 'Well, that is settled, then. Now I must ask you for your help, Dr Kerr. One of my pupils is suffering from some ailment, and I must ask you to visit us tomorrow in order to examine her. I cannot make her mother understand that she is ill and not naughty. That is a frequent error, I find.'

'Indeed, Miss Langley. Heretical as it may seem, there are times when I think it a pity that women may not be doctors. They often demonstrate such a sound understanding of the cause of many human illnesses. It may be because they use their emotions, as well as their intellect, when trying to understand what ails those around them.'

'Most heretical of you, Dr Kerr,' Sarah riposted with a rueful smile. 'Think what I have endured for wishing to be a painter. I cannot begin to imagine how I should be treated were I to assert that I wished to be a surgeon!'

She looked so charmingly animated when she came out with this that Alan had to repress a terrible urge to kiss her on the spot, John or no John! Such an action would have had him drummed out of the Langleys' home nearly as severely as the English courts had treated him.

'True, but all the same, think how extremely capably you dealt with Nellie, without any training whatsoever.'

'Oh, that was common sense, Dr Kerr, and you forget that I frequented the stables as a girl and knew where and how foals were born—even though I shouldn't have done.'

Alan could not stop himself from coming out with, 'As a girl, Miss Langley? Why, you are only a girl still.'

His eyes were full of admiration. It was the most open admission yet of his true feelings for her, and its effect on Sarah was so strong that she was overwhelmed with shyness—she, Sarah Langley, who was never shy. She had never been backward in flirtatious interludes back home, before Charles had destroyed her confidence in herself, but she felt a strange reluctance to flirt with Dr Alan Kerr.

It was not the presence of John that was affecting her, though that was a factor, but rather that her own feelings for Alan, and his for her, were too serious for the frivolous exchanges that had amused her in England.

Their eyes met over the filled teacup which she was offering to him, and she was aware that her hand was shaking.

To change the subject to lighter matters she asked him if his attendance at the Banquet was certain, since he approved of it, and he replied that it was. His own feelings were struck, too, and were all the stronger for being repressed. He was becoming more and more certain that she was not indifferent to him, but to declare his love was impossible.

Their conversation had reminded him yet again that he was nothing more than a transported criminal, and that restoration of the standing he had once enjoyed in society was, despite John's generous offer, also impossible. Alan did not see the ardent looks that Sarah was directing at him, but John did, and putting his portfolio down—he had found his painting of the wombat—he wondered. for the first time whether bringing Sarah to New South Wales with him had been altogether wise.

Kerr was a good enough fellow, despite his sad history, but to consider him as a brother-in-law… No, that was impossible!

Chapter Eight

The Governor's Banquet saw Sarah, dressed in her turquoise gown, and with the mantilla trailing across her shoulders, sitting next to young Captain Stephen Parker at the dinner table. He was one of her many admirers. The dining room of Government House had frequently been called majestic, and certainly the ninety people who sat down at three o'clock to partake of what could only be called a sumptuous repast after the indifferent fare to which they were used could have been forgiven if they had assumed that they were eating in one of the great European capitals and not in a southern wilderness.

Sarah usually found colonial boasting irritating, but she told Stephen that, for once, the locals had not exaggerated. Governor Macquarie had excelled himself.

'True,' said Stephen. 'The only fly in the ointment, if you will forgive me for saying so, Miss Langley, is having to sit down with so many of these dammed Emancipists. I wonder at the Governor, I really do. He seemed to be a stickler for the proprieties back home. I can't think what has come over him since he arrived here. Doctor Kerr's presence is almost bearable, but to expect us to hobnob with Dilhorne is too much.'

'I believe,' said Sarah carefully—and not for the first time—'that he thinks that Dilhorne and his kind will still be here when we are gone, and that, to some extent, the colony's future will be in their hands.'

Captain Parker laughed. 'The colony's future! You're bamming me, Miss Langley! I suppose that all ladies are sentimentalists. What future is there in this little settlement on the edge of the world? I find Macquarie's pretence of a capital city with courthouses and hospitals a nonsense. I'm told that he's thinking of building a library. Here, among the black and white savages!'

With some difficulty Sarah held her tongue. The arrival of a great dish of pineapple saved her from an immediate reply. Why had she never noticed before the insensitivity of so many of the men who surrounded her? Stephen Parker was quite a good sort, but his attitude to the colony jarred on her. Apart from that, though, he was a pleasant dinner companion.

To avoid further conversation she toasted him with her half-filled wine glass—'To England and home, Captain Parker.'

'And beauty, madam,' he added gallantly.

And doubtless, thought Sarah, he thinks that he's converted me to his views because I haven't argued with him. And that's a new thing, too. A few months ago I would have argued with him. What can be happening to me? I must be adopting Lucy's defensive colouring.

One advantage of a Sydney gathering, so far as the ladies were concerned, was that there was a shortage of women so that any halfway pretty girl found herself surrounded by admiring young men. And old men, too, thought Sarah amusedly, having had some tricky encounters with elderly officers of the garrison who were tired of confining their amorous attentions to the various

ladies of the town in Sydney's slum district of The
Rocks.

Stephen, however, had noticed Sarah's tact and considered that the Governor could do with a little of it.

'You may not have heard, Miss Langley, that the Governor has made himself unpopular with most of the men
in the colony because he has closed down many of Sydney's seventy-five public houses.'

Sarah forbore to tell him that Dr Kerr had already
informed her of this latest hotly debated measure, and
had expressed approval of it. He considered drink to be
a curse, and not only because of his own unhappy experience of its dangers.

Drinking was not confined to grog shops, however:
drinking at the Banquet had begun immediately after the
mid-day review of the troops. On top of that, during the
meal no less than nineteen official toasts had been proposed, as well as private ones, such as Sarah's. The noise
in the vast room had risen to a roar, and it was obvious
that some of those whose toasting had been more than
merely token would have difficulty in joining in the
strolling round the lawns outside when dinner was over.

Sarah's enjoyment was unforced, particularly when,
once the company had streamed convivially outside, she
found herself next to Alan Kerr, who asked her gravely,
'I wonder what you think of a colonial celebration, Miss
Langley?'

Her green eyes shone at him. She had not overin-
dulged, but she had taken just enough wine to make her
feel that the day, the weather and the company were
magnificent, that the men were all witty and the women
all beautiful.

'Oh, it's beyond belief,' she said.

Alan, who as usual, had drunk only water, took her

arm and they walked up and down, enjoying the playing of numerous popular songs and operatic pieces by the Regimental band. He thought that Sarah had never looked so beautiful: the turquoise silk set off her vivid colouring, and enhanced her glittering eyes. The wave of desire that broke over him was as shocking as it was sudden.

'The gardens are lovely,' said Sarah, who was suffering herself from her nearness to a man to whom she was growing more and more attracted. She was, though, genuinely impressed by the profusion of flowering plants in the colony and frequently stopped to admire the many pretty cottage gardens on her walks through Sydney. At home the labourers on the Langley estates filled their plots with vegetables, mostly cabbages, with only a few flowers between the rows.

'Then you must meet the garden's creator,' said Alan, conscious that he must remove the temptation to him which she unwittingly presented, and that this could be accomplished by presenting her to a fellow Scot, Charles Fraser. He already knew that Sarah was a keen gardener back in England and he sorrowfully surrendered her to his friend and, apparently casually, drifted away.

He was also conscious of the fact that John Langley was not happy if he stayed too long in Sarah's company. He had no wish to distress his kind friend, even if leaving Sarah cost him more than one pang. He walked through a crowd of footmen carrying even more drinks for the official guests, anxious to serve them before the general public were admitted to the gardens when dusk fell.

Sarah was enchanted to discover from Charles Fraser, who immediately added himself to the growing list of her admirers, that the oranges in the boughs of the trees were illuminated by lamps specially hung there. 'It's a genuine fairy grove, Mr Fraser,' she told him. 'Your notion, I presume?'

Charles Fraser confessed that it was the Governor who had inspired the decorations. 'He's a remarkable man, Miss Langley. He's not properly appreciated. When I consider what the colony was like when he came, and what he is now making of it I am full of respect for him. By the time he has finished we shall have a true capital city here.'

Sarah agreed with him. They strolled round the flower beds, drinking in the perfumed dusk, until good manners dictated that she freed him to talk to other guests. Wineglass in hand, full of the joys of good company and good food, she came upon Sukie on the arm of John's man, Carter.

'Oh, Miss Sarah!' Sukie's eyes shone in the light from the flambeaux, made from great boughs of Norfolk Island pine. 'It's beautiful, ain't it?'

Her hair had been properly cut and dressed, and, wearing one of Sarah's old gowns, cut down to fit her, she was a pretty girl, hardly recognisable as the dirty slattern Sarah had first seen in her kitchen.

In the months since the birth of Nellie's baby Sukie had blossomed under Sarah's influence. She had learned to read and write and had been persuaded that washing herself was not something odd that the gentry did to pass the time. She had even been persuaded to try her hand at sewing, where her first efforts were nearly as clumsy as Sarah's had been.

Sarah smiled at the pair of them. She felt full of an infinite well-being. Carter smiled back at her. He, too, was well turned out and she wished that Alan had been

with her when she had found them. He would have been
pleased, she knew, to see them so happy together.

'Very beautiful,' she said. 'It's nothing like home, but
then, Sydney isn't.'

'Aye, that it's not,' said Carter, 'and all the better for
being different—if you don't mind me saying so, Miss
Sarah.'

No, she didn't mind, but it struck her that, back in
England, she would have resented Carter's cheerful
frankness. What was happening to her? Ever since she
had arrived in New South Wales her whole life seemed
to have turned upside down, as though being transported
so far across the wide globe had changed everything,
including herself. She no longer thought or felt as she
had once done.

It had not changed John, though, and a few moment
later she was pleased that he was nowhere in sight when
Tom Dilhorne came up to her. He had been at the banquet, but seated far away from her, and for a moment
she did not recognise him. He was wearing the clothes
of a gentleman, his hair had been brushed into a Brutus
cut and, for the first time, he was indistinguishable from
the officers and officials around him.

'Miss Langley,' he said, bowing. 'I have to congratulate you on the change you have brought about in Miss
Sukie.'

'Oh, she has done a large part of that herself.'

He looked keenly at her. 'You are generous, Miss
Langley. Most women would have taken all the credit
for her transformation, but then, as I am well aware, you
are not most women.'

His voice had changed, too. It also was indistinguishable from that of the officers around them. She remem-

bered that Alan Kerr had once told them that he was an excellent mimic.

'You flatter me, I think.'

'Oh, no,' he said, 'I never flatter anyone, it is not my way. Besides, there is something else I wish to say to you here, privately, where none may hear us. It is this: being the woman that you are, I trust that you will take care not to hurt my good friend, Dr Kerr. I believe that you are clever enough to understand what I am saying.'

Sarah, being Sarah, knew what he meant and replied, gently but firmly, 'And I, Mr Dilhorne, am I not to be hurt, too?'

His smile for her was a frank one. 'Oh, yes, Miss Langley, you are quite as clever as I thought you to be. Remember, though, that in affairs of the heart, cleverness is not enough, indeed, has little to do with them. Forgive me for raising this with you, but your bravery, as I well know, is not confined to your physical activities, it is also related to the manner in which you face the world.'

Sarah did not know what surprised her the most: Tom Dilhorne's understanding of the world of men and women, or his ability to speak in good clear articulate English, quite unlike his usual hard, if not coarse, manner.

He smiled again. 'By your expression I see that you have understood me. We shall not speak of this again, but I trust you to do the right thing, however much it might pain you.'

His bow was one of farewell. He had scarcely had time to leave her before Pat Ramsey was by her side.

'Was that commoner Dilhorne troubling you, Miss Langley? If he was, I will see that he never troubles you again.'

'Not at all, Captain Ramsey. I find that he has a fund of good sense, and if you ever cared to talk to him with any consideration for what I understand that he has accomplished since he arrived here, I think that you would enjoy his company rather more than that of many of the men in Sydney.'

She thought for moment that she had gone too far, but, like many people, she had underrated Pat Ramsey.

He gave a long low whistle and shook his head at her. 'Suitably reprimanded, Miss Langley. I have to say that in his borrowed plumes he looks a different man from the one who usually roams Sydney, so you may be right. I thought that for a moment he might have been troubling you with his intentions.'

To his surprise Sarah began to laugh. 'No, indeed, quite the contrary. You need have no fear of that.'

'Excellent. There is one thing that I ought to say to you, and here, where we are private among the many, is perhaps the best time to say it. My feelings for you are strong. Were I other than a poverty-stricken younger son who fears to be seen as a fortune hunter, I would pay the utmost attention to you myself. Because of my circumstances, however, friendship with you is all that I may aspire to. I hope that knowing this, you will not turn away from me. I also believe that all that you wish from me *is* friendship and, given that, let us be happy together without commitment.'

Sarah was secretly amused at how much Pat's introduction to his little speech resembled that of Tom Dilhorne. It was plain that he had more in common with the despised Emancipist than he knew. She could never love Pat Ramsey, handsome and kind though he was, since, without knowing how it had come about, Sarah had discovered that she was in thrall to quite another type of man. Nevertheless, Tom Dilhorne had asked her to be kind to Alan Kerr, so it also behoved her to be kind to Pat.

'Certainly we may remain friends. I have not so many that I can afford to turn one away.'

He bowed to her, reminding her of Tom. 'Then that is settled, and we may proceed as we mean to go on. There is to be a giant bonfire. Will you allow me to escort you to the little hill that overlooks the garden where we shall have a good view of everything? Frank is up there already, with Lucy Middleton.'

'I shall be delighted, and pray call me Sarah. As a friend I would like you to be Pat to me as you are to Lucy and Frank. Also...' and she hesitated a little fearing to presume too much, but it needed to be said '...I hope that, one day, you will find someone who will be only too happy to be Mrs Pat Ramsey.'

'That is most kind of you, and now, take my arm.'

They walked off together. Sarah told herself that she ought to be flattered by what has passed, but, she thought, what I mostly feel is that I must be careful not to hurt people's feelings. I'm sure that I never thought of such a thing before, but I must remember it in future.

Later, being driven home with John, he said, to her no small amusement, 'My dear, I must urge you to be careful. We are in a strange and exciting place and I feel that it would be unwise of you to become fixed on any of the men whom you meet here, because of that. Captain Ramsey is a good enough fellow, but he is not the man for you. I understand he has little beyond his pay and must therefore be beneath your consideration.

'I also trust that you see fit to talk to Kerr and Dilhorne after such a fashion that they get no false notions, either. These Emancipists do not seem to know their place, and they fail to know it most of all.'

'Come, come,' said Sarah, 'I have no intention of marrying yet—if at all—and certainly I am not fixed on anyone at the present.' Was she being entirely truthful in saying this? She was not too sure—but then, she wasn't sure of anything at the moment—only that Alan Kerr was having the most strange effect on her.

'I'm glad to hear it, my dear. Now let us leave this topic and talk of better things.'

'Such as?' Sarah could not help saying.

'Now, my dear, you are not to tease me. I have only your best interests at heart, you know.'

The trouble was that Sarah no longer knew what her best interests were!

More than that, quite unknown to her, Tom was not the only person present at the party who knew that Alan and Sarah were attracted to one another. Sukie, for one, approved entirely of the comfortable understanding that they had apparently reached. The military men she dismissed with scorn and she considered the officials to be a namby-pamby lot. Since Alan's care for Nellie and the baby he could do no wrong. After all, if the Doctor and Miss Sarah were to get hitched then she, Sukie, would not lose Miss Sarah.

She confessed all this to Carter on the way back home. 'You women are all the same,' was his only comment, 'matchmakers, every one of you. What you really want is to see us poor fellers get caught.'

Sukie ignored this. She had long made up her mind that she would do everything she could to see that George Carter stayed in New South Wales. Carter, however, needed little persuading. He had already decided that he would remain behind when the Langleys left. He liked the freedom of the colony and reckoned that he could easily find employment, or perhaps work for himself. He was useful with horses and was tired of being John Langley's man. George Carter wanted to be his own man.

'To what do I owe this honour?' Tom was twitting Alan Kerr who had just arrived in his store, his medical bag in his hand.

'Not to buy anything, that's for sure,' Alan teased back. 'Sarah Langley sent their kitchen boy to me this morning to ask me to come and examine Annie Bell. She's worried about her health, and thought that it would be a good idea for me to see her when her mother isn't present. Apparently the mother is consistently denying that anything is wrong with her.'

'Well, Sarah's class is present in the back today,' Tom told him, 'but if Annie is the thin child with the persistent dry cough she isn't there. But look in on them, by all means; I may be mistaken.'

As usual, he wasn't. Alan walked in to discover that the children were bent over some improvised desks, busily copying Sarah's beautiful handwriting set out on a blackboard—also improvised.

She walked towards him, her face unhappy.

'Could we speak in the shop? I wouldn't like the children to hear us.'

'Indeed.' Alan led the way to a niche behind the counter where Tom had a desk and a bookcase. He was busy serving a customer.

'Just as I was leaving home, Mrs Bell arrived to tell me that Annie was not coming to my class in future. She said, most rudely, that Annie was wasting her time bothering with book learning and that she had found work for her in one of the woollen mills near Jenkins Wharf. You may imagine how shocked I was. I'm sorry that I've brought you here for nothing.'

'Do not trouble yourself about that. Instead, tell me why the child worried you so much.'

'Oh, Alan—' and in her distress Sarah called him by his Christian name for the first time '—you should have seen her last week. She's painfully thin and has this horrible dry cough. She was scarcely strong enough to write on her slate. I would have thought she was more fit to be placed in a hospital rather than a manufactory—and so I told her mother, who immediately left, cursing me for a busybody. Do you think that Tom has any influence over her?'

Tom, who had arrived in time to hear Sarah's last few sentences, shook his head. 'Mrs Bell is the biggest damn fool in the colony, begging your pardon, Miss Sarah. Her husband died of trying to make her see sense. I'm not surprised that she took no notice of you.'

'So that's that, then,' remarked Sarah glumly. 'Annie is destined to be a hand at Dempster's Mill—for a short time, any way. I would wager that she doesn't have long to live. I'm sorry to have brought you out on a wild goose chase, Alan. I know how busy you are.'

'Don't apologise,' he told her again. 'You know that I'll always come when you call. If I see Mrs Bell, I might try to have a word with her.'

'Thank you for that, too,' Sarah said, offering him her hand like a frank boy. She was beginning to tire of curtsying and bowing. Their handshake lasted a fraction longer than politeness demanded. Sarah's eyes glowed and their manner to each other betrayed them again to the observant Tom before Alan left.

He sighed. The pull between them was so strong that

he could trust neither of them to behave sensibly. He was beginning to wonder if he would ever feel for a woman what Alan was plainly feeling for Sarah Langley.

Somehow, he doubted it.

In the days following the Governor's Banquet Sarah found that public life in Sydney became much less hectic—other than Lucy's birthday party there was, for the time being, little in the way of excitement. On the other hand, her private life was growing much more intense. Stephen Parker was tireless in his pursuit of her, ignoring her attempts to convince him that she merely wanted him as a friend. A fresh outbreak of trouble in the kitchen added to her woes. And then, if all this were not enough, there were her feelings for Alan Kerr to cope with.

Her hours in the back room where she taught the little ones became a haven of peace where she could forget everything, and so she told Alan one afternoon when he visited her, after most of her class had left, to look at yet another child, Bessie Machen, who was showing signs of starvation and neglect.

His examination ended, with the verdict that he would ask Tom to investigate what was happening in the child's home. 'It may be,' he said, 'that there is too little money going in to feed the family properly. By her manner with me, the child is not being mistreated—unlike poor Annie.'

He handed Bessie back to her and Sarah cuddled the poor wan thing. Alan looked thoughtfully at the woman he was coming to think of as his Sarah. She seemed more subdued than usual.

'Forgive me,' he said, 'you seem a little tired, Miss Langley. Is anything wrong? Are you doing too much?'

'Yes,' she told him in her usual frank manner, 'I do

feel a little tired, but not because I'm overdoing things. I'm having to cope with a lot of nonsense at home. John seems to disapprove of everything I do, and for the past few days Mrs Hackett has been worrying me with her constant complaints that someone is stealing our food.'

'Stealing your food!' Alan began to laugh at the mere idea of such a thing. 'You can't be serious.'

'Oh, but I am. It seems that first some leftover sausages and some vanilla blancmange disappeared. After this the elves disposed of various other tit-bits which La Hackett had been saving for herself or for us. I know that it must be annoying for her, but she acts as though John or I have been getting up in the middle of the night in order to eat them. I've had a word with Sukie and Carter but they profess to know nothing. La Hackett appears to suspect Katie, Nellie's successor, but she seems too simple to steal anything.

'Unfortunately I told Mrs H, rather frivolously, that the fairies must be responsible and now she's more angry with me than with the thief—if there is a thief.'

Her expression was tragi-comic, but Alan suspected that Sarah was finding the problem of running a small handful of servants in Sydney greater than that of managing a large one at Prior's Langley where the staff had numbered over seventy.

'On top of that,' she added, 'Mrs Hackett is being more difficult than ever with the result that Sukie has reverted to being flighty again. Nellie's replacement is proving quite inadequate and only Carter is his usual solid self. And all this just when I thought that I had everything domestic beautifully arranged—it's all falling apart.'

Alan smiled tenderly at her. She was running her hand through her chestnut curls while she spoke and he always found her most enchanting when she was at her most informal. The rapport between them was never greater than when he came to examine her small charges. She had suggested recently that, except when there was an emergency, he might consider visiting the children once a week to look for the first signs of trouble. This had been prompted by his remark that doctors were wrong to wait for illness to happen: they should do more to prevent it from happening at all by making sure that people ate the right food and were not compelled to work overlong hours.

'You know that I will always do everything I can to help you, but I fear that solving the problem of the missing food is beyond my powers.'

'That's not all,' Sarah continued, 'that is, if you can bear to hear any more. But this is the most serious thing of all. Yesterday Mrs Bell arrived on my doorstep, shrieking that she wished to speak to me at once. John ordered her to be turned away, but I intervened and asked her what the trouble was. Whereupon she began, in the vilest terms, to accuse me of having stolen Annie. It's quite ridiculous really—first Mrs Hackett seems to think I'm making away with the food and now I'm accused of kidnapping little girls.'

Alan would have loved to kiss away the worried frown on Sarah's face. Instead all that he was able to do was to say, as reassuringly as he could, 'Don't worry too much, Miss Langley I'm sure that there's a perfectly rational explanation for the food, and Mrs Bell can hardly be serious over Annie.'

'She seemed serious enough. I think that I succeeded in convincing her that I had not kidnapped Annie, if that is the right word, but it seems that the child has disappeared, and I can't help worrying about what might have happened to her. There are some dreadful persons about in Sydney—as we both know. If she has been taken to The Rocks she might never be seen again. John didn't help matters by telling me that I shouldn't put myself in situations where trollops can insult me in my own home.'

Her expression was so sorrowful that Alan could tell how much she was affected by Annie's sad tale. Her usual ebullient manner was quite gone. Greatly daring, he placed his hand over hers. 'You must not repine. There is little you can do, or could ever have done, for Annie. Once her mother had decided to send her to the mill the matter was beyond you. There is no law against the employment of eleven-year old girls and their work-ing for sixty hours a week in a manufactory. To be fair to her, Mrs Bell almost certainly needs the money Annie can earn there. Worse than that, Sydney needs the mill. It is necessary if the colony is to provide its own goods without relying too much on what is brought in from England.'

'Good God, you cannot be defending the use of chil-dren, Dr Kerr,' she flashed back at him.

'No, but life is not just, as I well know. After all, I don't suppose you gave the matter a thought until you arrived here and saw what was happening to Annie your-self. Great Britain is full of mills employing children even younger than Annie.'

Sarah bowed her head in acknowledgement of the jus-tice of what he had just said.

'But I do know now, and I cannot pretend that I don't. I sometimes wonder what has been happening to me ever since I came to New South Wales.' She lifted her great green eyes to him in almost unconscious supplication.

'I never thought that I should care about such things.

Indeed, I doubt whether I ever had a serious thought at all before I came here. But none of this helps Annie. Could you look out for her when you are on your rounds? She must be somewhere.'

He lifted Bessie from Sarah's knee and offered her one of the comfits he kept in a screw of paper in his pocket in order to rid children of their fear of him.

'Yes, I promise to look for Annie, and I shall ask Tom to do so as well. You know, Miss Langley, before you came to New South Wales you lived a very sheltered life. But Sydney is relatively small, and it is not possible for you to be unaware of what is happening in the world around you.'

Alan did not add, 'The other women in the colony do not see what is happening around them, and never will. What distinguishes you is your compassion.' He did not want to leave her, would rather have stayed to comfort her, but his duty called, and it was one of the rules he had made since he had arrived in New South Wales that he would never resist that call, whatever the cost.

Sarah watched him go with more reluctance than she had ever felt before. She had tried to tell John something of her mental confusion and of her worries about Annie and the other unhappy children, but he had looked uncomprehendingly at her and advised her not to trouble herself about such things.

'They are not a woman's concern, Sarah, and that's the top and the bottom of it. There's no law to prevent a mill owner from hiring children, most of whom are the offspring of criminals and loose women.'

After her discussion with Alan, Sarah felt John's lack of pity even more deeply. Alan had told her much the same, but he had also demonstrated distress that matters should be so. She knew that he frequently attended the poor of Sydney without asking for payment, and that this was a matter for criticism among some of the Exclusives who felt it wrong that they should be asked to pay when others weren't.

When Mrs Middleton had complained of this to Sarah, she had pointed out that Dr Kerr lived a hard life himself, very different from that of most of the Exclusives, but had been met with the answer, 'Indeed, he's lucky to live a free life at all, never mind indulge in luxuries.'

Sarah was beginning to find it difficult to talk of such things not only to John, but also to many of the people whom she met in her daily round.

Chapter Nine

The day of Lucy's birthday party was as fine and bright
as any since Sarah had arrived in the colony. She had
not treated herself to a new dress, but had chosen to wear
one of those which she had brought from England. It
was a white muslin with pale blue trimmings and a parasol and a tiny straw hat to match.

She had debated on what to give Lucy for a birthday
present until Tom Dilhorne had taken her aside in his
store and shown her a fan which he had just unpacked.
It was Chinese and had delicate porcelain panels
mounted inside the cream feathers and intricate ivory
spokes. Each panel had a flower or a bird painted on it.
Sarah, entranced, bought it immediately and could
hardly wait to see Lucy's face when she gave it to her.
Tom spoke briefly to her of the missing Annie. He had
been unable to find any trace of where she might have
gone—or where she could have found refuge.

She was thinking of this when she ran lightly upstairs
that afternoon to dress herself for Lucy's party. Mrs Bell
had been round again and was finding an unlikely ally
in Mrs Hackett. Not that Mrs Hackett had any real sympathy for either Annie or her mother, but she was more

than happy to use them to show her disapproval of Sarah these days. She was always comparing her unfavourably with her brother. 'A proper gentleman he is, who knows a gentleman's place,' she was fond of saying.

Sarah tried to forget all her many worries. An afternoon and evening of innocent fun with Lucy and her friends were what she needed. She was debating which of her reticules was more appropriate for the ensemble she had just put on when she heard a door slam and the sound of running feet on the stairs.

As once before, Sukie burst into her bedroom in a state of ill-defined panic.

'What is it now, Sukie? I haven't time to engage in a new argument with Mrs Hackett. You really must learn to live with the woman.'

'It ain't that, Mum.' Miss Sarah and proper diction seemed to have flown out the window, thought Sarah in exasperation—as had Sukie's neatness of dress. She was nearly as flyaway as she had been before Nellie's baby had been born.

'Oh, Mum, you must come with me, now.'

'Indeed, no. I'm off to Miss Middleton's birthday party. I'm already late because of Mrs Bell's latest eruption. Tell me when I come back.'

'It'll likely be too late by then, Mum, I mean Miss Sarah. It's Annie.'

Sarah's heart gave a great lurch. She threw her reticule on to the bed. 'Explain yourself, Sukie. What do you mean by saying it's Annie? Annie is missing.'

'Oh, no, Mum, Miss Sarah, she ain't. Come with me and I'll show you.'

Dear God, thought Sarah. Mrs Bell is right. I *am* involved in Annie's disappearance, or Sukie is, which comes down to the same thing.

She seized Sukie by the shoulders. 'You know where Annie is, then?'

Sukie was suddenly in an agony of fear. 'Yes, oh, Miss Sarah, you must come with me. I think that she may be dying.'

'Dying!' Sarah picked up her shawl and threw it around her shoulders. Lucy's birthday party flew out of her head. 'If that is so, then I will come at once.'

'We'd best dodge old Hackett,' cried Sukie, 'she don't know about Annie. She'll be out of the house soon. She's visiting that friend of hers this afternoon.'

Again, as once before, she grabbed Sarah's hand and led her down the stairs, this time across the garden at the side of the house and towards the paved area before the stables where Carter stood waiting for her.

'Does this mean that Carter is involved in hiding Annie, too?' asked Sarah.

'Couldn't have done it wivout him,' declared Sukie, whose diction seemed to be deteriorating with every sentence she uttered.

'This way, Miss Sarah,' said Carter gravely. He escorted her into the stables and to the ladder leading into the hayloft. 'I'll help you up.'

There, in the hay, on an improvised bed, lay Annie, face ashen and eyes closed. Her breathing was rapid and shallow. Bloodstained cloths lay beside her.

'She were taken much worse this morning,' Carter told her. 'I fear that she's in a bad way.'

'How long have you been hiding her in the stables?' asked Sarah.

'Since she ran away,' Sukie said. 'She was very ill when she came here and asked us to help her. We knew that if we told anyone Mrs Bell would come to take her away and would send her back to the mill.'

Sarah knelt down in the hay with a total disregard for
her pretty gown, and felt Annie's forehead. Annie gave
no sign that she was aware of her presence. Even with
her limited medical knowledge Sarah could see that she
was dangerously ill.

She rose and, signing to Sukie and Carter to follow
her, made her way down the ladder.

'We shall have to send for her mother and for Dr
Kerr,' she said briefly, 'and even then we may be too
late to save her—if she was ever saveable, that is.'

'No, no,' gabbled Sukie, grabbing at Sarah's skirts.
'Don't do that. It'll be the death of her. Her ma will send
her back to the mill and I shall be tried and sentenced
to go to the Factory Farm for helping her. Carter will be
punished, too.'

'Even Mrs Bell can't send Annie back to the mill in
this state,' said Sarah angrily, although at whom her anger was directed she did not know. Principally at herself,
for her blindness in not connecting the missing food with
Annie's disappearance and the distracted Sukie's altered
condition.

'I wonder at you, Carter, for helping Sukie. Why did
you not tell me that you were hiding Annie? I might
have found some way out for you, but now…'

'The little maid didn't seem quite so ill when she
came to Sukie for help,' said Carter. 'She grew much
worse yesterday.'

'She was already ill when I last saw her,' Sarah
snapped. 'But we mustn't stand here idly gossiping. Carter, you must run and fetch Dr Kerr immediately. I can't
answer for Annie's life if you don't. We'll think about
saving you and Sukie from the law when we've done
something for Annie. Most of all, we mustn't let Mr
John or Mrs Hackett find out about this yet. We shall

all be sent to Sydney's deepest dungeons if either of them discover what we've been up to before I've had time to invent something that will save us.

'Sukie, go and sit with Annie. She shouldn't be left alone.'

Sarah went slowly back into the house when she had sent Carter on his way. There was no question of her setting off for Lucy's party until Alan had come. She thought of him as Alan almost unconsciously. Alan would know what to do. Alan would think of something that would save Carter and Sukie from punishment for the imbroglio into which their kind hearts had led them. Alan might even be able to save Annie.

How long had Sukie and Carter been hiding her? It must have been for at least a week, since it was about that time when Mrs Hackett had first begun to complain of the missing food. It was a little less than that when Mrs Bell had arrived at their door, breathing fire. Well, without knowing it, she had certainly come to the right place!

Sarah looked at her little fob watch. It seemed highly likely that Sukie, having ruined Race Day for her by involving her in the birth of Nellie's baby, was about to ruin Lucy's birthday party for her, too.

She shrugged her shoulders. Lucy would be wondering why she had not turned up by now, but she possessed no means of informing her that she might be delayed. It was a blessing that John was out on a painting expedition and was not due at the party until the tea board arrived. That only left Mrs Hackett to be avoided until she left for the afternoon.

Fortunately this time Alan Kerr was at home and arrived very rapidly. Carter, instead of taking him straight to the stables, had the good sense to bring him into the house where Sarah received him. On the way back to the Langleys he had also given Alan a brief explanation of what he would find there, before he joined Sukie in her vigil.

Alan's face was grave. 'So, all is explained—Annie's disappearance, the missing food and Sukie's odd behaviour.'

'Yes. It would appear that we have been unwittingly sheltering Annie. I fear that she is very ill indeed. As soon as Mrs Hackett leaves the house you can safely visit the stables to discover whether you can do anything for the poor child. By great good fortune John is also absent.

'Between us I hope that we can arrange matters so that we may save Sukie and Carter from the consequences of their folly. Good though their intentions might have been, they have put themselves in danger of punishment by the law.'

'Carter told me that Annie was very weak and already spitting blood when she arrived here and Sukie asked him to help her,' Alan said. 'I'm afraid that your brother is going to find that New South Wales has finally corrupted him. However, that is by the by. First we must do what we can for Annie.'

'Oh, Alan,' Sarah spoke his forename without thinking, 'I knew that I was right to send for you. What are we going to do?'

'Do, my brave girl? Why, you must sit down and compose yourself. It is Lucy Middleton's party today, is it not?'

Sarah began to wring her hands, saying, 'Yes, but I can't leave here until I know what is happening to Annie. Indeed, I doubt whether I will have the heart to go then. At the same time it's important that I attend her party and do not appear to snub her. I really am on the horns of a dilemma as you must see.'

'Of course I do.'

He leaned forward to try to quieten her by taking her hands in his. 'Come, Sarah, you must not fret. The case is hard, but you are doing all that is proper. We will find a way out for you if we can.'

We, he had said we, and by doing so had associated himself with her in her attempt to save Annie, Carter and Sukie. Before Sarah had time to thank him there was a knock on the door. He dropped her hands and walked to the window when Mrs Hackett entered, her hard eyes on them. Suspicion was written in every rigid line of her body.

'I'm off, now, Miss Langley. I can't find Sukie. I think that she must be idling somewhere with Carter. No wonder food disappears when the servants aren't under proper control.'

'Oh, I'm sure that I don't blame you, Mrs Hackett,' said Sarah giddily. 'Pray enjoy your afternoon with a clear conscience.'

'As to that, *my* conscience is certainly clear. I wish that I could say as much for others.'

She left in high dudgeon and Sarah turned with relief to Alan. 'Now we may go to Annie.'

Alan's examination of Annie was slow and methodical. More than ever Sarah was beginning to realise how different he was from most of the men she had met before. His care for Nellie and Annie was the same as for that of herself and John. She mentally contrasted him with the doctors at Prior's Langley for whom the servants hardly existed as human beings. A brusque examination and a recommendation for them to return to

work as soon as possible was the usual treatment pre-
scribed.

She watched Alan's gravely concerned face while he
knelt over the unconscious Annie, whose breathing
seemed to grow shallower by the minute. Sarah had seldom been so conscious of her own helplessness and
could tell by his expression that he was feeling the same.
When he rose to his feet, he told the sobbing Sukie to
continue watching over the dying girl before beckoning
to Sarah to follow him down the ladder. She responded
without a word.

Once down he spoke to her in a low voice so that
Sukie in the loft above them could not hear what was
he was saying. 'I fear that she is far gone, so far that I
am not certain that there is anything I can do to save
her. I will stay with her, but I am sadly sure that she has
been slowly dying as a result of consumption for some
time. Her mother should have called on me for help long
ago.'

Alan caught his breath when he saw Sarah's stricken
face. 'You are not to reproach yourself, Sarah,' he said,
using her Christian name in the middle of this sad occasion, for they were simply a man and a woman in the
face of death where all distinctions of rank disappear.
'There is little you can do, or, for that matter, could have
done, once her mother refused your help. What I am
about to say may appear heartless, but reflect: it is your
duty to go to your friend's birthday party.'

When Sarah made a sharp sound of demurral, he told
her, his voice as kind as he could make it, 'I know how
you must feel, but Annie will have Sukie, Carter and
myself to care for her. Lucy is your friend and I am
aware, if you are not, that she is already troubled by
Frank Wright's feelings for you.'

Sarah gave a start of surprise on hearing this. 'No, that cannot be! I have said nothing to encourage him and he has said nothing of this to me. I am sure that you— or she—must be mistaken. I would never, ever, do anything to hurt Lucy she is my best—and my only— woman friend in Sydney.'

Alan said gently to her, 'I don't think that you are aware of the effect that you have on men, Sarah, it is one of your nicest traits. Do not ask me how I know of young Wright's feelings for you, and that Lucy Middleton is disturbed by them, but that is the truth. Consider: if you do not attend her party without being able to offer her any reasonable excuse for not going—since we must, by all means, conceal what Carter and Sukie have done—what will she think? She might even assume that you are cutting her out in order to annex Frank. However hard it may seem, your duty is to the living, not here. Leave me to attend to Annie and to arrange that Carter and Sukie escape punishment. You may help me again when you return—if help is still needed.'

Sarah's trust that Alan would always tell her the truth was so strong that although her eyes filled with tears, she said to him, 'I know you well enough to be aware that you will always tell me to do what is right. I have never felt less like going to a party, but I see that I must, since Lucy may always mistrust me if I don't turn up today.'

She took a deep breath. 'You must know that I have never given Frank—or Stephen Parker—any encouragement. Besides, even if I had grown to love Frank, which I haven't, I would never injure Lucy by taking him from her.'

'I believe you, and I also believe that you will be brave enough to go to her party and give nothing away.'

Alan had never admired, nay loved, her more. He watched her walk away; he would have wished her to stay for his own sake, but he was adamant with himself. Ever since his disgrace he had tried to live his life by the highest principles and, valuing Sarah as he did, he could not ask less of her than he would have asked of himself.

Now he had Annie to care for—he dare not say save—and would have to do so without the grace of Sarah's presence. Well, he had been alone before, and doubtless would be alone again. He turned towards the loft ladder and to his duty to the dying child.

Sarah offered Lucy a concocted excuse for her late appearance, but was relieved to see that Lucy's enjoyment was such that she scarcely realised how late she was. That she had come at all was sufficient. The fan was given and admired and Sarah soon found herself the centre of an excited crowd of young men and women. The guests in the Middletons' comfortable parlour overflowed into the garden where, for once, she did not find Stephen Parker's attempts to monopolise her tedious, since they enabled her to dodge Frank Wright who, perforce, satisfied himself with Lucy.

She was relieved that the party was not one to which Tom Dilhorne would ever be invited, so there was no shrewd eye to note her pallor and her withdrawn air. She even managed to find a quiet corner away from the noisy gaiety where Lucy's little brother and sister had been left, and kept quiet by teaching them a card game that she and John had played long ago at Prior's Langley.

Somehow the afternoon and evening passed. She refused both Frank and Stephen's offers to drive her home.

John, she said, was due to arrive soon and he would see
her safe. Lucy did wonder a little at Sarah's subdued
mood, so unlike her usual flash and fire, but she put it
down to the fact that Annie Bell was still missing, and
that John was late.

His excuse when he finally arrived was one that Sarah
and the Middleton's could not argue with: the Governor
had come upon him in the grounds and had detained
him over tea.

'More likely port,' said Lucy, privately and shrewdly
to Sarah when John and Major Middleton retired into
the garden to smoke an early evening cigar, forbidden
in the house.

Sarah had already exercised her mind over what to
tell John when he finally decided that it was time to go
home. In the event, since he was so full of both the
Governor's and the Middletons' port, she decided to say
nothing—which proved wise. They arrived home to find
it brilliantly lit, Mrs Hackett in full cry, and a sobbing
Mrs Bell being comforted by Dr Kerr in the Langleys'
drawing room.

Alan's shrewdness in sending Sarah away was fully
justified. It was he who explained to a bemused John
what had happened and why Mrs Bell was in his drawing room, exonerating Sukie and Carter while he did so.
After Sarah had left that afternoon, they had found Annie
dying in the street, he said, and had taken her in. They
had sent for him, and after that he had sent for Mrs Bell.

'And Annie, what of her?' asked Sarah, although she
already knew the answer, for both Mrs Bell's behaviour
and Alan's gravity told her that the worst had happened.

He turned to her, his manner as kind as he could make
it. 'Oh, Miss Langley, I'm so sorry, but there was noth-

ing I could do for the poor child. She was so ill that her death from consumption was certain. She breathed her last in Sukie's arms scarce half an hour ago.'

Sarah ignored Mrs Hackett, the hysterical Mrs Bell, who was acting as though she were the most loving mother ever to be bereaved, and John. She had enough self-possession to realise that she must deceive him if the true facts were not to be revealed, but she felt compelled to say, 'I must see Annie before she is taken away. Where is she?'

'Really, Sarah,' exclaimed John. 'She was suffering from consumption, is this wise?'

'She is in the hay loft where Sukie and Carter put her when they found her. They dared not hide her in the house for fear that she might be discovered. By the time we realised how ill she was it was too late to carry her indoors,' offered Alan smoothly. 'Of course, you may see her, Miss Langley, if that is your wish.'

'She was my pupil and I did not wish her to go to the mill, which has been the death of her,' said Sarah steadily, ignoring both John and Mrs Bell, who had begun protesting at her last words.

Alan said nothing further, but took her arm and led her out of the room and finally to the hay loft, where she sank on her knees beside the dead child. Sukie was there, sobbing, but tried to speak to her.

'Hush,' warned Sarah. 'The less said the better.'

Her own hot tears fell on the shawl around Annie's shoulders, an old one of hers that she had given to Sukie, who had used it to cover Annie. She slipped the nosegay of flowers, which Lucy's little brother had picked for her from the Middletons' garden, and which she had pinned to her dress, into Annie's hand where it lay on the horse blanket, Carter's last piece of practical help.

Alan, looking at her, thought that Sarah had never looked so beautiful as she did now, grieving for poor Annie whom they had been unable to save.

'I will come back for you,' he said, not wanting to leave John Langley alone too long with Mrs Hackett and Mrs Bell. Sarah hardly heard him. She was past caring what John, or anyone else, thought.

Her world had shrunk down to Alan, Sukie, Carter and the dead girl; she could hardly imagine what would come after.

Life, of course, went on. The death of one poor mill girl was nothing in the great scheme of things, even in a world as small as Sydney's. Alan told John to let Sarah grieve when John expressed his impatience at what he considered Sarah's undue concern for the servant class.

'The less you say in disapproval, and the more you leave her to her feelings, the sooner she will recover,' said Alan firmly.

Lucy came round to see Sarah and in her warm-hearted way she comforted her. 'How dreadful for you to return from my party to find such awful goings-on in your absence. Oh, Sarah, when I heard that that poor child had run away I never thought that it was going to involve you.'

'Nor did I, and to think that I was making silly jokes and enjoying myself whilst she was roving round Sydney's streets and dying in them.'

The explanation, which Alan had concocted and had pledged Carter and Sukie to sustain, had been accepted by everyone and Sarah had kept up its fiction by stealing the odd tit-bit from the kitchen, so that Mrs Hackett should not connect the thieving of food with Annie's disappearance and Sukie and Carter's harbouring of her.

Lucy swallowed the story like all the rest and sympathised with Sarah. The only heretic was Tom Dilhorne, who stopped Sarah in the street, offered her his sympathy for Annie's death, rather than for Sarah's lacerated feelings, and then murmured, 'I hear that you are still losing food, Miss Sarah, and old Hackett is still complaining.' The Langleys' mysterious thief had become part of Sydney's folklore.

Sarah looked him full in the face and smiled. 'Some disappeared yesterday, Mr Dilhorne.'

'A wise move that, Miss Sarah. Your thief has an apt sense of timing.' His expression was as angelic as he could make it. 'I hear that you managed to attend Miss Middleton's birthday party...' he paused '...after all.'

Sarah's grief was not so great that she could not be amused by Tom's prevarication, and by his knowledge of everything that went on in the colony.

'Oh, yes...' she paused, too. 'It was my duty to attend, and it was a great shock to return to discover what had been going on in my absence.'

His expression was blander than ever. 'Indeed, it must have been. I gather that your brother's man, Carter, is Miss Sukie's beau these days. That must be very useful.'

'Very useful, I agree,' Sarah responded, as bland as he.

If he had tried to distract her from her misery he could not have done better. She almost laughed aloud at his skilful fencing, while also enjoying his masterly impudence, so much more subtle than that of the officers of the Regiment.

'Annie's death made me think on, Miss Sarah.'

'Oh, in what way, Mr Dilhorne?'

'That it's bad business as well as a bad thing for a mill owner to drive young children to their deaths. I made Dempster an offer for his mill that he couldn't refuse, so it's mine now. I shan't employ very young children, and for the rest I hope that my good friend, Dr Kerr, will come in and look at the young 'uns now and then.'

'Why, that is most kind of you, Mr Dilhorne.' Sarah wondered why it was that Dempster couldn't refuse Tom's offer!

'Good business, not kindness. I leave kindness to the ladies, Miss Sarah. You've enough for most.'

After they had parted Sarah felt happier than she had done for some days. Perhaps there would be no more dying Annies in Sydney. So much was she invigorated that Alan Kerr, coming to meet her after catching sight of her talking to Tom, said, 'I am happy to see you looking so well again, Miss Langley.'

'Sarah,' she said. 'It was Sarah last week, Dr Kerr, and it cannot be Miss Langley again after what we shared then.'

He bowed, more overwhelmed by her than ever. 'If so, it cannot be Dr Kerr. I am Alan to my friends, although I do not know what your brother will say when he hears us speak so informally.'

For the first time in days Sarah laughed. 'Oh, Alan, he can say nothing. I am my own mistress here as I was in England. More and more I understand why Carter likes his life in New South Wales. Despite the presence of convicts everywhere there is a sense of freedom in the air. The Exclusives find this shocking, I know, and poor Annie found little freedom, but I am convinced that times will change.'

He smiled at her. She presented more of a temptation to him than she had ever done before. Her green eyes shot fire at him while she came out with her frank opinion on the life around her.

'I must confess, Sarah, that I share your belief in future change. Governor Macquarie, I know, thinks the same. However, you may be underestimating the time that it will take. For the moment it is the military and the Government servants who control the colony, but the time will come when the those who are born here will take over—and they will be the children and grandchildren of the Emancipists.'

Sarah found him easy to talk to. Only with Alan, and Tom Dilhorne, was she able to express herself so freely. Besides that, the secret of Annie that she shared with him had brought them closer together. She found herself telling him about her thieving from the kitchen in order to allay Mrs Hackett's suspicions.

'I am not certain, you see, that she fully believed your story about Sukie and Carter accidentally finding Annie, but if the thefts continue for a little while, why, then it will be difficult for her to prove that they harboured Annie far longer than you said and fed her from the kitchen.'

Alan could not but admire her. She was the woman he had always hoped to meet but had feared that he never would—and she was beyond him. My splendid girl, he thought, how I wish that I could tell you of my true feelings for you. For the moment it had to be enough for him to talk to her and feel the rapport that was growing between them, day by day.

'What did Tom have to say to you?' he asked her, for he knew his friend of old, and also knew that he admired Sarah greatly.

'Oh, it was a strange conversation. I'm sure that somehow he is aware of the truth about Annie, Sukie and Carter. Did you tell him?'

'No, the fewer who know the truth the better. But Tom's a downy cove, as they say in The Rocks. Nothing escapes him. That's why he's such a good business man. He knows people's motives better than they do themselves.'

'He's always been kind to me,' said Sarah, 'but I shouldn't like to get on the wrong side of him.'

She found it a great relief to speak to a man so frankly, ignoring all the conventions that dictated that such a conversation should be politely vapid. She tried to imagine what Charles would have made of all the adventures in which she had been involved. If he thought that her painting was unwomanly, what would he have made of her birthing Nellie and trying to save Annie? Such people did not exist for him.

'I trust that you will feel well enough to attend the Governor's Musical Soirée,' said Alan, desperate to find some means of remaining with her.

'Oh, yes, I have been asked to play and sing. I cannot think that those who asked me were aware of what an amateur I am. How strange it is that it should be considered unwomanly of me to paint in oils, but perfectly proper that I should perform in public at the piano!' Her face lit up. 'Our customs must seem odd to the aborigines, that is, if the poor creatures understand that we have customs. Theirs certainly seem strange to me.'

Had she but known it, Alan was helpless before her. Her combination of wit and insight when she spoke of the world around her displayed a singularly rare talent that showed her to be quite unlike most of the men and women whom he knew. He found it difficult to reply to her sensibly because he feared that, if he stayed talking to her much longer, he was in danger of proposing to her on the spot!

'I shall see you there, then,' he managed at last. 'The Governor knows of my love of music.' He bowed, and, with the greatest reluctance, they parted.

Sarah walked on, only to be stopped again, this time by Frank Wright. Since Alan had told her how much he was attracted to her she had been wary of him, giving him no opportunity to speak to her alone. Now, caught in the street, she had no chance of avoiding his company.

'Sarah,' he said, 'I am so happy to have met you. I would be most grateful if you would offer me some advice. I have known Lucy Middleton ever since the Regiment came to Sydney, but it was only when I saw her at her birthday party that I realised that she has turned into a doosed pretty girl—and jolly with it. You know much more about these things than I do, but do you think she would look favourably on me if I...well...if I proposed to her?'

Relief that, if he had ever fixed himself on her, he no longer did, had Sarah saying swiftly, 'Yes, indeed. I imagine that Lucy would listen to an offer from you most sympathetically.'

'Oh, splendid,' he exclaimed. 'Apart from yourself, a fellow might do much worse than have Lucy Middleton for a wife.'

He was rightly named Frank, Sarah thought, amused, and Alan had been right. Frank had thought of her as a possible wife, but had doubtless considered that she was beyond his touch while Lucy wasn't. She was probably better than he deserved but, from everything she had said, Lucy wanted him and bless her, thought Sarah sentimentally, she looked like getting him!

Whoever would have thought that Sydney, a town at

the other end of nowhere, would prove to be such an exciting place in which to live? Every day brought along something new. Never a dull moment in the Antipodes, and even if some proved to be painful there seemed to be quite a few happy ones to make up for them.

Chapter Ten

'Frank's asked me to go to the Governor's Soirée with him,' Lucy told Sarah excitedly on the day before it was due. 'Oh, Sarah, do you think that he might be thinking about proposing some time soon? I believe that Mama thinks so, too. When I asked her if I could have Frank for an escort instead of going with the family party, she said yes immediately. That made me wonder if he's already asked Papa for permission to speak to me.'

'Possibly, and I shall be so happy for you if he does,' said Sarah. She wasn't surprised that the Middletons approved of his suit. He came from a gentry family and report said that he had a good income of his own beside his Army pay.

'And you, Sarah, who are you going with, John? Or perhaps Stephen Parker. He's a good fellow, too, you know.'

'John, of course. I like Stephen's company, you understand, but I am not *éprise* with him and so I have told him—and Pat Ramsey, too.'

'Is there someone waiting for you back home?' Lucy asked. She had often wondered why Sarah, so beautiful, clever and rich, should still be unmarried at twenty-two.

'Back home? Oh, no, not at all,' replied Sarah almost too quickly, so that Lucy wondered a little at why such a question should upset her.

Wisely she said nothing other than, 'I can't wait for tomorrow night. Not only because of Frank, but because I understand that I am going to hear you sing and play. I'd no notion that you were accomplished on the piano, too.'

'Only a little,' Sarah said, with shrug, and turned the conversation to other things. She didn't really want to be reminded of Charles Villiers with whom she had once thought that she had been in love.

Like all the other functions over which Governor Macquarie presided, his soirée was well organised and well attended. It was held in the vast dining hall, which had been lit with hundreds of candles. When Sarah walked to the piano, dressed all in white, with silver ribbons in her hair, she was rapturously received by her uncritical audience.

She played a short piano piece by Haydn before turning to her audience and announcing, 'I am going to sing two short songs by our immortal bard, William Shakespeare, which I hope will remind you of home. The first is ''Where the bee sucks, there suck I'', and the second is an Aubade, which is better known by its first line, ''Hark! hark! the lark at heaven's gate sings''.'

More rapturous applause followed this announcement until Sarah raised her hand for silence, turned back towards the pianoforte and began to sing and play.

Her voice was sweet and true, like herself, thought more than one of the men in the audience, including the Governor, who had heard tell of Miss Sarah Langley's exploits. At the end there was silence before clapping and shouts of 'encore, encore' rewarded her performance. The Governor walked towards her when she rose from the piano stool and prepared to leave.

'Come, come, Miss Langley, I know that you will not disappoint us after we have given you such an enthusiastic reception.' He beckoned to Alan Kerr, who was sitting in the front row next to the his own chair—an honoured position that had already met with some criticism from the Exclusives who were present.

'Doctor Kerr, I already know that you possess a good singing voice. I wonder, Miss Langley, whether you know that fine Scots song, ''Sweet Afton''? If you do, I trust that you will agree to accompany him so that he may favour the company with it.'

There was no denying the Governor. 'Yes, I do know the song,' she told him, 'although I do not have its music with me, so I hope that Dr Kerr will forgive me if my rendition is not completely accurate.'

Alan's look told her all. However reluctant they might be to perform together in public, the Governor's personal kindnesses to both of them demanded no less than obedience to his wish.

Alan had a good, if untrained, baritone voice, and Sarah's own performance was sufficiently competent so that when the last strains of the song died away there were few in the audience who remained unmoved by this memory of the home that they had left so many thousand miles away. Raising her hands from the keys, Sarah, her eyes full of tears, turned to look at Alan and it was obvious that he was equally affected. The rapport between them was plain for all to see.

Their audience called for more from them both, but Sarah was so moved by the song, and by Alan's response to it, that she did not wish to continue. Nor did he, for

he shook his head gently before bowing it in acknowledgement of the continuing applause.

Sarah rose from her stool. 'You must forgive me,' she
said, after bowing herself, 'I must not monopolise the
evening's entertainment. Another time, perhaps.'

She was aware that she and Alan had had almost certainly given themselves away, and she thought that he
was aware of that, too. Pat Ramsey had whistled between his teeth when he saw Sarah's response to Alan
Kerr. Now, he wondered, how long had that been going
on? The society beauty tamed at last by the convict doctor! It was no wonder she had shown no interest in poor
Parker or the officers of the Regiment.

He kept these thoughts to himself, but once the concert was over and the company was drinking tea, or, in
the gentlemen's case, port, he carried his glass over to
Sarah, who was surrounded by congratulatory admirers.

'Sarah, my English rose, who is still flourishing in
these distant seas, I must add my compliments to the
rest. I had no notion that our dour Dr Kerr could sing
so well, or that you would be quite so happy to accompany him.'

Sarah's look for him when he had finished was as
sharp as she could make it. Patrick Ramsey, whatever
else he was, was no fool and it behoved her to be careful
when she answered him.

'It would have been churlish to refuse the Governor,
would it not, Pat? Do you sing? If so, we must make a
duo at the Governor's next soirée.'

'Bravely said.'

He put down his glass to applaud her gently. 'Well,
no one doubts your courage, Sarah, myself least of all.
You have given the colony enough opportunities to admire it. I wonder if you have the courage to embark on

the greatest adventure of all. Knowing you, and your
brother's position in society, I would have thought that
you would settle for nothing less than a Duke—but I
believe that I may be wrong.'

Sarah's stare at him would have cut glass. How
strange that Pat Ramsey should be fencing verbally with
her in much the same fashion as Tom Dilhorne. Did he
know how much he had in common with the Emancipist
he despised? She would treat him as she had treated
Tom: coolly, giving nothing away.

'No Dukes for me, I fear, Captain Ramsey. The ones
I met in London were fat and middle-aged to a man—
and married already, thank goodness. As for great adventures, I used mine up in one go when I agreed to
accompany my brother here.'

Pat's smile for her was unforced. He took her hand in
his and kissed it before she could stop him. 'No more
fooling from me, Miss Sarah Langley. As you must
know, I admire you and your courage more than I can
say. Had things been otherwise...but they are not. That
being so, I can do no more than wish you well.'

He released her hand and bowed, saying, 'Now I must
go and quiz someone else.'

Sarah was left in the strangest mood. Had others also
seen what Pat Ramsey undoubtedly had? Or was he clev-
erer, or more perceptive, than most? She felt that everyone's eyes were on her and that the heat of the room
had suddenly become overpowering. She walked
through the crowd, automatically accepting the compliments of those about her.

She needed air. One of the French windows was open
and she stepped into the grounds, bathed in moonlight.

She walked away from the house, down a shrub-lined
path, the night air cool on her hot cheeks. She saw that

another person beside herself had found the company tedious.

It was Dr Alan Kerr.

He saw her at the same moment that she became aware of his presence, and said, his voice low, 'Did you find the crowd unendurable, too?'

'Yes,' and then in a rush, 'oh, Alan, whatever could the Governor have been thinking of? I am sure that everyone saw…'

Sarah ran out of words as the implication of what she had just said struck home.

Alan took both her hands and kissed them. 'What did they see, Sarah?'

She lifted her eyes to his. 'You know what they saw, Alan.'

He kissed her hands again. 'Yes, I know what they saw. I half-think that what the Governor did was deliberate. If so, he may have done us a favour. We were both afraid to speak of what lies between us. Oh, Sarah—' and this time his kiss found her lips, before he raised his head and said, 'I so hoped that you felt as I do. Tonight I am sure of it. Tell me that you do.'

Sarah's answer was lost as her arms stole around his neck and she returned his kisses with an ardour that she did not know she possessed. She felt as though she were drowning in a sea of passion, and as his embrace became more urgent and his kisses travelled down into the decolletage of her low-necked dress she gasped and clung to him the harder.

It had never been like this with Charles, never. The fire that swept through her was consuming Alan, too, and what might have happened next she did not dare to think—both of them had gone beyond sense and reason.

The strange affinity that had been present since their first stormy meeting was reaching its inevitable conclusion.

The French window was thrown wide, and John's voice could be heard calling, 'Sarah? Sarah, where are you?'

They broke apart. Sarah turned away and tried to restore her dishevelled hair and replace the shoulders of her dress, which had slipped down in the passion of their embrace.

John had seen them and came down the path towards them.

'Oh, there you are, Sarah. Kerr, is that you?'

Sarah's immediate presence of mind surprised her. She might have spent her life prevaricating after being almost caught in a compromising position.

'I was overheated,' she said calmly. 'I needed fresh air. Doctor Kerr evidently felt the same.'

John glared suspiciously at them both. Sarah's colour was high, her eyes glittered, and her hair had tumbled from its confining ribbons. Alan, whilst endeavouring to remain outwardly composed, despite the fact that he had been thoroughly roused, felt like a man who had been caught red-handed—and rightly so.

He was deeply aware that John Langley did not approve of the friendship between him and Sarah, and would have been horrified to discover that Alan had been on the verge of seducing his sister—and that his sister had been perfectly willing to be seduced.

In the face of Alan's silence and Sarah's steadfast refusal to be embarrassed, there was little that John could say beyond, 'Well, I advise you both to return to the dining room before idle tongues begin to gossip. You have provided enough fodder for the tabby cats already, Sarah, without providing more.

'Come, take my arm, it is perfectly proper for a brother and a sister to enjoy an evening walk in the gardens together. Doctor Kerr will excuse us both, I am sure.'

Alan watched them go. There was no doubt that Sarah's brother suspected the truth of what had recently passed between them. It had been a moment of madness in which the iron control which he usually kept over himself had slipped completely.

Useless to grasp that John's arrival had been fortunate for both of them. He knew how badly he wanted his tempestuous Sarah—and now he also knew that her feelings for him were equally strong.

No! He was wrong. It was not fortunate! However the scene had ended, one thing was for sure: he would have declared himself and won her without a doubt. Now he must wait to see to see her again and hope to win John Langley over to the idea of having the renegade Dr Kerr as a brother-in-law.

Sarah woke up the next morning to a whole new world, a world in which she knew that Alan felt for her as she felt for him: that, to put it plainly, her love was returned. It would surely not be long now before he declared himself. John would not be pleased if she accepted his proposal, but it was her decision to make, not his.

The Governor, by inviting them to sing together, had, wittingly or unwittingly, removed the last barrier between them. Her only regret was that others must have witnessed their joy, but that was no matter, either. What *did* matter was what had happened afterwards. If anything further had been needed to convince her how wrong she had been to lament the loss of Charles Villiers for so long, those few rapturous moments in the moon-drowned garden had finally supplied it.

Her cheeks burned at the memory of how abandoned she had been and how little she regretted it. Did Alan feel the same? She was sure that he did. He was due to visit her little school that afternoon, and she could scarcely wait to see him again. Would he propose then?

Alan's thoughts mirrored Sarah's. What he had dared to hope had come true: she loved him. All that remained was for him to ask for her hand in marriage, and he set out on his weekly visit to examine her pupils with every intention of doing so. Alas, when he arrived there he found John Langley was present!

He had accompanied Sarah after saying that he wished to see what in the world she was doing with the colony's brats. He had brought his sketchbook with him and was entertaining the children by drawing them.

Sarah looked ruefully at Alan. She had spent the morning eagerly looking forward to his visit when they would be alone together again, but it was soon apparent that John would not leave before Alan did.

Indeed, when Alan departed, John made some excuse to leave with him, and this watchdog activity persisted over the next few days, helped by the fact that Alan's medical duties were such that they kept him away. The inevitable gossip about them both after the musical evening made John even more determined to guard Sarah by ensuring that she rarely met Alan.

Fortunately for him, the next social evening, two days later, was one to which Alan was not invited. John and Sarah were guests at a ball given by the officers of the 73rd Highlanders solely for those considered to be part of Sydney's elite. Colonel O'Connell had once boasted, 'No damned Emancipist will ever set foot in any activity which I arrange.'

For Sarah, lacking Alan's presence, the only thing that interested her in it was that Frank Wright proposed to Lucy between the cotillion and the quadrille.

The following day Lucy flew round to the Langleys as soon as she decently could to show Sarah the seal ring that Frank had given her in lieu of a lady's half-hoop.

'Frank says,' she told Sarah breathlessly, 'that Tom Dilhorne has promised to order a diamond one from Macao by the next boat.'

Sarah's pleasure was genuine. She admired the ring and said everything that was proper about Frank. She told Lucy, quite truthfully, that, except for a few disappointed young ladies, the entire Exclusive tribe would rejoice with the happy lovers. She could not help contrasting the approval that Lucy had received with the reception which awaited her when Alan declared himself, as she felt he surely would, the moment that he could get past John!

John came in while they were celebrating Lucy's news. He opened a bottle of wine that the three of them drank, with John and Sarah toasting the happy couple. The wedding would take place in three months' time to allow Mrs Middleton to provide as grand a send-off as possible.

'So that's Lucy settled,' said John when she had finally departed after a flurry of kisses from Sarah. 'I thought at one time that young Wright had a *tendre* for you.'

'No such thing,' said Sarah, 'it's always been Lucy

for Frank. I think that he was a little fearful of her mother.' She did not want John spreading the notion that Lucy had been taken as second-best.

Later she walked round Sydney, dreaming of her own future with Alan, an expression of beatitude on her face that was not lost on Tom Dilhorne when she patronised his store. She had gone there the day after the news of Lucy's engagement to look at dress materials and wonder what Mrs Middleton had in mind for her chief bridesmaid—for so Lucy had asked her to be.

'Happen it won't be the only big wedding this year,' remarked Tom slyly.

Sarah blushed a delicate pink and shook her head at him. The idiot's not asked her yet then, thought Tom.

He made a point of being present at Dempster's Mill—as it was still called—when Alan paid his weekly visit there.

He walked in just as Alan was packing his bag to leave and regarded his friend with a certain amount of worldly cynicism.

'I hear that you and Miss Sarah entertained the Governor's Soirée no end t'other night.'

'You might say that.' Alan was short.

'Oh, *I* don't say it. It's the only topic of conversation in Sydney these days. I sometimes think that the officers of the garrison are bigger gossips than their wives. Comes of not having enough to do.'

'No doubt.' Alan thought that this was one of the few occasions when he was shorter than Tom.

'I shouldn't like to see Miss Sarah hurt. That brother of hers has no more sense than a koala.'

Alan was amused. Tom's conversation was even more

cryptic than usual. Did he mean that he approved of his involvement with Sarah? Or did it mean that he was aware of John Langley's opposition to any marriage between himself and Sarah, and disapproved of that?

He threw out a feeler. 'I think that John Langley wants the best for Sarah, although I am not sure that he knows what the best is.'

'True.' Tom made his shoulder more comfortable against the wall. 'The Governor seems to know his mind, though.'

Alan's laugh at that was genuine and hearty. 'It's not only the officers who are gossips, Tom. You do surprise me.'

Tom uncoiled himself lazily. 'I doubt me that I do, Kerr. Now, *you* surprise *me*. I thought that you were a deal more determined than you have turned out to be. Sarah Langleys don't grow on trees.'

This speech told Alan more about Tom himself than he thought that he wanted to know. He wondered how many scruples about John Langley or, for that matter, anyone else, Tom would show if he were in Alan's shoes. The word scruple probably didn't exist in Tom's vocabulary. But he was right. He, Alan, should have found some means of approaching Sarah before now.

His friend's parting shot was the information that ships from England had been sighted out at sea, 'And some of us are as slow in our ways as the letters coming from there!'

Tom's right, was Alan's inward response. I must not let fear of what John Langley might say stop me from proposing to Sarah. The Governor is giving a little dinner on Friday to which we have both been invited, and if I know Lachlan Macquarie he'll be matchmaking as hard as Tom. John Langley can't stop me from talking to her there!

The ships from England arrived the next day. They carried not only reinforcements for the 73rd's garrison in the shape of a Captain Jack Cameron, a couple of lieutenants and a large number of private soldiers, but also supplies of all kinds and letters.

Like the rest of Sydney John and Sarah were, for quite different reasons, excited by the prospect of letters from home—Sarah because she missed news from her many women friends, and John because the advent of the ships raised the prospect of his own return home.

It was not that he was disappointed by the Antipodes, but that they had not had quite the profound effect on him that he had expected. England, which had seemed tedious while he was there, was infinitely more attractive now that he had left it.

There were times when Sarah would have agreed with Tom's scathing verdict on John, if only she could have heard it. She often thought that all his brains were in his paintbrush, and, looking at his conventional oils, which showed the wild landscape of New South Wales as a tame version of the country back in England, she sometimes wondered how much of a brain he had there.

Her own paintings, by contrast, were becoming more and more untamed, as wild as the bush, the distant mountains and the sea. She occasionally found John staring at them with disapproval written all over his face, whereas Alan, visiting them one day before the Governor's Soirée, finding her at her easel, had again commended her for her truthfulness.

'But I haven't John's technique,' she had said.

'There's more to painting than technique,' he had replied, and had asked her to allow him to buy this latest study—she had refused and given it to him, instead.

Her wish for letters was to be granted. After the ship had docked the postman, who was on his rounds from the Post Office in George Street, delivered a small pile of mail to them. Some of them were business letters and some were personal. Among hers were two in hands that she immediately recognised—one, indeed, which she would, eighteen months ago, have longed to see. Now Charles Villiers's handwriting seemed to come from another world. He was a man whom she now understood she had never really known and had certainly never really loved.

She set it down by one from her old friend and John's long-term sweetheart, Emily Hazeldean.

John, who had been eagerly ripping his letters open, looked up in surprise.

'Aren't you going to open yours?'

'Later. I mean to save them until this afternoon when I shall have time to enjoy them. The pleasure will be longer-lasting,' Sarah replied, well knowing that she was not telling John the entire truth.

She was, in fact, surprised to discover how often she was shading the truth for him. She had not told him that, for the first time since the soirée, she had seen Alan alone in the street.

He was on his rounds and had only had time to take her by the hand, to tell her that he, too, was engaged to be part of the Governor's dinner party and that he hoped to speak to her at length then. His manner had been so ardent that she could only conclude, dizzily, that he was about to propose there. At such a moment Charles's letter seemed an intrusion, and even Emily's no longer appeared as desirable as it would once have done.

They could all wait until after nuncheon when she could spare a minute from her thoughts of Alan, her involvement with her little school, the sewing lesson which she was due to give Sukie and the expedition to the cliffs that evening when she was expected to chaperon Frank and Lucy. Her life had never seemed so full or so interesting. All this activity was in addition to the problems to be worked out in her latest oil painting. She had decided that she wished to paint some of the aborigines and was considering enlisting Tom Dilhorne's help.

Despite having wished for them, it was almost with reluctance that Sarah finally began to open her letters. John was preparing to visit Government House; Lachlan Macquarie had sent for him, asking him to bring along his sketchbooks and watercolours for inspection. The Governor was a patron of the arts and had already commissioned, and paid for, a series of oils by John. He had not yet seen Sarah's work, although Alan Kerr had told him that he considered it to be impressive.

While Sarah was beginning to read Charles's letter, John was assembling his portfolios. He was far more interested in what Charles had to say than Sarah was. He wrongly assumed, knowing how distressed Sarah had originally been over the breach with Charles, that she would be hoping for some kind words from her former fiancé, and was ready to tell her so. She had, however, refused to discuss with him what might be in the letter, contenting herself with eating her nuncheon in silence.

Sarah read the letter in a condition of total disbelief. She had to go over it twice before its impact struck home.

'Dear Sarah,' he wrote, 'at least I hope that I may still

address you as Sarah. After all that there has been between us, I fear that Miss Langley would be far too cold. I am writing to tell you that I now know that I have made a truly dreadful mistake. Barely a day goes by without my reproaching myself for the wrong which I did you, and without my regretting your absence and the reason for it.

'Sarah, my own dear girl, when I think of the happiness which we enjoyed together I wonder at myself for ever letting you go. You had scarcely left England before I realised that my involvement with Caroline Wharton had been a gross error of judgement. I will say nothing against her. Suffice it that every time that we met I found myself recalling you and understanding that I had thrown away a pearl of great price.

'My circumstances have changed. It is enough to say that Caroline and I are no longer betrothed. We have mutually agreed that our marriage would have been a mistake and we have parted without rancour in the hope that we might find happiness elsewhere.

'Sarah, I know that I did you a great wrong. Will you allow me to repair that wrong? It is my dearest wish that you should return to these shores and consent to be my wife. I repeat, nothing could give me greater happiness than to be reunited with you. I know that your brother was saddened by our parting and would rejoice in our coming together again.

'I know, too, how long it will be before I can see your dear handwriting again, and that we must lose even more precious time before you return. When that happy day arrives, know that you have no more devoted servant than your misguided Charles. My love flies to you across the vastness of the seas between us. Would that I had never given you occasion to go!

'Farewell, my dearest love. I trust that your generous heart will forgive me.

'I remain, ever your willing slave, Charles Villiers.'

Sarah put the letter down on the polished cedar of the table and looked at it with a mixture of disgust and disbelief. Of all the tricks and turns of fortune she might have foreseen, this was the last that would have sprung to her mind.

She could not but think with what joy she might have received this letter once. Now, reading it, Charles, who had become a shadowy figure, was suddenly before her, and she did not like what she saw. How ill he contrasted with Alan! His letter was full of himself, for all his protestations, whereas Alan, Alan always cared for others before himself—one of the reasons why he had ended up in a penal colony at all. His scruples in holding back from declaring his love for her for so long were plain to see.

How could she ever have cared for such a shallow pleasure-seeker as Charles Villiers? She wondered why, and how, his engagement to Caroline had ended. She could not believe a word he had written. He had tricked her once, and he would trick her again if he could.

She picked up the crumpled letter and was re-examining it when John entered, having discovered an errant portfolio of his among her possessions in the room which did duty as a studio.

'I must go, Sarah. Tell me, quickly, what Charles has to say.'

Sarah broke into incredulous laughter. 'It's the strangest thing. He has broken with Caroline Wharton and has asked me to return and marry him as soon as possible.'

John paused with his hand on the doorknob. 'Good, excellent. I always knew that the silly quarrel which threw you apart would somehow right itself. I am so glad for your second chance at happiness. Congratulations, Lady Amborough.'

He held up a hand as she began to speak, to tell him that she would as soon marry a kangaroo as Charles Villiers.

'No, no, my dear, leave it for now. I am already late,' and she heard him whistling merrily as he dashed through the door and made for the stables.

Sarah sank back into her chair. Time enough to tell him the truth when he returned. Through the window she watched Carter carrying John's impedimenta for his visit to the Governor, a small smile playing at the corner of her mouth.

John hurried to Government House. He urged Carter on: his journey could not be made quickly enough. Pleasure at Sarah's news had driven everything else from his mind. He had liked Charles Villiers, had been sorry when Charles and Sarah had parted and Charles had gone off with Caroline Wharton. He had always wrongly assumed that the rupture was much more Sarah's fault than Charles's. After all, he knew what a firebrand Sarah was and had once thought of warning Charles that he must not allow her too loose a rein after they had married.

Now that was all over. Sarah could go back home again with him as soon as he could arrange a passage, and she could become Lady Amborough, as she should always have been.

Prominent among his thoughts was that this timely offer would prevent Sarah from making a fool of herself over someone unsuitable like Alan Kerr! New South Wales had done strange things to her, and the sooner she was homeward bound, the better. It might be some little time before they could leave, but the knowledge that she was going to marry Charles and take her proper place in society was surely bound to make her distance herself from unworthy suitors.

He was on time for his appointment, but the Governor's secretary, a young lieutenant, told him that Lachlan Macquarie was engaged with Dr Kerr, and that it might be a little time before he could see Mr Langley. The Governor sent his apologies for the delay. John sat in the anteroom, too happy at Sarah's news to feel piqued at being kept waiting while the Governor talked with an Emancipist.

It seemed that he was going to have the opportunity to tell Alan Kerr of Sarah's news sooner than he might have hoped. Despite his criminal record, Kerr was still enough of a gentleman to leave Sarah alone, once he realised that she was promised to another.

He was thinking this when the door opened and Alan emerged. The secretary left them together when he went in to tell the Governor of John's arrival. Both men smiled a little uncertainly at one another, but John was the more eager to speak.

'Oh, Kerr, I'm most happy to see you.' His pleasure was so great, indeed, that Alan looked at him in some surprise. John's next words left him in no doubt of the reason for his delight.

'We have letters from home and Sarah has received some welcome and long-awaited news. I am most pleased for her. Her troubles are at last ended. The misunderstanding that resulted in her parting from her fiancé, Charles Villiers, is over. He has asked her to marry him, and we shall be returning home as soon as possible. When you next meet her you will be able to congratulate her on the prospect of becoming Lady Amborough when old Amborough dies.'

Alan's congratulations were private, and were for himself in that he neither spoke nor looked as though a large pit had opened up before him. He had planned to ask Sarah to marry him after the Governor's dinner on the morrow, and, as John had correctly surmised, his strong sense of honour would not permit him to approach a young woman who was already promised to another.

He heard himself replying to John, and half-agreeing with him, that interesting though New South Wales, was, it would be a relief to return to Southern England's softer greenery. He was unable to express pleasure at Sarah's elevation to the nobility.

How could he, a man of sense, have deceived himself into believing that a fine young society lady could ever have shown any real intention of marrying him? He ought to have remembered that even though Sarah might have come to love him, in the end the call of her own kind, the status that such a marriage would offer her would, on mature reflection, weigh very heavily with her.

Besides that, was not *he* being selfish in wishing her to marry an ex-convict, and live at the far, barbarous end of the world? To sacrifice himself for her good, however hard that would be, was what, in all honour, he ought to do. It would also solve another problem that occasionally troubled him—her wealth.

If she had accepted him, and the news of it had then become public, there were sure to have been some who would have sniggered behind their hands at the convict doctor who had been cunning enough to marry an heiress. They would not have been aware that he saw

Sarah's wealth as an impediment and that it was the reason why he had not declared his love for her earlier. It had been necessary for him to be certain of the strength of their mutual feelings, which made the question of her wealth unimportant.

Alas, what he had just heard from John showed that her feelings for him had had their limitations. When a better offer from one of her equals had arrived, she had been prompt to accept it, never mind how sincere she had seemed to be in the scented warmth of Government House's gardens.

The harshness with which life had treated Alan prevented him from asking himself whether the story John Langley had told him was true. The memory of his encounter with Sarah in the gardens of Government House was not sufficient to stop him from thinking that it was all too likely that Fate had cut Alan Kerr down again, just when he thought that he had reached a smiling plateau where happiness awaited him.

He remembered with pain how his first love had treated him after his arrest. He had never heard a word from her again, and his father had taken pleasure in writing to him that she was to marry another. Nothing had changed. He must try to rebuild his life yet again, paying once more for the moment of drunken foolishness which had ruined him.

He bade John a brief farewell, leaving his best hopes in ruins in the Governor's ante-room. He was halfway down George Street before he realised that he did not know where he was going, or what he ought to be doing.

Worse, he further understood that John's evident pleasure in telling him the news arose from his disapproval of himself as a possible suitor for Sarah. There had never been any chance that he would have welcomed Alan

Kerr as a brother-in-law. He had always suspected this, but the truth hurt, nevertheless. An empty-headed fribble like Stephen Parker would have been approved of, he thought, but I, why, I destroyed my chances long ago.

He walked savagely down the road: dour Dr Kerr had been reborn, and this time he felt as though the ice round his heart, which Sarah had melted, had frozen again—for good this time.

Chapter Eleven

Unaware of what her brother was saying and doing at Government House, Sarah continued to read her letters. There was one from an elderly aunt in Cheltenham, and another from an old schoolfriend, telling of her forthcoming marriage. Finally she picked up Emily Hazeldean's, which she had saved as a *bonne-bouche*.

Emily's letter was long and full of news. She asked after John, wondered whether he had found an aboriginal beauty, enquired whether Sarah had fallen for some rough colonial, or handsome Highlander—she knew that the 73rd were in Sydney. She filled several pages with family news and finally she wrote of Charles Villiers.

'The *on dits* have been flying round town. It seems that Caroline Wharton began to cry off as soon as the wedding day drew near. You remember old St Mawr, the man who wanted a wife, but never cared to offer for one—filthy rich and mean with it? It appears that she met him at Badminton, decided he was a better bet than Charles, and before they parted he had asked her to marry him.

'It was the work of a moment for her to give poor Charles his *congé*. Why should I call him poor Charles?

Well, he treated you badly, throwing you over for greater wealth and now he has nothing. The *ton* is laughing behind its hand, while gravely commiserating with him. Meanwhile Caroline is set to become the Marchioness of St Mawr and is on her highest ropes. I am desolate that we cannot laugh at this together.'

For the second time that day Sarah could scarce believe what she was reading. Rage filled her. She rose and paced about the room. So that was why Charles had offered for her again! He could not know that Emily would write to tell her the truth—and by the same post, too. It was like a bad farce.

How dare he! She would answer him. She would not waste time, paper or ink on recrimination, nor let him know what Emily had told her. No, she would be as short and plain as…as…Tom Dilhorne. He must find another gull to fund his expensive tastes. How fortunate that he had cast her off before she had married him. What kind of marriage would she have had with such as Charles?

More than ever she thought with kindness of Alan, unaware that the black dog of despair was riding on his shoulders. She would tell John when he returned that she would not marry Charles.

She would not show him Emily's letter—he would think that that had fuelled her refusal, whereas she had resolved not to accept Charles before she had even read it. The letter had merely served to confirm her decision, to show that her judgement of him was correct. Not only was he vastly inferior to Alan Kerr, but also to Tom and a dozen others who were carving a life for themselves in the most difficult of circumstances.

She rang for Sukie and for tea.

'Tea, Miss Sarah? It's barely two of the clock.'

'Tea,' said Sarah firmly. She wished to toast her good luck. Had she been a man she would have tossed down a bumper of good wine, but tea would have to do!

'You may take a cup with me, Sukie,' she said when that handmaiden returned with the tea-board.

'Lawks, Miss Sarah, what for?'

'So that we may both drink to the future,' Sarah said, 'in the hope that we attain our heart's desire.' And if that sounds sentimental, she thought, then sentimental it must be.

Sukie's smile said all. She and Carter had reached an understanding, but he had told her that they must say nothing until Mr John decided to leave Sydney. Then they would inform him that Carter did not intend to return to England. To tell him earlier would only invite trouble, particularly for Miss Sarah, whom Mr John would be sure to blame for Carter's desertion and Sukie's share in it.

Lucy Middleton called for Sarah at five o'clock that afternoon. John had not returned from Government House, missing dinner, and Lucy needed Sarah to act as her duenna on a visit with Frank to the nearby cliffs— one of the favourite rendezvous for the elite of Sydney.

Frank joined them on his best black, dismounted, handed his horse to his groom, and the three of them took a turn on the strip of green far above the waters of the harbour.

Since his betrothal to Lucy, Frank had adopted an elder-brother manner towards Sarah, which she felt was both amusing and slightly touching. It was as though his brief, secret passion for her had never existed. He asked if she and John had received any letters from home and was there any news of general import in them which the Langleys wished to share?

'Very little,' replied Sarah briefly. 'Only about the war, of which I am sure that you know more than my correspondents. For the rest, mainly births, marriages and deaths.' She had told no one in the colony about Charles Villiers's desertion of her, so said nothing of him.

'I collect that your brother is now eager to return home,' said Frank, 'although I expect that you may have to wait some time for a passage. We shall be sorry to see you both go.'

Sarah did not reply, other than by a smile and a nod of the head. As Alan had not yet offered for her, she could hardly announce that she expected to stay in the colony. In any case with, or without that offer, she had no wish to leave, but she knew that, without marriage, there was no way in which a lady such as herself could remain. Her smile was therefore enigmatic, and she decided that she was growing nearly as devious as Tom Dilhorne. The idle gossip that had previously filled her days no longer satisfied her.

She looked about her to see whether Alan was present, but there was no sign of him. She was disappointed, but not surprised. He rarely socialised and she suspected that his presence at recent gatherings was partly in the hope of finding her there.

John arrived on horseback, waved to her and went over to speak to some officers who, as usual, had formed an animated group of their own where they held a kind of court. Were she not committed to Lucy she would have been expected to join them. On the whole she was grateful that she did not need to. The empty badinage, the whole way in which men spoke to women, had al-

ways grated on her, and was responsible for her reputation as a firebrand. Of late such treatment had come to
seem intolerable.

Alan always spoke to her as though she had a mind
as well as a pretty face, though she remembered something that a wise old aunt had once said: men did not
marry women in order to talk to them.

But what happened when the honeymoon was over?
She knew of many marriages where, once the first passion had gone, husband and wife turned into polite
strangers and went their separate ways. She looked
across at Lucy, who was smiling at Frank. Perhaps there
was more for her than most women. Frank seemed kind
enough, but who knew what might happen once the knot
was tied?

Despite the warmth of the day Sarah shivered a little.
Had she really needed to come to New South Wales to
find a man whom she could love and respect? What
would John say when he knew that Alan Kerr was to be
his brother-in-law, and what would he think of her determination to remain in the colony with him and not try
to influence him to return to Great Britain?

All this was to anticipate. Alan had not yet proposed,
but surely after the understanding they had reached he
would: his words to her about the Governor's dinner
could have no other meaning. She smiled and was rewarded by Frank telling her that he had rarely seen her
look so happy.

This state of contentment stayed with her throughout
the evening. Later, John told her the details of his meeting with the Governor, and the Governor's pleasure at
his work. He said nothing to her of having met Alan.

When he had finished he smiled and said, 'Now you
must tell me more of your own splendid news. I collect

that Charles has come to his senses at last, and that you will therefore marry him. I told the Governor that my mission here was ended and that we should be seeking a passage home as soon as I had finished my last series of oils. I did not tell him of Charles's renewed offer. I knew that you would not want me to.'

Sarah was surprised and pleased by his delicacy, which was most unusual for John, who always took it for granted that her wishes were the same as his.

'Oh, I am so happy that you did not. You must understand that I cannot possibly marry Charles. I should never be able to trust him again. What's more, I no longer love him. I think that I never did. I loved his good looks and his charm, not the man himself. No, I shall never be Lady Amborough.'

His face fell. 'Reflect, Sarah, on all that you are giving up. By the time that we reach England you will be past your first youth, and cannot hope for many better offers. After all, Charles is a good fellow at heart. He is not perfect, but who is? More than that, to be Lady Amborough is not a poor ambition. You will be the responsible chatelaine of a great house, which is no small thing.'

Sarah shook her head. 'I am sorry to disappoint you. I know you like Charles, but it is of my life we are speaking. I am fortunate enough to be able to please myself. I have no need to marry for money and would prefer to marry for love or companionship. If I cannot find either, I would rather not marry at all.'

'I cannot say that I am other than disappointed but, of course, the choice is yours. You are of age. I cannot compel you. I can only advise.' He paused. 'I should not like you to make a foolish marriage that you might later regret.'

She ignored his final hint and replied only to the first part of his speech.

'Good, then that is understood. There is one further thing. You said nothing to the Governor of Charles's proposal. I must ask you to tell no one else of it. I do not wish my affairs to be part of the gossip of Sydney.'

John's reply was studied. In the mistaken belief that Sarah would be only too willing to accept Charles, he had told Alan Kerr that she had done so, and had told him that for a purpose. He made a rapid decision. He would not tell her of his conversation with Kerr, but neither would he undeceive Kerr by informing him of Sarah's refusal.

After all, Kerr was not a fit and proper husband for Miss Sarah Langley of Prior's Langley. Neither was New South Wales a fit and proper place for her to live. He quietened his conscience by telling himself that he was deceiving Sarah and Alan for their own good. He had not intended to mislead Alan, but now that he had done it was all for the best.

Once Sarah had returned to England it was exceedingly likely that she would change her mind and accept Charles. The advantages of doing so would be plain.

So it was with a Judas kiss on her cheek that John told his sister that he would respect her wishes, however much he deplored her decision. He felt sure that Kerr would not be able to reveal his double-dealing unwittingly by speaking to Sarah about her supposed marriage to Charles. Kerr was as proud as the devil and it would be unlikely that he would speak much, if at all, to Sarah now that he believed that she had rejected him for another man.

Sarah, completely unaware that with a couple of sentences her brother had destroyed her dreams of a future as Alan Kerr's wife, was pleased and moved that he has made so little effort to change her mind over her decision to refuse Charles and had shown her such a wealth of loving consideration.

Before she went to bed she wrote her answer to Charles, and tore up his letter and Emily's in an abnegation of her life in England, and as a pledge that her only interest lay in the future, not the past.

Sarah dressed herself for the Governor's dinner in a state of extreme anticipation. She knew that it was a relatively small one, confined to the immediate circle of the Governor's friends of whom she and John were now a part. There would be few of the military there, although Colonel O'Connell would be present as the senior officer, despite his disapproval of some of the other guests. These included Dr Alan Kerr and Tom Dilhorne.

The dinner was due to begin at four o'clock and Sarah had forgone nuncheon in order to do justice to the Governor's table. Her own sense of personal happiness was so great that she did not notice that John was less forthcoming than usual.

He was suffering from pangs of conscience. It was all very well telling himself that he had misled Sarah for her own good, but he was neither insensitive enough nor hardened enough not to realise what was causing Sarah's happiness, and he reproached himself for his own want of honesty with her.

His conscience was not sufficiently stirred, however, for him to say anything to her, or to Kerr should he meet him. When she took his arm on entering Government House he only had to look at her to be sure that such a handsome sight should not be wasted in the desert that was New South Wales. Happiness improved her brilliant good looks and her playful manner charmed the Governor, already her great admirer, and caused more than one middle-aged man to wish himself young again.

Sarah looked around for Alan whilst she waited to go into dinner, but could not see him. Another who was doing the same was Tom Dilhorne. He was a little surprised that his friend was not already there, and even more surprised when the Governor took him on one side and told him that Dr Kerr could not be present.

'Called away?' enquired Tom, and the Governor shrugged eloquently. Tom could only conclude that some really desperate medical emergency must have occurred for Alan to have absented himself to deal with it rather than send the tall lad whom he had recently hired as an assistant.

The butler came in to tell them that dinner was served: an announcement that came as a great shock to Sarah since Alan had still not arrived. She comforted herself with the thought that he had probably been called away and he might even arrive late—this was all part of a doctor's life, which might in future be part of hers.

The meal was a good one, but Sarah ate little of it since Alan's continued absence appeared to suggest that his late arrival might be turning into no arrival at all. For the first time a little worm of doubt wriggled into her consciousness. Surely he would have forewarned her if he was to be delayed, or was not intending to come to the dinner at all. She remembered his ardent looks when he last spoke to her and concluded that she was probably reading too much into his absence.

The ladies retired to the drawing room while the gentlemen lingered over their port and cigars. Sarah endured the idle conversation of the women present with even less interest than usual, and sat up eagerly when the men finally arrived—but Alan was not with them.

The glass doors on to the terrace had been opened and many of the company promenaded outside. Sarah took advantage of the general dispersal to approach Tom, who was staring at a singularly inaccurate oil of several kangaroos that was prominently displayed over the fireplace.

After a little chit-chat she said, apparently carelessly, 'I understood that Dr Kerr was to have been present this evening, but I must have been mistaken.'

'No mistake, Miss Sarah. He sent his last-minute apologies to the Governor.'

'Called out again, I suppose.'

'Can't say, no explanation offered.'

Good manners demanded that she said no more, even though she gained the impression that Tom was a little troubled, too, by Alan's sudden crying-off. She must at all costs avoid the appearance of desperation or disappointment. John, seeing that Sarah was talking to that rogue Dilhorne, made haste to join them. It was no use getting rid of Kerr—he, at least, had read Alan's absence correctly—if, instead, Sarah turned to Dilhorne, who was an even worse choice for her than Alan Kerr was.

'Happy to see you, Dilhorne,' he said, ignoring Tom's sceptical expression when he came out with this totally untrue statement. 'I hear that you are increasing your investments in the whaling trade.'

'Aye,' returned Tom, who was always at his most uncouth when talking to John Langley. 'Happen that some of the Yankees are running short of funds and need new agents in Sydney as well.' Typically he made no attempt to explain or enlarge. 'Seeing that I've to be up early to speak to their representative, I'd better leave now.'

This remarkable statement, seeing that it was not yet seven of the clock, almost provoked Sarah to mirth, and John's eyebrows rose alarmingly at the sight of Tom ambling across the room in order to take his leave of the Governor. He thought to take advantage of the shining hour by stressing Tom's total unsuitability for civilised intercourse by remarking, 'Off to see that widow of his, I suppose.'

Sarah was sweetness itself. 'You mean Mrs Mahoney?' she trilled.

John was surprised, 'You know of her, Sarah? Really, you shock me yet again.'

'Oh, don't be such an old woman, John. Everyone knows of Tom's Mrs Mahoney. Even Lucy Middleton knows. Sydney's a goldfish bowl. There are no secrets here, though gentlemen don't like their ladies to know of their bits of muslin and their excursions to Madame Phoebe's house.'

Disappointment made Sarah indiscreet. She usually took a proper, ladylike tone with John and tried to avoided revealing to him that her knowledge of the seamy side of the world was a great deal deeper than he thought it was.

'All I can say, my dear, is the sooner that we leave these latitudes, the better. They obviously have a bad effect on gentlewomen.'

Sarah shrugged impatiently. After her disappointing evening it was the outside of enough to be lectured by John. She was almost tempted to let him know how much of his life was in the public domain and how little right it gave him to admonish her about her own language.

Wisdom prevailed. She turned away. 'If you are finished here, John, I am ready to go home.'

'Then I will instruct Carter to drive you there. O'Connell, some of the officers and myself intend to go on to the Mess and make a night of it.'

It took her all her strength of will not to make some acid comment on the nature of the night of it which he hoped to spend. What began in the Mess would most likely end at Madame Phoebe's. She made her adieux to the Governor, and waited, a disappointed woman, for Carter to come and drive her home.

Sarah did not enquire at what time John returned there. He did not come down for breakfast in the morning. She and Lucy had arranged to go shopping for further trifles needed for Lucy's wedding, which loomed nearer and nearer. They walked down George Street laughing and talking together.

'Look, Sarah,' Lucy exclaimed. 'Doctor Kerr is coming towards us on his big grey.'

Sarah's heart gave a great leap. He would stop, he would get down and talk to them, and all would be well again: last night's absence would be explained. She let down her parasol and composed a welcoming sentence in her mind.

Alan, however, did not bring his horse to a halt. He swept off the large felt hat that he was wearing, and his words to them both were as cold and formal as he could make them. 'Miss Middleton, Miss Langley, your servant, ladies,' and in a moment he had ridden by them and was turning the corner at the end of the street.

The expression on his face had been as hard and unwelcoming as it could be. It was as though the last few months of their camaraderie had never been. Even at their most quarrelsome, in her early days in the colony, he had never been so indifferent. Even Lucy was struck by his manner.

Sarah stood as though frozen. It could not be. She could not be treated thus for the second time. When Charles had betrayed her she had been hot-tempered, voluble. She felt now that she never wanted to speak again. She could have been sick on the spot.

No, she must be wrong. They must be reading into his behaviour something which was not there. He could not have changed so much in three days. She would see him on the morrow when he came to examine the children and all would be well again. She was sure of it. How could she wait until then?

Oh, to be a man and be able to go freely to him and ask him what was wrong—if there were anything wrong. A woman could only wait and wonder.

Lucy was speaking to her and she must answer. She must not expose her feelings of betrayal before others. Her reply was mechanical and somehow she managed to sleepwalk her way successfully through the morning as though nothing had happened, even though her seething brain was full of suppositions, questions and conclusions.

If Alan, too, has cried off, she thought, then there must be something wrong with me. John is right. Men cannot endure a woman who is other than their echo. I should have encouraged Stephen Parker in his suit. There would have been little real love for him on my part, but I could have managed him and I should not be feeling this dreadful hurt. Her mind went round and round like a mouse on the wheel in its cage. She remembered John being given one when he was a boy.

She was so distrait when she reached home that she found herself unable to swallow her dinner, or take part in any of the occupations that filled her evening. John noticed her white face and wondered uneasily whether it was the result of Kerr's non-arrival at the Governor's dinner. He comforted himself with the thought that it was all for the best and in the bustle of going home she would soon forget her unsuitable lover.

When she finally reached her bed Sarah could not sleep, and tried to comfort herself with the thought that she must not mope without reason. She was sure to see him tomorrow when all would be explained. Yes, that was it, by tomorrow all might yet be well.

Sarah was not the only one who could not sleep. Seeing her in the street, looking at her most charming, had reinforced in Alan the sense of her goodness: the goodness that she had shown in looking after first Sukie and then Nellie, when most of the women in the colony would have shrugged their shoulders and left fate to settle the matter.

It had almost broken his heart to treat her so coldly, but it was all for the best, her best, was it not? He must, at whatever the cost, avoid her, lest he forget himself. True love often demanded a sacrifice for the loved one's benefit. The pain it brought him was a sharp one, but he had lived his life since his downfall by the strictest principles and it was these that were guiding him now. The one thing that surprised him was, given that he was so sure of Sarah's goodness, why was it that she had never approached him herself—or mentioned that she had left a prospective husband back in England?

For the first time he asked himself whether John Langley had been telling the whole truth—but he dismissed it as the whim-whams of a sleepless man in the middle of the night. Nevertheless, the seed had been sown.

It was only in the early hours that he fell asleep at last, and then it was to dream of loss and loneliness, telling himself when he awoke with the dawn that he must be strong and bear all that life threw at him without complaining.

By the morning Sarah reproached herself for her panic-stricken folly of the previous day. She felt positively cheerful after nuncheon when she changed into an old dress, laid out her brown Holland apron and helped Sukie to pack some of the toys which she had bought to take with her to her little class.

In her renewed state of happiness the afternoon flew by until the time for Alan's arrival drew near. She was seated at her desk, watching the children copy down some words on their slates when she heard him arrive and rose to her feet to welcome him.

The door opened and it was a moment before she realised that it not Alan who stood before her. It was Drew McMaster, the boy whom he had taken on as his assistant. He was carrying a little black bag, and there was a proud, but diffident, expression on his face.

'Where is Dr Kerr?' Sarah demanded before she could stop herself.

Drew advanced into the room. 'He's sent me, Miss Langley. He says that I am now capable of looking after the little ones and it will free him for more duties in the hospital. I shall be coming in future.'

Sarah was so shocked that she found it difficult to speak. 'Did Dr Kerr send me any message?' she finally managed.

Drew looked puzzled. 'Why, no, Miss Langley. Were you expecting one?'

'No.' She turned away to see Sukie's surprised face, and turned back again to avoid it. Was I expecting a message? she thought. Of course I was. I expected one two nights ago—and more than a message, a proposal. Oh, Alan, what can have happened?

She could no longer deceive herself. He wanted to have no more to do with her. He was removing her from his life. He had missed the Governor's dinner. He had virtually cut Lucy and herself, and now he had sent Drew in his place without a word of explanation or regret.

His message was, however, quite plain. Yet another man had cast off foolish Sarah Langley! It was all that she could do to prevent herself from crying out loud.

She and Sukie helped Drew with the little ones. He was a good boy and deserved her undivided attention. She must not let her suffering prevent her from carrying out her duties. It was not Drew's fault that he was the bearer of ill tidings. It was her fault. She spoiled everything that she touched. She felt that she could no longer blame Charles from turning away from her. It was her fate.

The reclusive life that Alan had followed since he reached New South Wales, and which first Lachlan Macquarie and then Sarah had breached, claimed him again. He not only avoided John and Sarah, he avoided all human contact, other than with his patients, to whom his manner remained unfailingly gentle and considerate. Even Tom Dilhorne saw little of him.

Others beside Sarah noticed the change in him with surprise and regret. Lachlan Macquarie stopped him one day on his rounds and asked him where he was hiding these days.

Alan's reply was courteous but firm. 'The medical claims of the colony are taking up my time.'

He would not be drawn further and, after a few monosyllabic exchanges, the Governor walked on, no wiser than before. He was the only person in Sydney—beside Tom Dilhorne—to notice that the Langleys were included in Alan Kerr's ostracism of all social life. He was not the only person to regret that Alan's interest in Sarah seemed to have come to an abrupt end, but, like the rest of Sydney, he had no clue as to why this had happened.

The only person who could have told him—other than Alan himself—was John Langley, and John Langley was saying nothing. If he was a little concerned at his sister's descent into quiet misery, he still comforted himself with the thought that when she returned home she would soon recover.

Their demand for a passage had been noted, but it might be some time before they could leave. He had expected Sarah to protest, to ask for delay, but she was as apathetic about this as she was about everything else—other than Lucy's wedding.

'Sarah, I must ask you,' said Lucy one day when they sat sewing in the Langleys' parlour, 'are you quite well? Frank was saying yesterday that you haven't looked quite the thing for some weeks now. We both hope that you aren't going to be ill when the wedding is due. You are my chief bridesmaid—I positively *insist* that you must be well.'

'I fear I may be homesick,' said Sarah untruthfully, 'which is not helped by the heat.' They were rapidly running through the Sydney spring and to the anniversary of their arrival.

'Frank was saying that Dr Kerr has become a hermit again,' said Lucy, apparently inconsequentially. 'Have you any idea why he has abandoned society?'

'None at all,' replied Sarah, painfully. 'One moment he came out of his shell and the next he was back in it again. I don't think that I have seen him, other than in the distance, for weeks now.'

'He doesn't come to see the children in your little school, then,' said Lucy, contemplating a delicate rosebud which she had just finished embroidering.

'No,' said Sarah, trying to sound as impersonal as possible and fearing that she was failing. 'Drew McMaster comes now. Doctor Kerr has far too much to do at the hospital and the work there is beyond Drew.' She tried not to betray how desolate she felt.

Lucy decided not to pursue the matter further. Whilst unaware of how far Sarah and Alan had gone towards an understanding, she did realise that Sarah was missing him. She had asked Frank if he knew why Dr Kerr had withdrawn from society again, but Frank's answer was that while he thought Alan Kerr was a good fellow, his senior officers were only too pleased that they did not constantly have to meet him in the Governor's company.

'Frank was telling me,' Lucy went on, 'that the Governor is a little worried about the Irish prisoners. He thinks that lately they have been showing signs of rebelling again. He is concerned that we might have a repetition of what happened in 1804. What is particularly troubling him is that this time the ordinary convicts are behaving as though they might support them. Frank says that Colonel O'Connell is pooh-poohing the whole thing. He believes that the Governor spends far too much time thinking about the convicts and the Emancipists and far too little time thinking about the rest of us.'

'I know that Tom Dilhorne is worried about the Irish, and Tom doesn't take fright easily,' said Sarah.

'Tom Dilhorne—you talk a lot to him these days. What does John think of your being so friendly with him? I've wanted to ask you before, but I didn't like to.'

'Now, Lucy, you know that you may ask me anything. John doesn't like my friendship with Tom and that is one of the reason why he is so pleased that we are going home. I like Tom. I know that the military don't approve of him, but he has been so kind to Nellie and Sukie. After Annie's death, once he had bought Dempster's Mill, he arranged for Dr Kerr to look after the children there. There are worse men in the world than Tom Dilhorne.'

Lucy worked away at her rosebud. 'There was a time when I thought that you might marry Stephen Parker. We could have been Regimental wives together, but I collect that you showed no inclination to be his wife, so that dream was soon over. I do understand why you discouraged him. He's a nice enough fellow, full of charm, but he's what Frank calls a lightweight?'

Sarah agreed. 'He's like a man I knew back home. You'd never be safe with Stephen. Frank now, he's much more dependable. I once thought that you and John might have made a match of it, but I don't think that you are really suited.'

'Oh, I could never have been Mrs John Langley of Prior's Langley,' said Lucy decidedly. 'I haven't the right manner for that at all. I envy you when you organise things for John. I need a man to look after me, You don't.'

And that is the trouble, thought Sarah sadly. I don't

need anyone to look after me. Perhaps that put Alan off—although from something he once said, I thought that he liked my independence. Oh, it's useless repining. I must think of other things.

Chapter Twelve

Like Sarah, Alan Kerr was trying not to repine and, equally unsuccessfully, was trying to forget the past. To pass her in the street with only the coldest of acknowledgements had nearly broken his heart. He became a recluse once more because otherwise he would surely see her again and the sight of her would be like a blow to his already battered emotions.

He avoided his old friend Tom Dilhorne because he knew that Tom would be sure to query his reversion to his behaviour in his early days in the colony and that would cause him even more pain, more than he might be able to bear.

One afternoon he met Sukie in the street. He had tried to pass her by with a nod and an aloof smile, but she had stopped him by confronting him, arms akimbo.

'What d'you think you're doing, Dr Kerr, to distress Miss Sarah so?'

'Now, Miss Sukie,' he had said, gently, 'You must know that I cannot speak of this to you.'

Her eyes on fire, she sniffed at him, 'Oh, that's the sort of thing the gentry say. I take no note of that. Why not?'

'I can't speak to you of Miss Langley behind her back. It would not be proper. She would not be pleased if she knew that we were gossiping about her.'

Sukie began to whimper. 'You're fools, both of you, fools. Why don't you ever speak to her now? You used to.'

He could not say that he had been hurt too often. He still had bitter memories of the girl in Scotland who had thrown him off without a word and married another, and of his long-lost mother, father and sisters who had also disowned him. He seemed to be doomed by fate to suffer yet more hammer blows like those which had destroyed his past life.

He had watched Sukie wander desolately off, and if her words had affected him at all, it was to remind him that he was cutting Tom out of his life. Tom, to whom he owed so much. He deserved better than that. Briefly, for the first time in weeks he wondered what Tom was doing—and at the same time acknowledged how much he was missing him.

Sarah, in an effort to forget the past, applied herself to her drawing and painting almost feverishly. She discovered that her pain over the breach with Alan, far from destroying her abilities, had apparently served to enhance them.

One, afternoon, sitting with her sketchbook on the edge of town, the faithful Carter and the Langley carriage nearby, she was a little surprised to see Tom Dilhorne coming towards her. He dismounted, and after a word with Carter came over to where she sat and squatted on his heels in order to examine her work.

She was finishing a water-colour of the native rose whose fragrance could be smelled throughout Sydney when it was in full flower. She had begun to fill a folio book, devoted to the wild flowers of the region, some months ago, but her busy life and involvement with Alan had slowed the work down. Now she was painting as though her life depended on it.

Tom said nothing until she had completed the wash which she was busy laying down. Then, 'You're a talented lady, Miss Sarah.'

She smiled a little wanly. 'One does what one can, Tom.'

'Aye.' He said nothing further for some minutes while she mixed colours to her satisfaction. 'I hear that you and Mr Langley are leaving us shortly.'

'Yes.' She was as brief as he was.

'There was a time when I thought that you might be staying.'

Her smile was painful. 'Did you, Tom? John and I never intended to stay when we came here.'

'That wasn't quite what I said, Miss Sarah.'

Sarah grew tired of fencing with him. Once it had pleased her, but after Alan had deserted her, everything seemed wearisome, too much of an effort. Except for her painting, that was.

'I know what you said, and I also know what you meant. However, the reason why I might have stayed no longer applies, as you well know. Now shall we talk of other things?'

'We might if I were a gentleman, but I'm not a gentleman so that don't signify, as you people would say.' His idle drawl was even more pronounced than usual. 'What beats me, Miss Sarah, is how you can be so clever on that little piece of paper, and so stupid about your life. Why, I do believe that even poor Miss Sukie has more common sense than you.'

The scene before her, wavered a little. 'Good God,'

she reflected, 'I never cried until I came to this benighted place, now I am going to turn the waterworks on in front of Tom!'

She put down her brush and looked at his quizzical, brown face. She grasped suddenly that she had never really taken him seriously before. To her he had always been odd, dependable Tom Dilhorne, her rather grotesque friend. Could it be that she had always looked at the people around her as mere appendages of herself? What did she actually know of him, the real Tom Dilhorne who was the centre of his life as she was of hers?

'I know that I must appear stupid to you, Tom, but consider how difficult life is for a mere female. What can I do? I was never the sort to connive and deceive to gain my ends. I cannot lasso Dr Kerr and compel him to speak to me again, and it's not only my pride which prevents me from running screaming into the street to gain his attention. Believe me, in a case like mine, it would be easier for me to be Nellie or Sukie than Miss Sarah Langley of Prior's Langley.'

Tom's silence was even longer than usual. He rose to his feet and walked a little way away from her. Sarah continued to paint vigorously. She wondered whether he would speak again before he left her. Carter stolidly watched them both. It was typical of her changed way of thinking that she wondered what he was making of it all.

Tom returned to her side as suddenly as he had left it.

'I shan't plague you again, Miss Sarah. Believe me, I have only your best interests at heart.'

'I know that, Tom, but matchmaker is an odd role for you to play.'

'Aye, I'm sometimes a bigger fool than God made

me. Trouble is, I want my friends to be happy, and happy is plainly what you and Alan Kerr are not.'

Sarah was touched. 'One day,' she told him, 'before I go home, I want to paint your portrait—with the Blue Mountains in the background. Simply to see it when I am home again in the orderly fields of England will take me back to a place where I once thought that I could live my life. I shan't forget this afternoon.'

Tom believed her. She would have made a superb wife for his friend, who was busy throwing away his hopes of happiness with her for reasons which he did not understand.

'Nor I,' he said, and, tipping his hat to her he wandered back to his horse. If it was Alan she wanted, then she ought to have him, and by damn, if he could help it, then Alan she should get, even though she was more than he deserved after the daft way he was behaving!

Tom had stopped to talk to Sarah on his way to a meeting called by the Governor to discuss the likelihood of a rebellion by the Irish and the steps which might be necessary to deal with it, should one break out.

He had called together all the notables and leading lights in the colony including Tom and Alan. The officers, particularly their Colonel, were annoyed at the presence of so many Emancipists, even when Macquarie explained that it was important to discover what rumours were running around among the ex-convicts, and those who were dealing directly with the convicts themselves.

The general feeling was that Macquarie was making a great fuss about nothing. Most of the convicts' resentment, it was suggested, was the result of the Governor's own policies. His ambitious building and road-making plans were creating a great deal of gruelling hard work for them which they naturally resented. This did not necessarily mean, though, that they would support an uprising.

Colonel O'Connell even went so far as to say that if the Governor wished to avoid one, then all he had to do was scale down his supposed improvements. This, however, was not the general feeling of the meeting. Most, indeed, thought things ought to continue as they were. Major Middleton was particularly loud in his denunciation of doom-laden prophecies, quoting the experience of his fellow officers which gave this one the lie. Many nodding heads supported him.

Tom, who felt that the matter was not being taken seriously enough, interrupted the Major's lengthy speech to say, 'That's not what I have heard, Major Menzies. Happen my friends are different from Major Middleton's. They all seem to think that the Irish are planning a major uprising, like the one in '04, and that this time they are arranging to include the other convicts in it. Not all will want to join in, but as usual, the hotheads are the noisiest, and they will influence the rest and drag many of them along.'

'Your friends,' sneered O'Connell. His tone was one of pure disgust. 'Pray who might they be? Fine friends, indeed, if they know of treason and do not report it.'

Tom, having made one of the longest public speeches of his life, was equable. 'Well, I know that they aren't your friends, Colonel, and I wouldn't expect them to be. But they are in a position to know what's being said, and to tell me to pass it on. If you won't listen to me, then that's your choice—you certainly wouldn't listen to them.'

This was irrefutable, and Alan thought it right to add his voice to Tom's. 'There's a strong feeling among the Irish that if they don't rise now, they will never be able to do so again. Sydney is rapidly changing those who are sent here. Only the hard core feel loyalty to their Irish past.'

'Well, you're the expert there,' said O'Connell, sneering again. 'But a felon sent here for committing treason is the last person I should go to for advice.'

'Gentlemen, gentlemen!' Macquarie called them to order. 'This is not the time for recriminations.' The expression on Alan's face after O'Connell's comment told him that he must go carefully or worse might follow.

It was plain that in Kerr's current black mood he would not hesitate to call O'Connell out if he were allowed to continue to insult him. Consequently Macquarie said in his blandest voice, 'I brought you together to ask you for your advice over the possibility of an uprising. Since, however, it appears that there is a split between you, wariness must be the order of the day and it would therefore be best for actual planning for such an eventuality to wait until the arrival of more definite information. I hope, though, that you will all agree that those responsible for the maintenance of law and order in the colony must be put on their guard.'

'And that,' said Tom to Alan, who had been unable to avoid him after the meeting was over, 'is no more and no less than you might have expected. Macquarie's afraid of what might be said back in England if he spends too much money on preparing for a rising which never happened.'

Alan looked a little sideways at his old friend. If Tom owed much to him—for it had been Alan who had educated him on the long voyage out from England—then, he, too, owed much to Tom and educating him had been a small reward for the other man's saving of his life. He had been a raw young gentleman, inexperienced in the world of gaoled and gaoler, and Tom had enabled him to survive when he might have gone under. Yes, he owed him a debt of gratitude which he could never completely repay and he suddenly felt sorry that in his despair he had been avoiding his friend.

He put out his hand to clasp Tom's, and that cool customer fully understood what his friend was trying to tell him 'Aye,' he said, 'Ye've been dodging me, mate.' He had not called Alan 'mate' since their first days on the transport bringing them to New South Wales.

'I'm sorry, Tom. I've had the black dog of despair on my back again. I thought I'd lost it I when they transferred us from Norfolk Island but, recently, it sprang there again, without warning.'

'You'd not like to talk about it, mate?'

'Some day, not now. I feel ungrateful for not wishing to when I think of all that you have done for me from the very first day we met.'

Tom sighed. 'Oh, be damned to that. You saved me on Norfolk Island when you stopped that swine from having me beaten to death by claiming that I was your medical assistant and that the colony would suffer if I snuffed it.'

Alan laughed for the first time in weeks. 'Yes, and I didn't know then how little time it would take for me to train you to be one. You should have been a doctor yourself.'

Tom's laugh was genuine. 'Oh, aye, we could spend the rest of the day working out which one of us owed the other the most. I thought of training for a doctor when at last we arrived here, but the notion of making money, and showing the nobs what a poor convict could do if he put his mind to it, attracted me the more. As to confiding in me—well, if you don't feel inclined to, then that's that.'

He paused before repeating what he had said to Sarah, 'You know that I've only your best interests at heart.'

'I've always known that, so you will understand that there are some things of which I cannot speak.'

'True of all of us, mate, true of all of us. If ever I can help—you know where to find me.'

With that they parted and Alan found, almost immediately, that talking to his old friend had eased his mind. It was possible for him to think of Sarah without too much pain, although he still found it difficult to imagine ever speaking to her again. It was useless telling himself that he was being childish—it was as though everything that had happened to him since that fatal evening when he had drunkenly destroyed his previous life had led to this final rejection.

Nevertheless, after meeting Tom, something which had recently been troubling him took on a stronger force. As time passed he had begun to think that it was a little strange that neither John nor Sarah appeared to have told anyone in Sydney of the grand match which was waiting for her back home. Certainly Tom had given no indication that he knew of it.

On the other hand John was a gentleman, and he would surely not lie over such a matter. It would be against the gentleman's code of honour. Nevertheless this new notion that he might have been deceived would not go away, however often he told himself that he was now, in effect, deceiving himself.

One afternoon on a sudden impulse, he walked to Sarah's makeshift classroom in the hope of seeing her and setting his errant mind at rest. However short and bitter their conversation might be, he could at least wish

her well in her grand future and try to convince himself
that he would be better off without her.

Unluckily he had chosen the very day when Sarah was
having one of her rare absences and Sukie was busy
supervising the little ones, proud to show off her new
accomplishments in reading and writing.

'I'll tell Miss Sarah you called,' she told him eagerly.

Alan was brief. 'If you like.' He hardly knew whether
he was glad or sorry that he had missed her.

'It's Miss Lucy's wedding next month and Miss Sarah
is helping to make the bridesmaid's dresses.'

Alan knew that he was not welcome at the Middletons
and would be unlikely to be asked to the wedding. He
rather liked Major Middleton and was reasonably
friendly with him, but Mrs Middleton possessed all the
colonial wife's dislike of ex-convicts, however much of
a gentleman they might have been before their conviction and would certainly veto his appearance at the wedding as a guest.

He packed his bag and left, ruefully thinking that even
fate seemed determined to prevent him from speaking to
her again. Perhaps it was all for the best. What sort of
wife would she have made for a disgraced colonial doctor when she had been part of the highest society in
England and had run her brother's great house?

Sukie took the earliest possible opportunity to tell
Sarah of Alan's visit. Poor Sarah would rather have
missed a hundred meetings with Lucy's bridesmaids
than have missed one chance of speaking to Alan. Like
him she thought that fate was working against her. Well,
she would soon be gone and once she was home again
she might find it easy to forget a colonial doctor with
whom she had thought herself in love, and who had

seemed to love her before he had dismissed her from his life forever.

She might think that—but she did not believe it... Instead, she tried to concentrate on making her last days in the colony as full and happy as possible She spoke to John about a visit to Nellie and the baby before she left, and although he considered this as yet another example of Sarah's new and reprehensible weakness for consorting with servants, set about arranging it. After all, she would soon be home again, mixing only with her equals.

Chapter Thirteen

The incident that sparked off the Rising—or, rather, encouraged some of the convicts to join the Irish—was, as these things often are, a minor, indeed rather silly one. Sarah learned of it from Lucy Middleton on the last afternoon she spent with her before visiting Grimes's farm.

'It's really the funniest thing,' she told Sarah when the tea-board was brought in, 'I only heard about it this morning from Papa. You'd not guess what it was, try you never so hard.'

'Then don't keep me in suspense, tell all,' Sarah said.

'Well, it seems that one of the convict gangs was working on the barracks at the edge of town. Since they were sent there, several of them have tried to escape into the bush, but the soldiers guarding them have always succeeded in stopping them. One of the convicts was an actor transported for forging a bank draft when he couldn't get work. Georgina O'Connell says she's seen him about and that he's a handsome fellow. He kisses his hand at all the ladies he sees.' She paused.

'And that's the story?' asked Sarah, disappointed.

'Oh, no, there's more to come. Papa said that the convicts secretly caught a kangaroo when the soldiers weren't watching them very carefully. They killed the poor thing and then skinned it.'

This time Sarah was incredulous. 'Caught a kangaroo without the soldiers knowing? You must be funning, Lucy.'

'Well, the poor things aren't very clever,' said Lucy knowledgeably. 'Papa often says that they're nowhere near as bright as most of the convicts and, looking at Tom Dilhorne and Will French, you can see what he means. Anyway, they cured the skin and gave it to the actor. Yesterday, when they were bricklaying and the soldiers were having yet another chat, the actor put on the skin and started to jump away—in order to escape, of course.

'Unfortunately the soldiers thought that he was a real kangaroo and began to shoot at him. You can imagine his fright: there he was, hopping and jumping away, freedom beckoning, when balls started to whizz around his head. Finally the poor fellow felt compelled to pull the skin off and beg for mercy.'

Sarah could scarcely speak for laughing. 'Lucy, I vow that you must be making this up!'

'No such thing.' Lucy was comically indignant. 'It seems that when he threw his skin off one of the soldiers thought that it was aborigine magic, and fell on his knees, howling for God to save him from the devil. It took some time for his fellows to convince him that it was only a poor escaping convict he was frightened of.

'The rest of the story isn't so funny. Papa says that the actor has been sentenced to a flogging for trying to escape, and will be put permanently in irons. He says that the sentence is deserved, but that there is a great deal of bad feeling about it. All the other convicts believe that the sentence is too harsh and inappropriate and it's even rumoured that they have begun to mutter about joining the Irish in an uprising. Papa says that at the moment it would have been wiser for the Colonel to be merciful.'

'I think that the actor ought to be given a pardon for inventiveness,' said Sarah. 'It certainly makes a change from all this fretting about the Irish and the goings-on of the Emancipists.'

'True,' said Lucy, 'my own feeling is that everyone's getting worked up about nothing. I do so wish that I could go with you to Grimes's farm tomorrow, away from all the silly gossip, but Mama would never hear of it, so I didn't ask.'

Sarah told John of Lucy's story about the kangaroo when, much later, he came home, having dined at the Officers' Mess again.

'A cup of tea only,' he said, waving away Sarah's offer of a light meal. Over it he suddenly remarked, 'I saw Alan Kerr today.'

Sarah, answering him, was surprised to find how steady her voice was. 'And did you have occasion to speak?'

'Yes, I told him that I hadn't seen much of him lately, and he explained that he has been infernally busy. It seems that he has been engaged in a battle with O'Connell over the treatment of the convicts. Kerr has told the Governor that he doesn't think it is sufficiently humane, and of course, Macquarie has agreed with him. O'Connell is saying that he won't be instructed by an ex-felon on the proper way to deal with criminals. I suppose that he has a point. After all, Kerr did come here as a convict.'

'You used not to think that. You used to like Dr Kerr,' returned Sarah a little bitterly.

'I still do, but he is sadly lacking in tact. A typical Scot. He asked after you, though. I told him that you were well and were looking forward to going home.'

'Then you did not tell him the truth. I do not want to go home.'

Unspoken were the words: and I do not want to leave Alan for good. If I do not marry him, then I shall never marry anyone.

'Oh, come, Sarah,' said John easily, 'you know that you don't mean that. Of course you want to go home. Think of what is waiting for you there.'

Sarah rose abruptly and looked out of the window. The blue and red cockatoo hanging in the veranda of the house opposite could be heard screeching its boredom.

'Nothing is waiting for me there. The trouble is, there's nothing waiting for me here, either. Only Lucy's wedding; once that is over, my life will be a desert.'

John shrugged his shoulders. There was no talking to her these days. He said, trying to sound amused, 'I see that you are determined to be contrary. When we were in England you wanted to be here. Now that you're here you don't know where you want to be.'

'I think that I would like to be at Grimes's farm, help-ing in the fields, or even at the hospital, doing something useful. I am sick of idleness.'

'Come, come,' said her brother. 'You know that in your station of life these things are impossible. Ladies don't work.'

'Then perhaps they ought to,' said Sarah, and, unable to bear being with her brother and constantly being told what she ought to do and think, she left him and walked upstairs to her bedroom. She could not tell him what she really wanted.

She wanted to be with Alan. Her whole body yearned after him. Until she had met Alan she had never known that she possessed a body. Now it had taken her over quite ruthlessly, so that the cool lack of interest which she had always shown to her suitors, and which she had partly maintained with Charles Villiers, had disappeared as though it had never been.

She ached to be with Alan, to see him again, to be in his arms, to learn from the book of love with him... For the first time she felt that she understood what the marriage ceremony meant when the groom addressed the bride with the words, 'With my body I thee worship.' She knew now that such a statement held true for the bride as well. No etiquette book, no novel that she had been allowed to read, had ever hinted at such a thing. Love had been a mental, not a physical, attribute and to express it through the body had not even been an idea to discuss. The heroes and heroines were bloodless creatures.

Downstairs her brother, unaware of how his sister really felt, was telling himself that once she was home again all this would be forgotten. Kerr would be forgotten. To that end it was convenient that she wished to visit Grimes's farm. By the time that she returned their passage to England might be assured and, in the excitement of packing, her foolish *tendre* for Alan Kerr would disappear. More than that—he had embroidered his original lie to Alan by informing him that Sarah's pallor these days was because she was pining for Charles Villiers and was finding their wait for a passage home intolerably long.

* * *

Afterwards both Alan and Tom were to regret that, while John and Sarah were going ahead with her visit to Nellie, they had had no opportunity to warn them of the dangers and urge delay. At the one function that the Governor gave before Sarah was to leave—another dinner for the notables of both sides—neither John nor Sarah was able to attend.

Not that John would have taken any notice of them. He had spoken to O'Connell about Sarah's visit and the Colonel had assured him that the journey would be safe—but that Carter should carry a case of pistols with him. As a result, Sarah was packed into a carriage with her luggage, her painting equipment, a rag doll from Sukie for the baby and a parcel of baby clothes that she and Lucy had made from the scraps of delicate material which were the off-cuts from Lucy's trousseau.

Lucy and the entire Langley household, including Mrs Hackett, gave her a truly royal send-off. Sukie was in tears at the prospect of losing Sarah for a fortnight. Sarah's own feelings about her short holiday were mixed. In the last few days, while walking around Sydney, she had looked for Alan in an attempt to speak to him, but had never had the luck to see him. Carter, who appeared to know everything, had told her one day, apparently idly, that 'Dr Kerr is working at the Hospital these days'.

Tom's dismissal of John's intellect—or rather lack of it—was never more just than when John was using it to consider Sarah and Carter's future. He had no inkling that Carter had already decided not to return to England and had arranged to take up employment with Tom as a useful man of all work when he moved into his new villa on The Point.

* * *

Alan Kerr was sadly amused, but not surprised, to learn that one of the *on dits* running around Sydney was that part of John Langley's reason for sending Sarah away was so that he would be able to live a more free and easy social life. For the first time he would be able to sample the various delights that the fancy ladies in the Rocks offered, without having to lie to Sarah about the reason for his returning home shortly before breakfast.

His carefree fortnight was crowned by his invitation to a party in the Officers' Mess to celebrate Major Stewart's thirty-fifth birthday and his survival as a bachelor to that great age. After dinner the company adjourned to Madame Phoebe's, where such a good time was had by all that John finally arrived home, completely fuddled, around four of the clock, and then managed to sleep through all the early excitement of the Rising, as it was always to be known.

Alan Kerr had worked late at the hospital on the previous evening. It was fortunate, he thought, that he was so busy, because otherwise he might have forgotten his rule about not drinking. To drink himself senseless would at least have the merit of enabling him to forget about Sarah, but would render him incapable of being useful when he was most needed.

Early the next morning he was woken up by the sound of men shouting outside. He ran to the window to see half a dozen soldiers, bayonets fixed, running along the street. In the distance a trumpet sounded. Suddenly a volley of shots coming from the centre of Sydney rang out, to be succeeded by more shouting and the sound of a bugle.

In the middle of this brouhaha Drew McMaster arrived to pound on his bedroom door, bellowing, 'Wake up, wake up, sir. We shall be wanted. The Irish have risen and they are fighting the soldiers in the streets.'

Alan, who had begun to pull on his clothes, shouted back, 'One moment, and I shall be with you.' He picked up his medical bag, which lived on his washstand, and flung the door open.

'What time did this begin?'

'Recently,' Drew panted back at him. 'It started under my bedroom window and then the fight moved on. There are dead and dying lying outside—mostly Irish, I think.'

'No doubt,' said Alan wryly. 'They can't expect much mercy from O'Connell now that they've proved him wrong. Which way do we go?'

'George Street,' said Drew, who was carrying his own medical bag, eager to put into practice what Alan had been busy teaching him. They ran down the stairs and into the street. The noise of firing grew louder and louder until, suddenly, before they reached the corner of their road, which led into George Street, it stopped and a ghastly silence fell.

Once they turned the corner it was plain that the attempt at a rising was already over. The small group of Irish rebels, and the even smaller one of dissident convicts, which had set up a makeshift flag and some crude barricades in George Street, were either lying dead or injured around the flag, or had already run through the streets leading to the bush with the soldiers in hot pursuit after them.

The long volley that Alan had heard had disposed of their leadership: in particular the main organiser, Francis Xavier Ryan, who, realising that the Rising had failed, had called for quarter from the military. He was now lying dead in his own blood, shot down as he spoke. The looked-for support had not materialised and his dawn foray had failed miserably. To this extent both the Governor and his critics were right: the Governor in his belief that an uprising was likely, O'Connell and his officers claiming that it was unlikely because it stood no chance of success.

Alan, joined by Tom Dilhorne, who had left his bed on hearing the noise of the brief battle, walked over to Pat Ramsey, who was one of the officers called out at short notice to deal with the rebels and who had ordered the series of volleys that had disposed of their leaders.

'It's all over, then?' Alan asked.

'Yes,' said Pat briefly, gesturing at the wounded rebels lying around their dead leader, and at those who were not vitally injured and were trying to drag themselves away. Their arms were lying scattered on the road. They consisted mainly of old fowling pieces, improvised pikes and scythes and a few wooden staves whose ends had been cruelly pointed. It was hardly an arsenal that could have given them victory against O'Connell's disciplined men.

'May I treat the wounded? With your permission, of course.'

He looked at the soldiers, some of them leaning on their muskets and others who were helping their fellows to improvise bandages for the few wounds that they had sustained in the hand-to-hand fighting which had preceded the final skirmish. Drew was already in action, helping them. Pat followed Alan's gaze, and wondered whether there was censure in it.

'I didn't join the Army to shoot down stupid, barely armed peasants,' he said stiffly. It was not the sight of men dead in action that affronted him, but the sheer pointlessness of the whole business. Useless to say that he was not a butcher when O'Connell had ordered them to refuse quarter—that is, surrender without further loss of life when the rebels called for it—until the leadership had been disposed of. It might make good military sense, but was distasteful for all that.

'I also,' Pat told them, 'have orders that you are to attend to our own men first. The other poor fools must wait their turn. I must also warn you that some disgruntled rebel might take a pot shot at you at any moment, so be careful.'

Pat was completely different from the cheerful, light-hearted, friendly fellow that both Alan and Tom had always known: he was transformed into the complete soldier, doing his job impersonally and dispassionately.

'Very well,' said Alan, 'but by the look of it, Drew is capable of looking after your men's light wounds. With your permission I shall, with Dilhorne's assistance, take charge of the rebel wounded. Tom, I wonder if you would be good enough to help me.'

'Can Dilhorne help you?' queried Pat.

'Indeed. He was my medical aide on Norfolk Island and a good one, too.'

'Go ahead. I shall organise some stretcher-bearers to carry them off to prison when you have said that they are fit to be moved—or to the cemetery. You may simply be prolonging their lives so that they may be tried and executed—but you have your job, as I have mine.'

Alan and Tom laboured together as they had not done since Norfolk Island. It did not take long. Some of the wounded had died before they reached them. Tom said when they both straightened up at last, 'I was told on the way here that the rebels broke immediately and that the majority of them deserted at once and fled to the bush. They have a camp there—or so I was told.'

'Is there anything going on in Sydney which you don't know of, Tom?'

'Not much, and the rest I can work out. Come home with me and have some breakfast—we've earned it.'

They began to leave when the first stretcher-bearers arrived and with them the soldiers who were ready to chain and march away the walking wounded.

They had barely left George Street when, of all people, they saw a frantic Sukie running down the road, tears streaming down her face.

She stopped when she saw them. She was so short of breath that she couldn't speak properly, but began to pant incomprehensible words in their direction. Alan took her by the shoulders and said gently to her, 'Wait a moment to get your breath back, Miss Sukie, and then tell us what is wrong.'

'Oh, I'm so glad I've found you both,' she managed at last. 'It's Miss Sarah, Miss Sarah... In the whole of my life she was the first person ever to be kind to me and through her I met George, I mean Carter, and you and Mr Tom, and you were all kind to me, too.' She stopped and began to sob uncontrollably.

'Miss Sukie,' said Alan, taking her by the hand. 'Think a moment. What is it that you are trying to tell us about Miss Sarah?'

'That she's been visiting Grimes's farm and that George took the carriage there yesterday afternoon to drive her home this morning and, oh, I'm afeared for them both. The road leads back through the bush and they might be caught by the rebels running away from the soldiers to the camp they've built there—and what will happen then?'

She had, as once before, begun to wring her hands. This time it was Tom who took them. 'Sukie, have you

spoken to Mr John about this?' He was not surprised
that Sukie almost certainly knew more about the details
of the Rising than the military and her betters.

'Oh, yes, and that's why I came looking for you now
it's over. He won't listen to me. He says that Colonel
O'Connell said that Miss Sarah would be safe and that
I'm making a great fuss about nothing. He sent me back
to the kitchen with a warning.'

In all the years he had known him, Tom had never
heard Alan swear, not even in the depths of his misery
on the transport and at Norfolk Island, but when Sukie
had finished he let off a volley of oaths about John Langley that left both Sukie and Tom dumb.

'I'm sorry,' he said, wiping his face with his handkerchief. 'I shouldn't have said that before you, Miss
Sukie.'

'I've heard worse most days.' She shrugged. 'What
are you going to do?'

'Visit John Langley first,' Alan told her, Tom nodding
agreement, 'and then we shall set off to try to find
Sarah—you will come with me, Tom, won't you?'

'Aye to both proposals,' Tom said.

John Langley, a fuddled expression on his face, never
even allowed them past his front door. He stared at Sukie, saying, 'I suppose that she's been filling you up with
her nonsense about Sarah.'

'Is it...' asked Alan, trying not to let the anger that
filled him cause him to set about Sarah's brother immediately, 'is it true that George Carter is driving Sarah
home from Grimes's farm this morning?'

'Yes, what of it?'

'You mean that you aren't afraid that they might be
in danger?'

John Langley shrugged his shoulders. 'Why should

they be? The Rising was a damp squib, is already over and, in any case, O'Connell said—'

He got no further. Alan, his usual calm face purple with anger, seized him by his cravat and began to shake him.

'You damned short-sighted fool. Miss Sukie here has more common sense in her little finger than either you or O'Connell in your whole bodies. How dare you palter with your sister's safety by claiming that she's not in danger? Don't you know that when the military dispersed the rebels they fled into the bush in the direction of Grimes's farm? I've a damned good mind...' and he began to shake John, who was only able to splutter back at him while his face turned purple.

Tom interrupted his friend and put a calming hand on his shoulder, saying equably, 'Let go of him, Alan. You'll strangle him if you're not careful, which would help neither you nor Sarah. Let's away to do that since her brother has no mind to save her.'

Alan, recalled to sense, loosened his hands from John's throat and stood back from him. 'You're right as usual, Tom, but mark my words, Langley, if ill has come to Sarah through your inaction then be sure that I shall come back and make dog's meat of you—and if I swing in consequence it will be worth it.'

With that he turned to Tom. 'We've no time to lose. Miss Sukie, if you're in any trouble, go to my lodgings and ask my landlady to look after you until I return.'

She nodded agreement and ran into the house.

'Well said,' Tom told Alan with a grin, 'and I might as well put in my pennyworth before we leave.'

He, too, leaned forward and took the shaken John by his cravat. 'Now let me tell you this, John Langley, you're not only an excuse for a man, but you aren't a patch on your sister as a painter, choose how!'

Alan was still laughing at this last sally as they almost ran to Tom's home over his office to collect what Tom described as the necessary armaments before they took horse for the bush, Sarah and Carter. They stopped to speak to Pat Ramsey on the way. He told them he couldn't release any of his men yet to accompany them on their mission—O'Connell's orders.

'We can only hope that Sarah is safe,' he said, 'and that your journey is unnecessary.' He looked hard at them both before adding, 'Take care of yourselves, particularly you, Dilhorne—there's some of those who've risen today who don't exactly love you.'

'Aye and I don't care for them, either,' retorted Tom, 'and as for Sarah being safe, she'd never have been anything else if O'Connell and that brother of hers had any sense between them.' And on that he and Alan rode off to try to find her.

It was almost mid-day when the rutted road that led out of Sydney turned into a track through the bush along which a carriage might just make its way. It was plain by its condition that a large party of men had recently used it. They passed one body, dragged into the bush and left behind in the rush for safety. There were no signs that soldiers had come this far. Later they were to learn that O'Connell had ordered that the rebels were not to be followed very far into the bush on the grounds, that when previous malcontents had escaped there, it had been almost certain death for them.

At the point where the track turned sharply to the right they saw the Langleys' carriage standing across it, apparently empty. There was no sign of John's matched pair of horses.

The further they had ridden, the more Tom and Alan had feared it might be so. If Carter had left the farm early—which had been his instructions—they should have come across him and Sarah some little time ago.

There was no sign of either Carter or Sarah. Sarah's luggage had gone—only her painting equipment had been left behind. There was blood on the driver's seat. Sarah's reticule was caught on one of the wheels. Alan, his face a mask of grief, picked it up and put it in his pocket, fearing that it might be the last relic of his apparently doomed love.

They looked at one another. Alan swore again. 'I had hoped,' he began, his voice breaking.

'Don't despair,' Tom said. 'They've apparently taken her and Carter with them—perhaps as hostages. One good thing is that we can easily follow their trail through the bush. It's plain that they've left the track. There's been talk of a camp in it, and they're probably making for that.'

'So,' said Alan, trying to dismiss the hateful image of Sarah as a prisoner and a hostage, 'what do we do now?'

'Follow their track on horseback until it becomes impossible to ride. Then abandon the horses.'

Alan nodded agreement and they set off, their pace slowed to a walk. They had not gone very far when they heard someone weakly calling. It was Carter, lying half on and half off the track. He had been left for dead, but had crawled out of the sun and into the relative shade of the bush. He was covered in blood from a head wound and a gentle examination by Alan showed that he was suffering from a broken leg as well.

'Thank God you've come,' he whispered. 'I thought

that I was going to perish here without telling anyone that those devils have dragged Miss Sarah off into the bush with them. Now I may die easy.' He coughed and slid into half-consciousness.

'Not if we can help it,' Alan said. Tom went to his horse and found the spirits and a skin of water that he always carried with him. He handed them to Alan, who helped Carter to drink a little of the brandy to relieve his pain and then allowed him a small measure of water.

'Well, that's that,' said Tom, sitting back on his heels. 'You can take Carter back to Sydney—he'll die here else—and I'll go on to try to find Sarah.'

Alan shook his head. 'No, Tom, no. Sarah is my love. I lost her once, but I'm damned if I'm going to lose her again. It's my duty to try to find her, yours to go back with Carter so he can be treated—he'll die otherwise. Drew and old Wentworth will look after him. Tell the military to send a detachment into the bush after us— you can lead them here—while I go after her.

'Besides, it's my own folly that has partly caused this. If I hadn't hidden away from her when I heard that she was going home to marry her former suitor I would have urged her to delay her visit until the rumours of a rising were over.'

I should have let her marry whom she liked, he told himself, and stayed her friend—and now I might never see her again because I was stiff-necked in my hurt pride and love.

Tom demurred a little, but a glance at Alan's face checked him. 'It's right that you should be the one to go,' he said, 'even if you're not so used to roving in the bush as I am but, since that is your wish, I'll indulge you. I only ask that you be wary. I don't want to lose the only real friend I've ever had.'

The two men shook hands. Alan took the proffered skin of water and set off, his thoughts spinning round in his head. He could not pray, he dare not hope, that Sarah might yet be saved, if not for him then for the unknown man back in England. He told his God that he would be resigned to giving her up if only she were saved. More he could not ask of himself.

Tom watched Alan until he was out of sight, his own thoughts nearly as tormented. He could not have stopped his friend from going on an errand that might end in his death, nor could he go with him. There was Carter to save, John Langley to see, O'Connell to confront as well as the Governor.

He, too, set off, but in the opposite direction.

On the first part of her journey home from Grimes's Farm Sarah spent a great deal of time thinking about her own situation, and comparing it with Carter's. Shortly after they had started out—she was seated beside him— he had said to her in the quiet but respectful manner that he always used with her, 'I think that I ought to tell you, Miss Sarah, that I have finally decided not to return to England with Mr John. I have no family waiting for me there. I have asked Sukie to marry me, and Mr Dilhorne has offered me a post as his man of all work. He's a hard man, but I think that I shall enjoy working for him.'

'I can only say that I shall be sorry to lose you, Carter, but I fully understand your reasons for settling here,' she told him.

Oh, yes, indeed, she fully understood them, and she also understood how much simpler it was to be a man. Carter had made his decision and no one could stop him. She, however, was bound by all the conventions that surrounded an upper-class, moneyed woman. She could

not be alone in a room with a man before marriage—
that she had been alone on more than one occasion with
Alan, was, she knew one reason for John's disapproval
of her and for his determination to make her return home
as soon as possible.

Home! She had no home—she might have had one if
she had not lost Alan, and why she had lost him she
could not fathom. She looked sideways at Carter, that
man of sound common sense, and she might even have
asked him for his advice had not the whole world suddenly turned on its axis and presented her with a new
and different face.

They had heard the sounds of men shouting and
women screaming even before the escaping rebels, waving an assortment of weaponry, burst into their view just
at the point where the track swung to the left.

'What the devil...?' began Carter, turning the horses
to prevent the carriage from running the mob down. He
never completed the sentence. The leaders of the pack
sprang forward, while others tried to control the horses,
and attempted to drag Carter and Sarah from the carriage.

Shocked, barely aware of what was happening to
them, they both put up as valiant a resistance as their
dreadful circumstances permitted. Carter managed to
pick up one of his pistols but, before he could use it, he
was knocked down by a big, burly fellow, who took it
from his lax hand and shot him with it. Sarah, struggling
spiritedly, marked the face of one of her attackers with
her nails before a sharp slap on her own face knocked
her sideways, so that she hung, half-stunned, over the
side of the carriage.

One of the men, believing her to be comatose, dragged
her out of the carriage, but as soon as she was on her

feet she managed to break free for a moment to kneel beside the body of her faithful servant, who had been thrown out of the carriage to lie in the dirt against one of its wheels. She was immediately pulled upright by the burly man who seemed to be the mob's leader.

'None of that,' he shouted, 'you're coming with us, you'll make a useful hostage if we ever need one.' He flung her towards his applauding followers, reviving in her all the painful memories of the assault upon her on the cliffs.

A hostage! And what else? The feral expression of both the men and their women, and what they were shouting at her, told Sarah that they must be part of a rising which had failed—with the result that they were fleeing into the relative safety of the bush. They also told her—in blunt and hateful terms—what her fate would be once they had reached their camp.

Only the need to continue their flight at top speed, so that they could get as far away from Sydney as soon as possible, was stopping them from raping her on the spot. For the moment dishonour, and perhaps death, were not immediate things—but in the future, what then?

She had no time for further thought. The rebels renewed their headlong flight through the bush, leaving a trail of destruction behind them. They smashed their way through the abundant vegetation, brilliant with flowers, occasionally shadowed by giant eucalyptus trees. They stopped once to eat and drink from the packs that they carried with them.

Sarah sat a little apart, panting and exhausted, her head sunk apathetically on her breast. One of the younger men, kinder than the rest, took pity on her and offered her a tin cup of water.

'Fancy her, do you, Stevie?' the burly fellow called

to him jovially. 'Well, you can have your turn later. For now let's get the goods safely back to camp before we have our fun. The damned lobsterbacks might capture us if we don't get a move on.'

Coarse laughter followed his little speech before they turned to discussing why the Rising had been so easily put down and cursing those convicts, the overwhelming majority, who had not seen fit to join them. She could only hope that the men in her life were safe, had not been killed or wounded in whatever fighting there might have been.

It seemed strange to think that she might never see Alan, Tom Dilhorne or her brother again. Her throat closed when she thought of Alan and the last few wasted weeks apart from him. She should have damned convention, gone to him and found out what was wrong, why he had been avoiding her. In danger, lost in the bush, the polite rituals of her world had never seemed so petty.

If by some chance she survived this, her life would be different. Alan or no Alan, she would not go home. If Carter could have stayed, so could she. Carter! Her worries for herself seemed selfish when she feared that he might be lying dead beside the carriage. At least she was still living, though whether that was a blessing only time would tell.

Whatever else she must not give way, she must be brave—though God knew how hard that was already, even before the rebels finally reached safety. The world swam about her: shock and the exhausting run through the bush had made her drowsy. Stevie came over, took the cup from her and shook her gently. She thanked him politely. Even in this dire situation the good manners

that had been drilled into her were still part of her behaviour—but they could not save her.

He avoided looking at her directly, but she was
touched to notice that during the subsequent forced
march through the bush he frequently found an opportunity to come to her side and to help her when she
stumbled. Her stockings were already torn, her neat kid
shoes were ripped beyond repair and her feet were blis-
tered and bleeding.

Cool, collected Miss Sarah Langley looked as though
she had been pulled through a hedge backwards, a
phrase her old governess was fond of using whenever
Sarah's appearance deviated ever so slightly from a ladylike norm.

If only the dear woman could see me now, was
Sarah's bemused thought.

Exhaustion, the lack of food and water, for after the
first stop she was not given anything to eat or drink,
combined to make her slightly light-headed. Heavy exercise was something that ladies never took. A quiet
walk down the road, or along a country lane, a turn about
the room, or in a shrubbery was as far as one usually
went. Being hurled at speed across country, sworn at,
struck and pushed if she faltered was alien to everything
that Sarah had experienced before.

Consequently, when they arrived at the camp Sarah
resembled Nellie and Sukie as she had first seen them,
rather than her usual charming self. Her face was red,
she was soaked in sweat, her clothing stuck to her body
and her hair had come down, giving her an abandoned
appearance, much appreciated by her captors, or so they
told her.

'Not such a fine lady now,' one of them jeered at her
when they stopped for the last time. They had reached

a clearing full of makeshift shacks and lit by home-made lanterns gleaming in the gathering dusk.

'Look what we've found,' the party's leader called out boisterously, 'a fine lady of our own to play with and to barter with for our lives if we're caught.'

Ragged men, women and a few children emerged from the huts. They fixed their fierce eyes on Sarah.

'That's a fine lady?' sneered one of the women, pointing at Sarah's ruined appearance.

'Well, she was when we caught her,' shouted one of the men, a statement that was greeted with ironic cheering and which confirmed Sarah's sad belief as to the destruction of her usual cool charm. The women surrounded her. One of them tore off the brooch at her throat, another the fichu which it had held in place. The third removed her shawl, which had somehow not been lost on her breakneck journey.

She began to shiver with fear that the rest of her clothing might follow suit, a fear reinforced by the comments of some of the men. She was beginning to grasp that the miniature camp was composed of more than the Irish rebels. There were also the more hardened of the ordinary convicts who had joined the Rising to escape from the restrictions placed on their freedom, imposed by reason of their violence. They were fiercer and more dangerous than the political prisoners.

She found that she could no longer stand and sank to the ground, only to be dragged to her feet and told to let everyone have a good look at her. Facing the laughter and the repeated promises of her fate, she could only hope that God would let her bear what was going to happen to her. She could not pray that she might be spared: that would be too much to hope for.

Light-headed from exhaustion and fear, she seemed to

stand outside of herself so that when deliverance came she was hardly aware of it. As soon as they had arrived, a group of her captors had gone into one of the shacks where they were joined by other rebels who had come from a different direction. From what had already been said she grasped that nothing would be done to her without the permission of the leaders.

Sarah swayed as she stood, but each time that she threatened to fall she was pushed upright with ungentle, and sometimes cruel, hands. Her arms were pinched and when her head began to droop it was slapped erect again. She was saved from further indignities when a number of men emerged from the shack.

One of them, a tall man, better dressed than the others, took her chin and tilted her face towards the rising moon.

'I've met you before, have I not?' he asked.

Sarah was so far gone that he had to repeat his question. She looked at him dazedly before saying, 'I can't remember.' There was something familiar about him. 'Perhaps you did.'

He shook her slightly. 'You'd best think. Your honour and your life might depend on it.'

'My honour!' This struck her as so absurd that she almost burst out laughing.

The hand that held her chin dropped. 'I see that you are near collapse. Best you tell me your name.'

'My name?' She lifted her head, suddenly proud. 'Why do you wish to know my name? What is my name to you?'

This sudden outburst of haughty spirit caused some of the onlookers to shout, 'Leave her to us, Kevin. She'll tell us her name soon enough then.'

The name startled Sarah into awareness. 'Kevin! I met a Kevin once. Nellie Riley had a brother called Kevin.'

She paused and then added as an afterthought, 'I was on my way home after visiting Nellie and her baby Sarah when you kidnapped me.'

Her captor drew a deep breath. 'I thought that I knew you. You're the sister of John Langley, the painter. You saved my sister Nellie's life—and her baby's, too. Sukie Thwaites told me all about it.'

He turned to the waiting crowd. 'I'll not have her harmed. You understand me. She did my sister the greatest favour a woman can do. She may be a fine lady who is now our prisoner, but I can't let you hurt someone who went out of her way to help one of us—when many wouldn't have done.'

An angry roar went up. 'You promised, Kev, you know you did,' shouted the man who had jeered at Stevie for giving Sarah water in the bush.

'I know what I promised, but that was before I knew who she was. I told Nellie when I visited Grimes's farm that no harm would come to her through me. It was bad luck that you found her, but I gave my solemn promise to my sister nigh on a year ago.'

Sarah listened to them wrangling over her: her kindness to Nellie, given almost idly at the time, was going to be the means of saving her from dishonour and a likely death. For the first time since she had been kidnapped she was roused from her apathy and began to hope that the worst might not befall her.

Kevin was their leader and his will prevailed. Sullen agreement was given that she should be left unharmed, but that she would be used as a hostage, if necessary.

'She's no fine lady, here,' called one of the women. 'She'll have to do her share of the work.'

Sarah would have walked back to Sydney on her knees to save herself from shame so that being made to

work did not distress her. She tried to thank Kevin, but
he silenced her with, 'Thank yourself, woman. Had you
not cared for Nellie I'd have thrown you to them without
a thought.'

He motioned to the shack, which was apparently his
headquarters, as well as a home to several other men and
women, and indicated that she was to follow him inside,
after saying, 'You'll have to work your keep and be
careful where you go. There are many who are not best
pleased that I've spared you.'

He could be as harsh as he liked. He had saved her.
Sarah bent her head in the low doorway and entered the
ill-smelling, dark and grimy room. He called to one of
the women, the thin one who had baited and slapped
her, 'Fill her up with whisky, Moll. I don't want her
trying to escape, she's valuable to us as a possible hostage.'

Moll went to the corner of the room and came back
with a large pannikin full of yellow liquid.

'You heard him, drink this.'

There was no point now in defiance—and the evil-
looking stuff might help her to sleep. The strong liquid
scorched her throat so much that she almost gagged on
it, but pride reasserted herself. She would not be cowed
or show fear or dislike of what was happening to her,
so she drained the pannikin to its last disgusting dregs
and handed it back to Moll, thanking her for the drink.

She had hoped that the vile stuff would help her to
sleep and so it did, but not before, her head buzzing and
reeling, she had an apparently incongruous memory of
Governor Bligh's portrait. The puzzle as to why she
should remember such a thing was solved when she recalled saying to Alan Kerr, on that night months ago in

Government House, 'I'm not likely to partake of that, Dr Kerr,' when he had told her, while standing before Bligh's portrait, about the convicts' habit of brewing illicit whisky.

Chapter Fourteen

Ever since John Langley had told him that Sarah was going home to be married, Alan Kerr had tried to believe that either he had never loved her or he loved her no longer. He had steeled himself, as her departure grew more imminent, to a lonely future in which his work, and his work alone, would have to satisfy him. After all, he now had a role in life, a duty to perform for the people of the colony, and this would have to suffice— but he knew in his heart that it would not.

The day before the Rising he had made up his mind that he would try to see Sarah for one last time, to repair the breach between them that he had created, and to make one last effort to propose marriage to her. Never mind that she was already promised to another and that it was not a gentleman's part to trouble her with his own offer. Well, I'm no longer a gentleman, he had thought, I'm an ex-felon, but I have my rights and one of them is to make an offer to the woman I love.

Alas, the following morning had brought the Rising and Sukie's news that Sarah was in danger. The thing that had distressed him most was all the time which he had wasted by refusing to see her—and now…and

now…he might never see her again. This dreadful
thought ran through his mind over and over again while
he followed the trail through the undergrowth that her
kidnappers had taken.

He rode along it until the bush became so thick that
it was impossible to continue on horseback. Prince Charlie, his big grey, had helped him to make good time, but
now he must dismount, and leave him to try to find his
way back to Sydney. His horse might deserve better of
him, but he had no choice. Alan slapped Prince Charlie
on his rump and started him on his way.

He slung the pack containing the rest of his food and
water on his back, resting for a few moments before
setting off on foot. The moon was high in the sky when
he breasted a gentle rise and saw before him a clearing
where a fire was burning before a number of shacks.
Two men were acting as sentries and patrolling the sur-
rounding area. He had reached the rebels' camp.

Was Sarah there, still alive and hopefully untouched,
or should he journey on? He had come so far that, if he
were to return to Sydney to get help, Sarah might well
be dead before a rescue party could reach her—or the
rebels, taking Sarah with them, might have moved on.

No, as with his horse, Prince Charlie, he had no
choice. He must remain and try to save her himself.
There was also the hope that Tom might have managed
to persuade the military to come after them. He dropped
to the ground, and crawled nearer to the shacks, using
the remains of the bush as protection. A number of the
rebels were sleeping in the open, but he was too far away
to tell if any of them were women.

He crept on towards a cluster of small trees, which
stood at some distance from the sentries, where he would
be able to lie down and sleep without being seen. There

was nothing he could do until daylight when he might be able to discover whether or not these were the rebels who had kidnapped Sarah. Hard though it would be, he must try to sleep himself in order to be ready for anything in the morning.

In the early dawn the noise from the little camp aroused him from his uneasy slumber. In the hope of seeing Sarah, he crawled forward once more but, again, not so close to the shacks that he might be detected.

He recognised many of the men whom he had seen around Sydney. Kevin Riley was particularly prominent, and it was was clear, from the scraps of conversation which floated across, that he was the leader. His hopes for Sarah's safety rose a little: he knew Riley to be basically decent. On the other hand, pushed to the limit as the rebels were, mercy for any man, woman or child might be in short supply.

Lying hidden and unmoving in sight of the camp, he kept watch and tried to work out how he might save his love—if saveable she were.

Back in Sydney, Tom's return with the injured Carter and the news of Sarah's capture had caused an immediate furore. He drove straight to the Langleys' home and confronted John with Carter, whom the pair of them carried to bed. A crying Sukie was sent for Mr Wentworth, the surgeon who had been helping Alan and Drew to care for the injured soldiers.

'And Sarah?' John asked hoarsely.

'Captured,' said Tom, briefly. There was no point in wasting his breath on a man faced with such dreadful news.

John sank into a chair, his head in his hands. He

looked up at Tom. 'God forgive me. What will they do to her?'

'Kill her—or worse. Probably both. She'll be a hostage, but when they hear that Ryan was shot in cold blood...' He did not finish.

John rose. 'We must see O'Connell at once and ask him to send some of his men into the bush after her.'

Tom pushed him back into his chair, walked to a side-table with a tantalus in it and brought him a tumbler of spirits. 'That's been done. I saw Pat Ramsey on the way here. He's gone to tell O'Connell. The trouble is that he's likely to set Sarah's needs against the safety of the colony. He won't send any of his troops into the bush until he's sure that the Rising's over and all the leaders are smoked out.'

If John had not been so distraught, he would have noticed how much Tom's speech had changed. The slang, the Yorkshire mannerisms, the thieves' cant had all disappeared and he spoke to John as Alan or one of the officers would have done.

John swallowed his brandy in one convulsive shudder. 'But the Rising is surely over now.'

'They're searching the town for rebels, house by house. O'Connell's pride is involved. He'll take a terrible revenge on all those whom he thinks are involved. They've captured one of Ryan's lieutenants, Quinn, and they've been flogging the names of the dissidents out of him.'

John shuddered again. 'I owe you an apology, Dilhorne—and Kerr, too.'

Tom turned to go. 'I don't want it, Langley. Remember what I said to you earlier. If aught has happened to Sarah I'll see that you pay for it—and there's more. Alan

Kerr has gone into the bush after her and you'll pay for his life, too, if he doesn't return.'

He was bone weary and to deal longer with John Langley would only tire him more. He had other errands. There was O'Connell to see; if he would not do anything to rescue Sarah then, by damn, he would raise a small force himself and go after her and his friend.

All through the long hot morning. Alan lay in the shade, just outside the camp, waiting to catch a glimpse of Sarah. He was rewarded when she came out of one of the shacks, carrying a bucket of slops that she slung into the bush not far from where he lay. A few yards further on and he would have been drenched in ordure.

He was relieved to see that, although she was hot and dishevelled, quite unlike the Sarah he knew, she did not look or behave as though she had been mistreated. Far from it. She appeared again, a little later, carrying a basket of washing. A thin, shrewish woman followed her, berating her for some supposed misdeed.

To Alan's amusement Sarah dropped the washing basket, put her hands on her hips and fired a volley of words back at the woman. He was not near enough to hear what she was saying. The thin woman thereupon aimed a slap at her, which Sarah neatly dodged. Their embryo brawl was stopped by Kevin Riley, who pulled them apart and shouted at them impartially.

Neither woman looked at all abashed. Sarah picked up the washing, carried it to some bushes not far from where Alan was hiding and started to spread it out on them. When Sarah moved nearer to where he lay, he decided to make use of this opportunity by wriggling his way forward as stealthily as possible and tossing a small stone in her direction.

When the stone hit her foot Sarah looked about her in alarm, mixed with anger, thinking that it had been thrown by one of the women intent on making her life a misery. When a second, larger one struck her ankle she looked down—to find herself staring at Alan, lying prone on the dust.

Fortunately she was so surprised to see him that, rather than cry out, she was rendered speechless. Alan put his finger to his lips to warn her to be silent while rapidly running over means of safe communication with her in his mind.

Once she had recovered from her surprise Sarah's quick-wittedness stood her in good stead. She continued to spread out the washing very slowly while moving to a spot where she stood between Alan and any possible watchers.

Thanks to a good night's whisky-induced sleep, she had recovered a little from the previous day's shocks and was beginning to hope that she might yet escape from her dreadful predicament. The hostility of the other women was disturbing, but she would not quail before it, not she! She might be a fine lady, but she would give as good as she got. The tough, fighting spirit that had made her life so difficult in polite society stood her in better stead in this enclave of outlaws.

What a wonderful surprise it had been to see Alan's beloved face peering up at her through the undergrowth. How in the world had he managed to find her? No, she would not waste time thinking about that: for the present she must concentrate on what he was whispering to her. She could hardly hear him because he dared not speak up for fear of being overheard, but she managed to make out that he was telling her that she must not try to escape until nightfall.

Because Sarah was taking a long time over what was a simple task, the watching Moll decided that she must be practising a form of mute defiance. She ran towards Sarah, began to scold her for her slowness, and then attempted to drag her away. Sarah, partly out of anger at being man-, or rather, woman-handled, and partly to direct attention from Alan, reacted by fighting back with renewed vigour.

She wrenched herself out of Moll's grasp and slapped her face. Moll thereupon screeched at her and caught her by the hair. The two women wrestled together again, Sarah pushing Moll further and further away from where Alan was hidden, until Kevin Riley, attracted by the noise and the ironic cheers of the watching men, burst out of the shack where he had been working.

'Are you two cows at it again? If you don't stop it at once, I'll give you both a beating.'

'Come on, Kev,' called one of the watching men. 'Don't be a spoilsport. Let the two Jills carry on with their mill. My money's on the fine lady.'

'I don't want the goods damaged,' shouted Kevin. His angry glare took in a defiant Sarah, her hair now down to her waist, her face red, who had taken the opportunity of his intervention to aim a last defiant slap at Moll before she was pulled away from her.

'By God, madam, I thought that we'd caught a lady, not someone who'd go ten rounds with The Game Chicken. I can see why Nellie thinks so highly of you— but we've no time for tantrums here. Remember what I said. The next time you two hens start a mill, it's a beating for both of you.'

Alan, lying in the undergrowth, was full of admiration for his fighting Sarah. He guessed, correctly, that she had started the brawl to divert possible attention away from him. He could only hope that she would not go too far and try Riley's patience too much. He lay quite still until the crowd dispersed before wriggling back into full hiding again.

A couple of the men bundled Sarah into one of the shacks and Moll into another. Neither of them were allowed out for some time. Sarah, sitting on the floor and told to be quiet, now had time to wonder when Alan had discovered that she was missing and, after that, how he could have found her, seeing that she and her captors were deep in the bush. Was it possible that Carter had not been killed after all, but had somehow managed to send word to Alan that she had been taken prisoner by the rebels?

She was not foolish enough to believe that her salvation was assured now that Alan had found her, but for the first time she allowed herself a little real hope. Mingled with that hope was her fear for him. What the rebels might do to him if, by ill chance, they found him, did not bear thinking of.

The day seemed endless. In the late afternoon she was allowed out of the hut to help to prepare the dinner over an open fire. Her tender hands—further softened by doing the wash—made this painful, and Moll, who had become her chief persecutor, cuffed her around the head when she was slow to lift the hot and heavy cauldron from the fire.

Mindful of Kevin's threats, Sarah accepted this abuse in order to avoid a beating that might weaken her and make escape impossible. Every time the sentries paced around the edge of the clearing, which they did at infrequent intervals, often passing near to where Alan was hiding, she was fearful for him.

Unknown to her, while dinner was being ladled out, he had inched even further away and was now lying concealed in a gully where he had hidden his reserves of food and water to shield them from the heat. His thoughts were not all of Sarah, although she was never far from them. He was hoping that Tom would have alerted the military, and might even have enlisted some of his own men so that either, or both, might be on their way to save him and Sarah. He dozed a little in the afternoon heat, hoping that Sarah, too, had had an opportunity to rest, preparatory to an attempt at escape.

After the meal and in the cool of the gathering dusk Kevin Riley called all the inhabitants of the camp together into the open to tell them that he was resolved that they should all avoid capture for as long as possible.

'We would have moved on before,' he announced, 'but we have been waiting for O'Brien and Power to come from Sydney to tell us what happened after you were compelled to retreat to our base camp.'

These two, together with several others, had been left behind, pretending to be among those who had refused to join in the Rising, with orders to follow with the latest news.

'If necessary,' he went on, 'we shall move to quarters further into the bush, and then, if further danger threatens, we shall make for the Blue Mountains and try to cross them.' This last was the counsel of despair. Many convicts had made for the Blue Mountains, but none had ever returned.

Alan, who had crept back to the spot where Sarah had hung out the washing, heard this in some dismay. He could see her standing quite near to him. She was obviously being guarded by Moll and another woman, which made it unlikely that she would find an opportunity to escape. Worse than that, if the rebels made for the Blue Mountains then the chance of their being caught by the military were greatly reduced, but their hopes of ultimate survival were low.

While he was trying not to let these dismal speculations trouble him too much, Alan heard the noise of an approaching party hurrying along the trail by which he had come. For a moment his hopes soared. With any luck this might be the military coming from Sydney to rescue Sarah, but the nearer the noise grew it became apparent that the newcomers were few in number so it was more likely that what he was hearing was the arrival of the rearguard from Sydney which Riley was expecting.

He was right to think so. Half a dozen men ran past him, shouting urgently. The camp, grasping that they were friends and not enemies, shouted back at them. Riley called vainly for order. It was plain to Alan that his control over his followers was diminishing, throwing Sarah into even greater danger. Riley's cries were at last heard and obeyed and the rearguard's leader, Finn O'Brien, began a coherent account of the latest news from Sydney.

'It's all up, lads. They shot down poor Ryan and flogged Quinn to death, but not before they'd whipped the names of many of us out of him. That swine, O'Connell, damn him to hell, has rounded most of us up. We just managed to get away before they found us and before we left we heard that he's sending soldiers to catch those of us as is hiding in the bush. That bastard Dilhorne and a blackfellow are tracking for them.'

The reception of this news was what might have been expected. Confusion reigned for several minutes as shouts for vengeance and curses against the military mingled with the calls of Riley for order so that their instant departure might be organised. The whole party milled about, shaking their fists and waving their weaponry—such as it was—cursing God, the military and Governor Macquarie. For a moment even Moll and her partner forgot Sarah in the general cry for vengeance.

The moment that she grasped that the uproar, allied to the gathering dark, offered her an opportunity to escape, Sarah slipped backwards into the bush, making for the spot where she had last seen Alan. When she reached him he put out his hand and together they ran away from the camp as fast as the bush would allow them, hoping that it might be some time before it was discovered that she was missing. Their only delay was when Alan picked up his iron rations, praying that in the general mêlée the rebels would have little idea of the direction which Sarah might have taken.

It was just as well that Sarah disappeared when she did. Riley continued to question O'Brien, asking why it was that the military were so soon aware that the rebels had a camp in the bush.

O'Brien shouted back at him, 'It was that bastard Dilhorne again and his bloody friend, Kerr. They went looking for Sarah Langley when they heard that she was coming from Grimes's Farm yesterday morning. They found her half-dead driver and Dilhorne took the news of her capture straight back to Sydney. Have you still got the bitch, and what are you going to do with her?'

The anger over the military's treatment of Ryan and Quinn was now transferred to Sarah. She would provide them with an opportunity for revenge on their hated oppressors by sacrificing her. Riley neither could, nor would, save her now. Alan and Sarah heard the roar in the distance that followed O'Brien's last words, followed by the repeated shouting of her name.

The roar also reminded Moll of her duties. She looked around for Sarah to find her gone. Her screams of thwarted rage gave the general alert and the whole camp began to search for her—to no avail. Fortunately for the runaways, the rebels' first consideration was for their own safety. Sarah had been a useful hostage and might also have been a useful vent for their anger but, in the end, the realisation that they might share Ryan's and Quinn's fate if they did not move on quickly proved a powerful incentive, and the search was abandoned.

'It's no use, lads,' shouted Riley when it became apparent that Sarah was not going to be found. 'We can't waste time running round in the bush looking for the bitch. She'll not get far on her own. Let's leave her to rot in it. We can't kill her any more dead than New South Wales will.'

He had to raise his voice to be heard above the clamour. 'It's vital that we leave here soon. Let's sleep now, and move on as soon as daylight comes. If we don't we're gallows-meat—or the whipping post will do for us. You know the drill, men—aye, and women, too. You're soldiers of Ireland, not a mindless rabble.'

'We should have done for her last night,' shrilled Moll.

'Stow that—let's ready ourselves to be up and away in the morning before the soldiers find us.'

Once they were some distance from the camp Alan and Sarah began to hurry through the night without caring how much noise they were making. Alan had already decided that they ought not to worry overmuch about whether they could immediately rejoin the trail by which they had come, in case the rebels decided to follow them down it.

He knew that Sarah possessed enough common sense to follow his lead without questioning it. What did trouble him was how far she could walk or run without becoming exhausted. He tried not to hold her hand too tightly, but when he loosened it she tightened her own grip on him as though she would never let him go. He had wondered if she knew how much it meant to him to be with her again, even in these dire straits, but that tightening clutch told him everything.

Whatever her brother had said of her wishing to return home, her manner to him had not changed... He stopped himself. Why should he think of that here? Survival was all. They were alone in the bush, far from the rebels who would slaughter them if they were caught, but also far from Sydney. As soon as he thought that they were safely away, he pulled Sarah down beside him in the undergrowth so that she might rest. It was now his duty to prevent the bush from doing the rebels' work for them by bringing about her death.

Once she had stopped running Sarah sank down on the ground to lie there, supine, her eyes closed, white to the lips and breathing heavily. He had noticed quite early on in their flight that she was limping and that running was painful for her, but, gallant as ever, she had never complained. His love for her overflowed. He could not, would not, lose her now to this new enemy.

'My darling,' he said tenderly, 'I ought to examine your poor feet. They are obviously paining you.'

Darling! He had called her his darling. For that she must sit up and let him do as he asked. Sarah looked down at his dark head while he carefully removed her battered slippers to reveal how much damage their headlong flight had done to her feet, on top of the wounds inflicted by the forced march on the day before.

'You must be in great pain, my love, and I fear that, out here, there is little that I can do to relieve it.'

'They are already beginning to feel better,' she murmured, while he peeled off her torn stockings as tenderly as he could, and used a little of their precious water to bathe her bleeding feet.

'Rest a little,' he said, 'before I try to bandage them. The air will help them to recover.'

'I can't pretend that they are other than painful,' she said, steadfastly, 'but seeing you was an antidote for pain. I cannot tell you how much I have missed you, and this time I thought that I was truly lost, not only to you, but to life. What would have become of me if I had still been in the rebels' power after the news of Francis Ryan's death had arrived?'

Despite the warmth of the night she began to shiver violently. Alan put his arms around her to warm and comfort her.

'Hush, my love. Do not think of it. You are safe from them now. Think only that we are together again and of how we may find our way back to Sydney.'

He kissed her grimy cheek before she turned in his arms and hid her face on his broad chest. Gradually her dreadful shuddering stopped when the shock created by her suffering began to diminish. She pulled away from him with regret and began a futile attempt to pin up her streaming tresses. Alan was wearing a thin black ribbon around his stock and he tied her hair back with it.

Then, as though it were the most natural thing in the world, he put his arms around her again and held her to him. In her exhausted condition it behoved him to be as gentle as possible with her so that she would feel safe

from harm or mistreatment. For the moment neither of
them wished to think, or to speak, of the cruel past,
either before or after she had been captured.

'Is it safe enough for us to rest here a little?' she
asked. 'I fear that it is weak of me, but I am so tired
that I am not sure how long I could keep going if we
started off again immediately.'

Alan rose to his feet and looked back along the way
that they had come. All was silent.

'I don't think that we've been followed. I don't suppose that they even know that there is a ''we''. They've
probably decided that you are on your own and consequently doomed. At the moment we're safe enough for
us to sleep for a little now. Lie down and I'll keep
watch.'

Sarah did as she was bid.

'Before you try to sleep,' Alan told her, 'I feel that it
is only right that I should be frank with you. I know that
you are both brave and resourceful. Our chances of survival are good, but they depend on our not becoming
over-exhausted, on being as sparing as possible with our
food and water, and finally on not losing our direction.
Now that the moon and stars are coming out I think that
I know enough about the night sky to navigate our way
towards Sydney.'

Sarah felt drowsily that so long as she was with Alan
she could bear anything, even her aching feet and her
fear of dying in the wilderness. She dozed for a little
and then sat up suddenly to find that Alan was keeping
watch a little way away from her.

'Alan,' she said, her voice stronger than it had been
since they had run away from the camp, 'do you think
you could sit by me for a little while before we start
again? I should so much like to know how poor Carter

is, how you found out that I had been captured, and what
has been happening in Sydney. Is John safe? I collect
from what was said back at the camp that the Rising
failed.'

Alan came over to sit beside her and take her hand in
his. 'Of course, you know nothing of what happened.
Yes, the Rising failed badly and rapidly. Many of the
rebels were wounded and their leader, Ryan, was killed.
John and all your friends are safe. I saw Pat Ramsey just
before Tom and I left to try to reach you on your way
home before the fleeing rebels did.

'We found Carter lying badly wounded beside your
carriage. To try to save his life Tom took him back to
Sydney and I came after you into the bush.'

'Poor Carter,' said Sarah faintly. 'I am so glad to learn
that he is still alive. I thought him dead.'

'Do not raise your hopes too high: he was far gone
when I last saw him. I am sure that the military and Tom
will come looking for us. The only question is, when.
Now let me bind your feet. We can use my neckcloth
and your petticoat.'

Together they ripped up their available linen and
bound Sarah's feet, retaining her light kid slippers beneath the bandages as some further protection before
they set off again in the direction that Alan hoped would
take them towards Sydney.

Their progress was slow, but before the night was too
far gone they had covered a reasonable distance. Alan
was privately of the opinion that they were successfully
making their way back to the place where Sarah had
been captured and which joined the track which led to
Grimes's farm. If they could find that, then their route
to Sydney would be a straightforward one. It was becoming increasingly plain to him that Sarah was not far

from collapse, but that her gallant spirit would never let her admit it: it was time for her to rest again.

They hid themselves in the shade of a stand of gum-trees, surrounded by small shrubs, and drank sparingly from Alan's water skin. Tired though she was, Sarah could not sleep. She lay against Alan, holding his hand.

'Oh, my darling,' she murmured drowsily, 'you do not know how pleased I was to see you. When I was captured all that I could think of was those wasted weeks when we never met one another. Worst of all, I could not bear to think that I was going to be killed in the bush without ever having seen you again.'

She began to shiver, and Alan took her in his arms again, saying, 'We are together now and that is all that matters,' He began to kiss her with a little of the passion that he had not dared to show before, and must keep muted now, for he wanted her to rest to be ready for the following day.

'I never thought to be in your arms again,' she whispered. 'All those long weeks I was so lost and lonely. What did I do to turn you away from me?'

'Oh, Sarah,' he said, his voice broken with an emotion that was so deeply felt he could scarcely speak, 'how can you say that to me when you are going back to England to marry Amborough's heir?'

Delight at finding his arms about her gave way to dismay. Sarah pushed him away from her. 'Marry Amborough's heir! Marry Charles Villiers! No such thing. From where did you get that strange notion?' She paused, appalled. 'Is that why you have been breaking my heart? Is that why you have been avoiding me?'

His face in the moonlight was nearly as white as her own.

'Your brother—' he began.

She interrupted him fiercely despite her near-exhaustion. 'My brother? John? John told you that I was going home to marry Charles Villiers? How could he tell you that? He knew that I had written to refuse him after he wrote proposing marriage to me again. Marry Charles Villiers! I would as lief marry a kangaroo—and so I told John. How could he betray me so?'

Aghast, the lovers stared at one another.

'How could he?' repeated Sarah. 'It must have been that day when he met you at Government House—and you have been avoiding me all these weeks because you thought that I had been toying with you to pass the time.'

Alan thought dizzily that the Fates could have contrived no more bittersweet ploy than for him and Sarah to find themselves in the wilderness, in danger of death from one of half a dozen causes, in order to discover what had parted them.

He gazed ardently into her great green eyes, luminous in her ashen face. 'My darling Sarah, so all the time that I have been playing the honourable fool and avoiding one promised to another, you have been thinking that I had discarded you. Tom was right. I am a fool.'

'What else could I think but that you had changed your mind?' Sarah managed painfully. 'I was looking forward to the Governor's dinner—and then, you never came. Besides, it had all happened to me before, when Charles Villiers betrayed me, so what was I to think but that I had been abandoned again? I thought that there must be something wrong with me—and all the time it was John. The worst thing of all is that even when I told him, again and again, that I would never marry Charles, even if we did go home, he never told you the truth.'

She clutched at him as though she never meant to let him go. 'No, that is not the worst thing, what is the worst is that I might have left for England without discovering the lie which John told to part us and I would always have thought that you were playing with me.'

As Alan heard this, his embrace of her grew tighter still.

'Oh, God, Alan…' and now it was Sarah's voice that was broken '…it may be forward of me to tell you this, but I love you so much. I cannot bear to think that we might never have met again.'

'Never forward, Sarah,' he told her tenderly, 'never forward, my gallant girl.'

Sarah had begun to sob, whether from pain or joy she did not know. 'I think that I know why John deceived you. He always wanted me to marry Charles and he was fearful that I would stay here and marry you. He does not like it here, while I…'

She fell silent. Alan kissed her hair—he did not dare to do more; the passion that he had always felt for her was beginning to consume him, here in the wilderness.

'Yes, Sarah, while you…?'

'I like it here. I think that I shall always like it where you are. The thought of England seems stifling to me after New South Wales.'

Alan was moved. 'I was a fool to doubt you, my darling—but I had reason, Sarah. Like you, I was betrayed once before. But let that pass. I understand your brother. He did not want you to marry an ex-felon, living at the end of the earth, and particularly one who had been convicted of treason, when you could go home and be Lady Amborough.'

She put her hand on his lips. 'Hush, that's done with. I know your story and you need not be ashamed of it. I love you, Alan. and I would not exchange you for a thousand Charleses. It is enough to say that he deceived

me once, and, were I to have married him, he would
have deceived me again.'

It was enough; they were together at last. All the mis-
understandings were explained and over. They lay quiet
in one another's arms—consummating their mutual passion would have to wait for another time. They were not
yet saved from their physical danger, even though the
emotional one had been overcome. Time, which had
stood still while they talked, was moving on again, and
was reclaiming them. Alan said at last, 'We must sleep
now so that we may be on our way early tomorrow
morning, in the cool of the day.'

'I know.' A smile touched her lips. 'You know, Alan,
when I was a little girl I used to plague my governess
about the Christmas Star. I thought that it was the Pole
Star, and she said, "No, that is not the Star of Bethle-
hem. It is Sarah Langley's star." But she was wrong,'
and Sarah pointed to the heavens where the Southern
Cross blazed far above them.

'*That* is Sarah Langley's star.'

'With God's blessing, Sarah Langley's star will watch
over us as we sleep and keep us safe from harm,' Alan
said.

And so it did.

Chapter Fifteen

Back in Sydney the Governor had been told by Tom of Sarah's capture, and that O'Connell was still hanging fire about sending a troop into the bush after her.

'I can understand his reasoning,' the Governor said. 'He probably feels that the needs of the colony come first but, from the latest news that has reached me, it seems that the Rising has been defeated and that most of the rebels still in Sydney have been rounded up. That being so, there is no reason for delay.'

'If he delays any longer I shall round up a party myself to go after her,' Tom said. 'With due respect, every moment that we delay puts her life and Dr Kerr's in greater danger.'

'Agreed,' said the Governor, 'but I'd rather you worked with O'Connell. He has no one skilled in tracking in the bush, while you, I know, have some talent in that direction. He'll need you.'

'Again with due respect,' returned Tom, who was wryly amused—he had never before been so diplomatic with anyone as he was now being with the Governor, 'my blackfellow friend, On and Off Abe, is far better at that then I am, and I will happily assist him to lead into the bush any party of which I am a member.'

'So be it,' said the Governor. 'Now you must wait while I send for O'Connell and give him his instructions. I want him to work with you on this—I'm not having any nonsense about him having no truck with Emancipists and aborigines—I agree with you that lives are at stake here.'

While the Governor was reminding O'Connell of his duty, John Langley was suffering the pangs of remorse over his lies to Alan Kerr. He had endangered not only Sarah's life but Carter's and Kerr's as well. The hours after Tom had brought Carter home with the dreadful news about Sarah passed agonisingly slowly. Word of her capture ran round Sydney's grapevine and more than one Exclusive called to offer him his sympathy.

His only practical visitor was Lucy Middleton. She defied her mother by visiting him on her own to find that, in his anxiety over Carter and Sarah, he had barely eaten since Carter's return. She invaded the kitchen, ordered Mrs Hackett to prepare something easy to eat and finally made John eat it by telling him briskly, 'Starving yourself won't bring Sarah back.'

She also told him that O'Connell, while grumbling over the Governor's interference in matters that were the province of the military, had put Pat Ramsey in charge of a contingent to go into the bush. He would work with Tom Dilhorne, On and Off Abe—the aborigine Tom Dilhorne had befriended, who worked for him on and off and was so nicknamed—and a group of Tom's men, on the grounds that all these were more familiar with the bush than the military were.

'It's a good thing that Pat's in charge,' said Lucy shrewdly, 'since he hasn't any silly notions about not

working with Tom. Frank's not with him, which is a
relief. I should hate having to worry about him as well
as Sarah and poor Dr Kerr.'

Now that she had persuaded John to drink tea and eat
something, however small, Lucy sought to distract him
by informing him of Sydney's latest piece of non-Rising,
non-military gossip.

'On top of all this, the rumour is that Fred Waring got
drunk the night before the Rising, fell down the stairs
and broke his neck, leaving poor Hester alone in the
world, God knows what will happen to her now. Pa says
that apoplexy would have killed Fred if he had lived to
hear that Tom Dilhorne was enlisted by the Governor to
work with the military to try to find poor Sarah, so it's
just as well he went when he did.'

This heartless comment wrenched a faint smile from
John, his first since Tom had brought Carter back.

'You will let me know at once if there is any news
of Sarah. I went into church on the way here and prayed
that she would be safe. It seems hard to believe that
someone as strong as Sarah could be lost forever.'

'I shouldn't have encouraged her to go to Grimes's
Farm. I should have listened to Tom Dilhorne...'

Kind Lucy told him not to worry. 'You weren't to
know that the Rising would trap Sarah. She could have
gone to the farm a hundred times without mishap.'

John could not immediately answer her. He could not
tell Lucy of the worst thing he had done—lied to Kerr
about Sarah going home. She might never want to speak
to him again. Indeed, the more he thought of it, the
worse his conduct seemed to him. It was this that was
making it difficult for him to eat or drink.

'Useless to tell me that,' he said at last, 'but next time

that you go to church, pray for me as well. I need God's forgiveness.'

She gave him her promise and left him to face the long lonely hours alone. He and Sukie were taking it in turns to sit by Carter who, a little after night fell, recovered consciousness for a few minutes, giving them both some hopes that he might yet recover.

Alan and Sarah walked steadily on, unaware that a search party was already on its way. Their progress through the bush that stretched around them was slow. They were walking beneath a rising moon, which on other nights Sarah would have admired for its beauty, but which she now valued for the help it gave them. They had rested in the worst heat of the day, but tiredness held them both in thrall.

Sarah's painful feet prevented them from keeping up a rapid pace; after they had travelled for some distance, Alan called a halt. He had noticed that she was walking more and more slowly.

'You're growing over-tired, I think, my darling.'

'No,' Sarah protested, 'I can keep walking a little longer.'

'I know,' he answered, 'but at a price that I do not wish you to pay—and I, too, need to rest.'

Despite her exhaustion she began, to Alan's surprise, to laugh a little when he helped her to become comfortable on the hard ground. Her reserves of strength were fast diminishing, but her spirit remained undaunted and, lying in his arms, she explained why she had laughed.

'It's odd. I was thinking of something that Frank Wright said to me not long after we first arrived in Sydney: that I did not need to know anything about the bush because I was never likely to be lost in it—and look at me now!'

Her laughter became unsteady when she considered their situation and the change in their appearance that their time in the wilds had created. They were both grimy and travel-stained: their clothes were in ruins and Sarah's hair was like that of a chimney-sweeper's boy, so dusty was it. Alan's cheek against her own was rough with a heavy growth of beard and she hardly dared to look at her damaged feet.

It was difficult not to think of them. Alan gave her a little more water and tried to get her to chew on one of the ship's biscuits that he had brought with him, but she gagged on it and he refrained from urging her further.

Despite his brave words to her he had little notion of exactly where they were, but if his rusty woodcraft were to be trusted they were nearer to Sydney than they had been. He had, however, still no idea of whether they were any nearer to the track to Grimes's Farm, which was their best hope of reaching safety.

'I'm assuming that a search party will come after us,' Alan said to reassure her while they rested. 'Perhaps Tom and his men, or the soldiers, or both. It's also likely that they started out some time late yesterday. I left your stockings near the camp and can only hope that someone saw them.'

He put his arms around her shoulders and kissed her gently, 'Come, my love, let us both try to sleep a little so that we might start again soon, a little refreshed.'

Alan slept in fits and starts, but Sarah fell into an exhausted slumber, her hand in his. He had often dreamed of being alone with her, telling her of his love, of protecting her even, but he had never visualised doing so in such circumstances as these.

* * *

He woke her just before sunrise, so that they could be well on their way again before the day grew too hot. The sun's position would tell him where they were. Sarah looked sleepily at him.

'Oh, Alan, I thought for a moment that this was all a dream and that I was waking up in my bedroom back in Sydney. How could I sleep as soundly as I did? It must have been exhaustion.'

She looked up at him. 'You do not look as though you have slept at all.' She laughed weakly at yet another sudden thought. 'You do know, my darling, that if we ever get back to Sydney you will have to marry me. I am quite, quite ruined. I have spent two nights in the company of a man without a chaperon—and what is worse, in the open! I shall have no reputation left—not that I had much before. Mrs O'Connell will say that this is a judgement on me.'

Alan sat down beside her to take her in his arms again. 'My dearest love, I would marry you with or without your reputation, with or without a dowry. What Mrs O'Connell or anyone else may think of you is of no consequence. Here, in the bush, there are only the two of us, and that is all that matters.'

'I know,' she said, closing her eyes and trying to smile at him: speech was becoming difficult.

He kissed her, trying to suppress the genuine passion that he felt for her. He could see that she was on the verge of collapse: her eyes and cheeks were glazed, her lips were cracked and he knew that he must do nothing to tax her overmuch. He dare not even propose to her for fear it would excite her too much and drain her of even more of the few reserves that she had left.

He moistened her lips again—noting sadly that their food and water were almost used up. What was important was that he must not push her beyond the limit of her endurance, and she was very near to that. He also knew that her gallant spirit might cause her to walk until she dropped. He remembered Tom's advice about surviving in the bush too well to knowingly allow that.

They walked on, but it was not long before Alan made her rest again. His own reserves of strength were running out, and this time he lay beside her, in the shade of a hedge of scented flowers, her hand in his again.

'My love,' she said drowsily, 'if we do not survive this strange adventure I shall, before I die, have only one regret: that we were never truly lovers, that we never shared in the grand passion of which the poets sing—and the birds, too. On the other hand, if we don't survive, we shall go into the great unknown together, and for that I shall be truly grateful—for I shall not be alone.'

'Nor I,' he said. 'But do not despair. I may be wrong, but I think that we are not far from our first destination and, if so, the search party may yet find us.'

She pressed his hand, whispered, 'I love you,' and then was silent. She had fallen into something between sleep and waking, aware that he was there, beside her, but of little else.

Alan looked down at her beloved face—it might yet be the last thing he saw. Once he would have railed against Fate, against the ill chance that had brought them together, only to lose one another again. But he could not, for to have known her was enough, and if this was all that they were ever to have, then that must be sufficient.

Like Sarah he fell into a light doze, but remained vaguely aware of his surroundings, so that when, suddenly, he heard the noise of men marching and the sound of their voices grew nearer and nearer, he jerked fully awake and sat up sharply.

Friends or enemies? Which were they? This time he and Sarah had lain down so that they might not easily be seen. He wriggled forward to peer through the undergrowth to find out who might be approaching them. It was the sight of On and Off Abe and Tom Dilhorne tracking ahead of the soldiers and reading the trail as they went that told Alan deliverance was at hand.

He rose, shouting, to his feet, waking up Sarah, who pulled herself unsteadily erect, reeling forward at the last minute to clutch at him, wondering what it was that was exciting him so. The moment that she, too, saw Abe and Tom, and the red coats of the soldiers, the fighting spirit that had kept her going for over two days fled completely at the prospect of safety and she fell against Alan, unconscious.

The effects of pain, fear and exhaustion, so long held at bay, overwhelmed her. At last Sarah could allow herself the luxury of collapse.

The luxury of sleep was to follow as soon as Sarah reached her own bed again. Lost in semi-consciousness, she remembered very little of the long journey back to Sydney, or of arriving home. Alan was to tell her later that the soldiers improvised a stretcher for her out of their coats and muskets, once it was realised that her exhaustion, combined with her damaged feet, made it impossible for her to walk any further.

She vaguely recalled John's relief and Sukie's crying over her. She thought that it was Tom who carried her up to her room, for Alan was also in a state of near collapse before the little party reached Sydney. Even when she opened her eyes after her long rest to find Lucy by her bed, she was not quite sure where she was, or whether she was still dreaming.

Lucy's robust reception of her left Sarah in no doubt that she was safe home at last. 'Oh, Sarah, you're awake again. You've slept for nearly twenty-four hours. Doctor Kerr came around a little while ago to find out how you were. He wouldn't let us wake you.'

Sarah ignored her bruised body and tried to sit up. She wanted, above all things, to see Alan. She wanted to be assured that she had not dreamed their reconciliation and that they had truly found each other in the wilderness. Alas, her head reeled and she sank back against the pillows.

'Is Dr Kerr here now?'

'Yes, he's with John. He said that he wouldn't leave until you woke up. You can't imagine how relieved we all were when we heard that you were safe home again. You can't imagine what it has been like here. First the Rising, then the news that you were coming home along the very path which the fleeing rebels were taking. After that, Tom Dilhorne and Dr Kerr went to try to reach you before they did, only for Tom to return with poor Carter and the news that Dr Kerr had gone into the bush to try to find you. The Governor then ordered Colonel O'Connell to send out a search party under Pat Ramsey to try to rescue you both and round up the rebels.

'Everyone began to cheer when the lookouts reported that Lieutenant Macleod, Tom and On and Off Abe were on their way back with you and Dr Kerr. Until then we had no idea whether you were alive or dead. Pat Ramsey had taken all of the soldiers, other than those carrying you, further into the bush to try to capture the remaining rebels—he's not back yet.'

'I'm not sure how alive I am at the moment,' said

Sarah cautiously, trying to smile. 'Every limb aches and my poor feet feel as though I shall never be able to walk again. You haven't told me yet how Carter is.'

'He's holding his own and both Dr Kerr and Mr Wentworth think that he will live.'

'I can't tell you how happy that makes me. I was so sure that the wretches had killed him. I kept thinking about poor Sukie and how she was to be married soon after you and Frank.'

She did not ask after John. The thought that he had wilfully and wickedly lied to Alan to keep them apart was too painful. She knew, as a Christian, that she ought to forgive him, but her proud spirit rebelled at the very idea. He should have known better than to play with her life and happiness so lightly—and so she would tell him. Perhaps, after that, she might feel a little more forgiving, but only time would tell.

Lucy was plainly curious about what had happened to Sarah's relationship with Alan Kerr once they were alone in the bush. She knew, without Sarah having said very much to her, that his sudden disappearance from her life had hurt her greatly. She had sometimes wondered how much John had had to do with Alan's behaviour, but it would not have been either tactful or *comme il faut* to question Sarah about it.

Sarah's wanting to know everything about everybody but her brother was another odd thing. Lucy decided on a direct question about the Doctor, who had been haunting the Langleys' home ever since Sarah had been carried into it.

'Sarah, I must say this—from his behaviour, have you become reconciled with Dr Kerr?'

When Sarah heard this, her face glowed, but all she felt it right to say was, 'I can't speak about that until I have seen him again. So much happened in the bush that I am not quite sure how much was real and how much I dreamt.'

'I'll go and get him for you.' Lucy turned at the door and said, shyly this time, 'You've been so brave, Sarah. From what Dr Kerr has said, I don't think that I could have borne what you did. He says that you might have died if you hadn't been so determined to survive.'

Sarah laughed again. 'As to that, my feet feel as though I *have* died. You know, Lucy, the most surprising thing is that what I remember most is not the dreadful things that happened to me, but my poor feet, and how much they hurt all the time!'

She waited for Alan half-expectantly and half-shyly. Perhaps she had dreamed all that loving time with him, too: their exchange of endearments once they had discovered John's duplicity. Her own declaration of love—and his. Had she really been so forward and he so caring of her?

When he did arrive John was with him, but Alan did not let that deter him. He dropped on his knees by her bed and took her hand in his, as he had done so many times in the bush.

'My own darling, you look so much better already. My heart failed me on the journey home, you looked nearly as ill as poor Carter.'

To her surprise Sarah was so overcome at seeing him, clean, shaved, in his good clothes, his dear face so full of love for her, that she found it difficult to speak. Before she could do so, John, who had been standing by the window, came over to the bed.

'Sarah, before we say anything more, I must ask you for your forgiveness.'

He did not say what the forgiveness was for and the

look she gave him was a painful one. 'What you ask, I must grant, but I cannot forget. I can only hope that time might yet soften my feelings towards you. Even if what you did was done out of mistaken love, you had no right to make my decisions for me without asking my permission. What was most unforgivable was that you should lie to Alan about my intentions so that he thought that I had been playing with his feelings. I hope that you have apologised to him, because he was the worst sufferer.'

'What has recently happened,' John replied painfully, 'has taught me how wrong I was. I cannot argue with your feelings. They are most natural. Now I must inform you that Dr Kerr has told me that he wishes to ask for your hand in marriage and hopes that I shall consent to be his brother-in-law. I have agreed to that, for God knows, that without him, you would not be here at all, but lying dead in the bush. I have also come to understand how miserable you have been since I led him to believe that you intended to return home and marry Charles.'

Sarah knew how much it had cost him to confess to this. Nevertheless, she could not forget that he had not only sought to part her permanently from Alan, but had also thoughtlessly sent her into great danger of losing both her honour and her life.

'You know very well that I do not need your consent to marry Alan,' she said coldly, 'since I am my own mistress, in control of my fortune, and may therefore determine my own destiny. His asking you for it is typical of the integrity that he shows in all his actions. What I would like is your blessing, and your active goodwill towards us both—not just to me. Only then may I be able to forgive you a little for the wrongs you have committed, which nearly lost both of us our lives.'

Alan looked up quickly. 'Langley, I must add my voice to Sarah's. Do as she asks and then we may all forget the past.'

John, his face working, stared at the pair of them. Most of all he stared at the man who had saved his sister's life. He would always believe that she demeaned herself by marrying Kerr, but he could not deny the man's courage—and the integrity of which Sarah has spoken so movingly. To deny Sarah what she had asked for—his blessing—after he had treated them both so badly would reflect on his own integrity.

'Of course, you have my blessing,' he said at last. 'How could I refuse it when you mean so much to each other? Moreover, I must also apologise to you, Kerr, for having deceived you so grossly. I am particularly pleased to learn that you did not propose to Sarah until you had spoken to me.'

He put out his hand to Alan, 'Let us shake hands on it. Kerr, and forget the past—as you suggested.'

Alan took the proffered hand reflecting that Sarah's plain speaking had brought about this revolution in her brother's behaviour.

'I could not offer for her in the bush,' he said simply. 'It would not have been right. I told her of my love and I knew that I had hers. To speak to you first was, it seemed to me, the proper thing to do, even if it were not strictly necessary that I should. I shall remedy that now. Sarah, my darling, will you marry me?'

His delicacy of feeling brought tears to Sarah's eyes. 'My dearest Alan, you know that you have my answer already—and besides, after two nights in the bush, you also know that you must make an honest woman of me,'

She was half-laughing and half-crying when he kissed her again on the cheek.

'Now, my own dear Sarah, I must leave you to rest for a little longer. I will visit you again when you are more restored.'

'No,' she said urgently, kissing him back and tightening her grip on his hand. 'You are not to leave me so soon. The more I see of you, the more rapidly I shall recover. I know that you will show me every consideration, and since you risked your life to save mine, and I've not yet really thanked you, this is a splendid time for me to do so before the busy world descends on us once more.'

John's smile at this sign that his sister was her own lively self again was a forced one, but Alan's was genuine. Alone at last, after John's reluctant departure, all that they both wanted for the moment was to feel their arms around one another. More than that, Alan wanted to be in the bed with her, showing her how much he loved her, but in her present condition that was impossible—he would have to wait. Merely to be with her roused him, but he would have to be resigned to that until they were married.

So he sat on the bed beside her and rested her head on his breast again, so that she could feel his heart beating, strong and true.

'Happy now, my darling?' he asked her tenderly.

She looked up at him, her face mischievous. She was very much the old lively Sarah, the Sarah that neither Riley's camp nor the bush could tame. 'Of course,' she said, 'but there is one thing that does worry me a little.'

His own face anxious, he said, 'Now what can that be, my love?'

'It's this, Alan. Now that I'm going to stay with you

in New South Wales, I do hope that you're not going to have to make a habit of rescuing me. I think that two such efforts are quite enough, don't you? Any more would be excessive and might cause unwelcome gossip, besides being exceedingly troublesome and time-consuming for the pair of us.'

His shout of laughter was spontaneous, as was his kiss.

Soon, quite soon, she fell asleep, with her head on his chest, as she had done in the bush, and this time no nightmares of death, loss and sorrow came to plague her.

The excitement created by the Rising continued even after Sarah and Dr Kerr had been brought safely home. Kevin Riley and his followers were never to reach the Blue Mountains. They were caught by Pat Ramsey's detachment of soldiers some twenty-four hours after Sarah and Alan had been found.

Alan brought Sarah the news: she was out of bed and was resting on a sofa in the Langleys' parlour. She had already told Alan, Tom and John that only Kevin Riley's intervention had saved her from rape or worse and that she wished to plead for mercy for him when he was tried. It proved useless to ask John to support her. His guilt over his own folly in sending her into danger had made him declare that all those who had captured Sarah should be hanged.

Sarah, still unable to walk without pain because of her wounded feet, listened to Alan when he described how the rebels had been paraded in chains after they had been brought back to Sydney.

'What is likely to happen to Kevin Riley?' she asked him.

'He is almost certain to be hanged. He was one of the

leaders of the rebellion and it was his men who captured you. There is a great deal of feeling about that.'

Sarah sighed. 'Had it not been for Riley I should not be here. He saved me from death and dishonour in return for what I did for Nellie, which was little enough in the great sum of things, and I did not do it for reward. Is there no way in which I can speak on his behalf?'

'I'm bound to warn you that the military want him to be hanged. Even Pat Ramsey is fierce against him, and Pat is not a bloodthirsty monster.'

'I do so wish that I could walk,' she exclaimed. 'What worries me is that I hear that there are plans for a summary execution. Can that be true?'

Alan did not like to tell her the truth, but respect for Sarah's integrity and courage had already made him resolve never to treat her as though she were a mindless doll.

'Yes, I fear that there is a real danger of that.'

She sat up. 'Then, somehow, you must take me to Government House. I am sure that Lachlan Macquarie would not want the full force of the law used against a man who risked the anger of his followers by sparing his victim when they called for her mistreatment.'

Sarah's strength of will had never been more plain, and, because by saving her Riley had indirectly enabled them to come together again and be reconciled, Alan agreed to do as she wished.

'I'm not sure that you'll achieve anything, though,' he warned her. 'The feeling against him is so strong.'

'But the Governor is the ultimate judge,' she said vigorously, 'and he is a fair man. He has nothing to prove, either, unlike John and O'Connell, who are trying to forgive themselves for their misjudgement by wanting the most condign punishments to be handed out.'

Alan gave his forthright love an admiring look. 'I do believe that you're becoming as shrewd as Tom. Very well, let me take you to Government House where you may practise your new-found skill on Macquarie—and who knows what might happen!'

He carried her in his arms into the Governor's office, despite John's disapproval. Macquarie listened to her carefully and considered the matter for a few moments before he replied to her.

'My dear Miss Langley, I can certainly make you one promise: there will be no summary executions without proper trial while I am Governor of New South Wales. I am here to uphold the law, not break it. As for Riley being spared hanging because of his merciful treatment of you, I will make sure that his behaviour towards you will be mentioned at his trial and will be borne in mind when he is sentenced. More I cannot say.'

It was exactly what Sarah had hoped of the Governor, given his known reputation, and so she told Alan and John. There was nothing more she could do for Riley.

Of them all, Sukie was the most annoyed by Sarah trying to save him from hanging. 'Miss Sarah's a deal too good,' she declared, for she could not forgive the rebels for what they had done to Carter, albeit that he was slowly recovering from his injuries and, despite his recent experiences, was still determined to stay in Sydney with her. Her usual diatribes on the subject always ended with, 'If I had my way I'd hang 'em all!'

'Even Nellie's brother?' asked Sarah, leaning on her stick when she entered the kitchen to hear Sukie giving Mrs Hackett a piece of her mind.

'I know he's Nellie's brother, but his lot had no business nearly killing my poor George.'

It was Sarah who got her wish, not Sukie. After much

grumbling from the military it was agreed that because of his behaviour towards Sarah he should not be hanged, but sent to Van Diemen's Land instead. Neither Alan nor Sarah was comfortably sure that they had done Riley any service by having his sentence commuted. Van Diemen's Land was the most cruelly savage of the penal settlements.

'Nevertheless, I couldn't see him hanged, it wouldn't have been right. It was his life in exchange for mine and Governor Macquarie saw it that way, too.'

She did not tell Alan that because she was happy she wanted others to be happy also. In the end none of the remaining rebels was sentenced to death. Clemency reigned as the Governor had wished.

'I think that this might well be the last of the Risings,' he told Sarah, John and Alan when he invited them to dinner after the trials were safely over. 'The colony is beginning to change. There was very little sympathy for the rebels this time. People are trying to build a new life here in a new land, the old life forgotten. Even the convicts and the Emancipists, or perhaps I should say particularly the convicts and Emancipists, feel like that.'

'That's what Tom Dilhorne says,' offered Sarah.

'Ah, yes, the man of common sense himself,' said the Governor, amused. 'Mark my words, Miss Langley, your future husband and Tom will be two of the mainstays of New South Wales when I am long gone. Are you aware that there is a proposal to call the new land Australia? The aborigines, its original natives, have always been known as Australians. Soon the name will describe all those who live here, regardless of their origin.'

If John looked down his nose a little at the Governor's forthright glimpse of the future, Alan and Sarah welcomed it. They were in the first glow of happiness that followed their official betrothal, although Sarah always privately maintained that their first real betrothal had taken place in the bush.

She had entered Government House still using her stick, and the Governor's wife, Elizabeth, had asked her if she would be recovered enough to act as chief bridesmaid at Lucy Middleton's wedding, which had been put off until all the formalities connected with the Rising were over so that they would not be allowed to spoil the year's most brilliant social event.

'I am nearly well enough already,' Sarah said. 'My feet have almost recovered. The worst thing of all is that I am still occasionally plagued by nightmares. I sometimes wake up thinking that I am back in the bush—but they are getting fewer and Alan says that they will pass, given time.'

So, when Lucy was married, Sarah was there and caught Lucy's bouquet as soon as it was thrown. 'As is only right,' said Lucy happily, 'seeing that your wedding follows so soon after.'

To the surprise of every Exclusive in Sydney, Alan and Tom Dilhorne were both guests as well. Lucy had put her foot down and, despite her mama's protests, had announced that it was only proper that the two men who had saved Sarah between them, Emancipists though they might be, ought to be present in order to support her. Lucy was slowly beginning to turn into someone far more formidable that the sweet young girl that her mother, and propriety, expected her to be.

Alan had persuaded Tom to buy yet another new suit in honour of the occasion. 'It will do for my wedding, too,' he told his friend, who was going to be his best man. Amid some grumbling from Tom, the Regimental tailor turned him out after such a fashion that he was, as at the Governor's Banquet, indistinguishable from all the Exclusive guests. He joked to Alan that he was now turning respectable in appearance and manner—except when it paid him not to be!

Alan and Sarah's wedding was, by contrast, to be a quiet one, with only a few good friends invited.

'I don't want a great brouhaha, and neither, I think, do you,' said Sarah to Alan. 'I know that many do not approve of our marriage, whatever they say to our faces. Besides, many secretly think of me as damaged goods after our nights in the bush. The only people I want to be present are those who truly care for us.'

They were seated in the Langleys' small garden behind the house, glasses of lemonade before them and Sarah's macaw screeching in the background.

'That is what I want,' said Alan his face grave, 'but I must say this now before it is too late. Are you sure that you are doing the right thing in marrying me? After all, what John said is true. You could have a splendid match back in England. Think of the difference between that and living here at the other end of nowhere with a half-ostracised doctor.'

She put his hand to her lips and kissed it. 'It's noble of you to say that, Alan, but I don't want a splendid match and a title: what I want is you. I want you so badly that I am having difficulty in not throwing myself at you, begging you to anticipate our wedding night. Oh, I'm not a fool, I know that it's not always going to be easy, that there may even be times when I shall regret what I have done. But in the end it all comes back to the fact that, rightly or wrongly, what I want is to live here with you, helping you in your medical practice.'

He took both her hands in his, saying hoarsely, 'Indeed you may help me, my darling, and so far as anticipating our wedding night is concerned, if you look at me like that much longer I am in danger of anticipating our wedding night in John's back garden, and that would never do. I burn for you, and yes, I know that you burn for me. I also know that there may be difficult times ahead for us, but, my darling, I have seen how you behaved in the most difficult time of all, and I know that we shall win through together.

'Now let us drink our lemonade and think of the Arctic wastes or of a snowy night in Scotland lest we both forget ourselves. Allow me only one chaste kiss on your cheek.'

'Granted,' said Sarah, 'so long as I may kiss yours.' She was rapidly discovering what she had only suspected before: that really loving a man meant that mind and body were both engaged. She no longer felt her body to be treacherous: it was telling her that her choice of Alan for a mate was a true one.

Consequently, there were few brides who could have looked more radiant than Sarah Langley did on her wedding day. The small company present, which went on to the Reception afterwards, was an exclusive one. Governor Macquarie, together with his wife, attended; Pat Ramsey and Stephen Parker acted as his aides. Frank and Lucy Wright—Lucy was Sarah's Matron of Honour—were also present on this extraordinary occasion, where Tom Dilhorne and all the Langleys' servants were included among the guests of honour. Even Mrs Hackett deigned to join in the celebrations, although she did sit at the back of the church, glowering at everyone. She had never quite recovered from the fact that no explanation had ever been found for the missing food.

Lucy's mother acidly commented, 'The only surprise is that On and Off Abe hasn't also been invited.'

Lucy replied mischievously, 'Well, he was, only he chose to go walkabout two days before the wedding.'

Sarah walked down the aisle on John's arm, with Alan and Tom Dilhorne waiting for her at the altar, to hear Sukie shrill out in a highly audible whisper to the recovering Carter, 'I allus knew that Dr Alan and Miss Sarah were made for one another.'

Unknown to both Alan and Sarah, Tom had already enlivened his own day by remarking to John Langley that he was relieved that he hadn't had to shoot him after all, and that seeing his friend and Sarah being married was a rare treat which he hoped that John was enjoying as much as he did!

Regardless of John, or anyone else for that matter, the two main parties in the wedding later agreed that the day seemed as if it would never end. At last all the celebrations were over and they were left to enjoy their wedding night in the house that she had shared with John. He was lodging with the Middletons until he left for England.

A radiant Mrs Lieutenant Frank Wright and her husband were the last to leave. Tom's departure was early. He announced loudly to anyone who would listen that it was time that the newly-weds were left alone to enjoy themselves: a hint of which few took notice, but with which the said newly-weds were in full agreement.

'The only good thing that I can say about our sojourn in the bush,' Alan remarked, when they were alone at last, 'is that I didn't have to share you with others. I thought that today was never going to be over. I will say one thing for Tom—he seems to have more fine feelings than all our Exclusive friends put together, even if he doesn't always express them in the most tactful or delicate fashion.'

'Are *you* going to be tactful now?' asked Sarah softly, leaning forward and beginning to untie his cravat. 'If so, I shall insist on carrying you up to bed rather than the other way round if that is the only way in which I can get there.'

'I suppose that is a hint as delicate as Tom's, so I'll do my best to oblige you, madam,' said Alan, sweeping her into his arms and carrying her up to her bedroom—which was now theirs, 'but only on condition that my cravat is not the only piece of clothing we shall be removing tonight.'

'What,' said Sarah, panting as though she had run upstairs with him and not the other way round, 'am I not to wear this truly elegant nightgown that Sukie made for me with her own fair hands?'

Alan, who was now kneeling on the bed after pulling off his shirt, leaned over her, murmuring, 'Later, perhaps—or perhaps not.'

'Now what kind of answer is that?' replied Sarah, while he was turning his attention to removing her wedding dress.

Once Alan had manoeuvred it safely over her head he tossed it on to her bedside chair, saying, 'An answer that depends on how much we enjoy ourselves.'

'I hope that there's no doubt of that,' she threw back at him, 'since I have spent the three weeks since we were rescued looking forward to tonight.'

'No more than I,' Alan told her; he was now off the bed and was busily divesting himself of his breeches. 'You have no notion of the state I have been in, too.

Delaying marriage is a matter guaranteed to try a man's body as well as his soul.'

When Sarah began to remove her petticoat and drawers, he threw himself on to the bed beside her before she had time fully to appreciate the sight of a naked man, fully aroused.

'No, allow me,' he told her. 'It's a husband's privilege to prepare his wife for the final act.' Which he did by transforming her into Lady Eve before the fall, lying alongside his Lord Adam.

'Oh, is there an etiquette in all this?' asked Sarah mischievously. 'I wasn't aware of that. Please do instruct me. I shouldn't like to be doing the wrong thing.'

They both began to laugh together. Later Sarah was to muse on how much mirth there had been in their mutual pleasure. Nothing that she had read, heard, or overheard, had ever led her to believe how joyful the whole business was.

Laughter over, Alan knelt over her where she lay, open before him. 'Oh, Sarah,' he whispered, his voice as soft and loving as he could make it. 'I shall try not to hurt you, but in the throes of pleasuring the woman he loves a man cannot always keep that promise.'

Sarah rose a little, put her arms around his neck and kissed him. 'No need to tell me that,' she said. 'Dear Alan, you are as gentle a man as I have ever met. All your patients bear witness to your kindness and how hard you try to save them from unnecessary pain.'

The look that she gave him was so loving that Alan's hitherto fine control was lost. He muttered something which she could not quite hear, and then his hands roved over her body, touching and stroking her, first gently and then more strongly, until he brought her to the point where she was begging him for more. What that more was Sarah did not completely know—only that she wanted it and would not be complete until she had it.

At last, aware that his bride was as ready for him as she would ever be, Alan entered Sarah to achieve the perfect union in which mind and body both share: a union that transcends and transforms the mundane acts of everyday living and loving. When both lovers climax together the two become one in that brief moment of time when the conscious self is lost so that, afterwards, it is hard to describe what actually happened in words which make sense.

Afterwards, lying there fulfilled, his arms around her and hers around him, Sarah murmured brokenly to Alan, 'I had not known…I could not imagine…or describe, now it is over, how wonderful that was… Is it always like this for everyone?'

She had imagined beforehand what it was about making love that set all the poets writing, which had so tempted many otherwise honourable men and women that they had relinquished everything—wives, husbands and children—so that they might be with a forbidden love, so powerful was it.

And now she knew.

Alan, exhausted, lying drained beside her, shook his head and said slowly, 'No, not always—with some it is never like this. We are among those fortunate beings who are truly two halves meeting. Philosophers argue about the nature of love and desire, but I do not believe that they can be rationally explained. We are among the blessed for we love one another in the truest fashion since we have no wish to hurt others by it.'

'Blessed, indeed,' said Sarah drowsily. 'Will *you* feel hurt if I tell you that what I most want now is to go to sleep? Preferably in your arms—and without my night-gown.'

'No, indeed, for that means that we have reached completion together—something else that is not always achieved. Besides, we shall enjoy ourselves all the more next time if we are not sated, and since this is your introduction to love-making, your body needs to rest a little before we enjoy ourselves again.'

Alan had never been a promiscuous man: he had taken his pleasure with women only infrequently, but he had never before experienced such a profound consummation as he had just reached with Sarah. If he had ever doubted that she truly loved him as much as he loved her, that fear had disappeared. The cynic who had said that in love there is always one who truly loves while the other merely turns the cheek was wrong.

Safe in one another's arms, they slept until it was almost dawn, whereupon they celebrated their marriage again. This time their love-making was slow, and sweetly long-drawn-out since they were now secure—the deceits and lies of the past, which had kept them apart, had disappeared.

Later, Alan was to tell Sarah that the perfection of love and fulfilment that they had then reached was because each of them sought to please the other as well as themselves, to give, rather than to take—thus they were able to achieve that transcendence of self in which loving becomes more than mere lust.

After their second love-making and its fulfilled sleep, Sarah awoke to the realisation that in her private life she was now travelling in an enchanted and unknown land. She had left the plateaux of ordinary living and had scaled the mountain tops. She was not foolish enough to believe that she and Alan could live permanently on these heights, but when they descended to the valleys again, the memory of them would always be there.

She had sailed to a New World from an Old One. She was now committed to that world and to the man who was sleeping beside her. England lay behind her, before her was the unknown—except for one important thing.

At this point in her musings Alan woke up and said, sleepily, when she gently stroked him, 'You are awake, Sarah?'

'Yes. I have been thinking.'

'How to please your lord and master, I trust.'

'That, too,' she told him, 'but do you realise, Alan, that we are, in the truest sense, guests in this land? If, however, we have a baby it will be born as—what was Macquarie's word?—an Australian. He or she will be a true native, not brought here in chains, or for the convenience of the government or of trade, or like me by curiosity—but here by right.'

Alan was silent for a moment, before replying, 'True, and their descendants—for I hope that we shall have more than one child—will not care how we came here, because this will be their land from birth. And now, Mrs Dr Kerr, since you have presented me with such a profound truth, how about setting to again, thus making sure that our own little Australians will not be long in coming?'

'Agreed, Dr Kerr, on the double, as the military say.' They turned into one another's arms again—and united to make Sarah's prophecy come true.

Australia, not Terra Australis, was coming into being with every baby that was born there.

Modern Romance™
...seduction and
passion guaranteed

Tender Romance™
...love affairs that
last a lifetime

Medical Romance™
...medical drama
on the pulse

Historical Romance™
...rich, vivid and
passionate

Sensual Romance™
...sassy, sexy and
seductive

Blaze Romance™
...the temperature's
rising

27 new titles every month.

Live the emotion

MILLS & BOON®

MB3

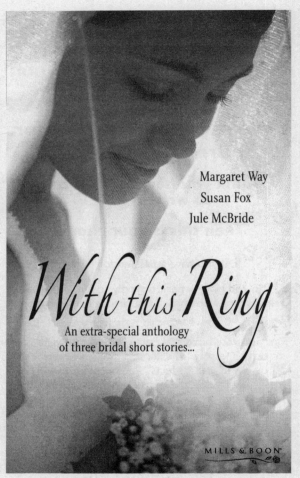

Margaret Way

Susan Fox

Jule McBride

With this Ring

An extra-special anthology
of three bridal short stories...

MILLS & BOON

Available from 18th April 2003

*Available at most branches of WH Smith,
Tesco, Martins, Borders, Eason, Sainsbury's
and all good paperback bookshops.*

0503/024/MB69

Don't miss *Book Nine* of this BRAND-NEW 12 book collection 'Bachelor Auction'.

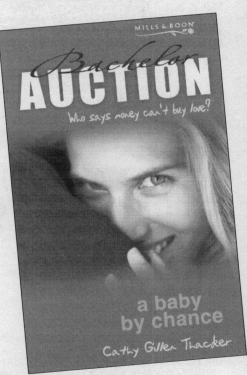

Who says money can't buy love?

On sale 2nd May

2 FREE
books and a surprise gift!

We would like to take this opportunity to thank you for reading this Mills & Boon® book by offering you the chance to take TWO more specially selected titles from the Historical Romance™ series absolutely FREE! We're also making this offer to introduce you to the benefits of the Reader Service™—

- ★ FREE home delivery
- ★ FREE gifts and competitions
- ★ FREE monthly Newsletter
- ★ Exclusive Reader Service discount
- ★ Books available before they're in the shops

Accepting these FREE books and gift places you under no obligation to buy, you may cancel at any time, even after receiving your free shipment. Simply complete your details below and return the entire page to the address below. *You don't even need a stamp!*

YES! Please send me 2 free Historical Romance books and a surprise gift. I understand that unless you hear from me, I will receive 4 superb new titles every month for just £3.49 each, postage and packing free. I am under no obligation to purchase any books and may cancel my subscription at any time. The free books and gift will be mine to keep in any case.

H3ZEA

Ms/Mrs/Miss/Mr ....Initials.....................................
BLOCK CAPITALS PLEASE

Surname ....

Address ....

....

....Postcode...............................

Send this whole page to:
UK: FREEPOST CN81, Croydon, CR9 3WZ
EIRE: PO Box 4546, Kilcock, County Kildare (stamp required)